Soul of a Bishop by H. G. Wells

Herbert George Wells was born on September 21st, 1866 at Atlas House, 46 High Street, Bromley, Kent. He was the youngest of four siblings and his family affectionately knew him as 'Bertie'.

The first few years of his childhood were spent fairly quietly, and Wells didn't display much literary interest until, in 1874, he accidentally broke his leg and was left to recover in bed, largely entertained by the library books his father regularly brought him. Through these Wells found he could escape the boredom and misery of his bed and convalescence by exploring the new worlds he encountered in these books.

From these humble beginnings began a career that was, after several delays, to be seen as one of the most brilliant of modern English writers.

Able to write comfortably in a number of genres he was especially applauded for his science fiction works such as *The Time Machine* and *War of the Worlds* but his forays into the social conditions of the times, with classics such as *Kipps,* were almost as commercially successful. His short stories are miniature masterpieces many of which bring new and incredible ideas of science fiction to the edge of present day science fact. Wells also received four nominations for the Nobel Prize in Literature

Despite a strong and lasting second marriage his affairs with other women also brought the complications of fathering other children. His writings and work against fascism, as well as the promotion of socialism, brought him into increasing doubts with and opposition to religion. His writings on what the world could be in works, such as *A Modern Utopia*, are thought provoking as well as being plausible, especially when viewed from the distressing times they were written in.

His diabetic condition pushed him to create what is now the largest Diabetes charity in the United Kingdom. Wells even found the time to run twice for Parliament.

It was a long, distinguished and powerfully successful career by the time he died, aged 79, on August 13th, 1946.

Index of Contents

"Man's true Environment is God"
J. H. OLDHAM in "The Christian Gospel" (Tract of the N. M. R. and H.)

THE DREAM

I

It was a scene of bitter disputation. A hawk nosed young man with a pointing finger was prominent. His face worked violently, his lips moved very rapidly, but what he said was inaudible.

Behind him the little rufous man with the big eyes twitched at his robe and offered suggestions.

And behind these two clustered a great multitude of heated, excited, swarthy faces....

The emperor sat on his golden throne in the midst of the gathering, commanding silence by gestures, speaking inaudibly to them in a tongue the majority did not use, and then prevailing. They ceased their interruptions, and the old man, Arius, took up the debate. For a time all those impassioned faces were intent upon him; they listened as though they sought occasion, and suddenly as if by a preconcerted arrangement they were all thrusting their fingers into their ears and knitting their brows in assumed horror; some were crying aloud and making as if to fly. Some indeed tucked up their garments and fled. They spread out into a pattern. They were like the little monks who run from St. Jerome's lion in the picture by Carpaccio. Then one zealot rushed forward and smote the old man heavily upon the mouth....

The hall seemed to grow vaster and vaster, the disputing, infuriated figures multiplied to an innumerable assembly, they drove about like snowflakes in a gale, they whirled in argumentative couples, they spun in eddies of contradiction, they made extraordinary patterns, and then amidst the cloudy darkness of the unfathomable dome above them there appeared and increased a radiant triangle in which shone an eye. The eye and the triangle filled the heavens, sent out flickering rays, glowed to a blinding incandescence, seemed to be speaking words of thunder that were nevertheless inaudible. It was as if that thunder filled the heavens, it was as if it were nothing but the beating artery in the sleeper's ear. The attention strained to hear and comprehend, and on the very verge of comprehension snapped like a fiddle string.

"Nicoea!"

The word remained like a little ash after a flare.

The sleeper had awakened and lay very still, oppressed by a sense of intellectual effort that had survived the dream in which it had arisen. Was it so that things had happened? The slumber shadowed mind, moving obscurely, could not determine whether it was so or not. Had they indeed behaved in this manner when the great mystery was established? Who said they stopped their ears with their fingers and fled, shouting with horror? Shouting? Was it Eusebius or Athanasius? Or Sozomen.... Some letter or apology by Athanasius?... And surely it was impossible that the Trinity could have appeared visibly as a triangle and an eye. Above such an assembly.

That was mere dreaming, of course. Was it dreaming after Raphael? After Raphael? The drowsy mind wandered into a side issue. Was the picture that had suggested this dream the one in the Vatican where all the Fathers of the Church are shown disputing together? But there surely God and the Son themselves were painted with a symbol—some symbol—also? But was that disputation about the Trinity at all? Wasn't it rather about a chalice and a dove? Of course it was a chalice and a dove! Then where did one see the triangle and the eye? And men disputing? Some such picture there was....

What a lot of disputing there had been! What endless disputing! Which had gone on. Until last night. When this very disagreeable young man with the hawk nose and the pointing finger had tackled one when one was sorely fagged, and disputed; disputed. Rebuked and disputed. "Answer me this," he had said.... And still one's poor brains disputed and would not rest.... About the Trinity....

The brain upon the pillow was now wearily awake. It was at once hopelessly awake and active and hopelessly unprogressive. It was like some floating stick that had got caught in an eddy in a river, going round and round and round. And round. Eternally—eternally—eternally begotten.

"But what possible meaning do you attach then to such a phrase as eternally begotten?"

The brain upon the pillow stared hopelessly at this question, without an answer, without an escape. The three repetitions spun round and round, became a swiftly revolving triangle, like some electric sign that had got beyond control, in the midst of which stared an unwinking and resentful eye.

II

Every one knows that expedient of the sleepless, the counting of sheep.

You lie quite still, you breathe regularly, you imagine sheep jumping over a gate, one after another, you count them quietly and slowly until you count yourself off through a fading string of phantom numbers to number Nod....

But sheep, alas! suggest an episcopal crook.

And presently a black sheep had got into the succession and was struggling violently with the crook about its leg, a hawk nosed black sheep full of reproof, with disordered hair and a pointing finger. A young man with a most disagreeable voice.

At which the other sheep took heart and, deserting the numbered succession, came and sat about the fire in a big drawing room and argued also. In particular there was Lady Sunderbund, a pretty fragile tall woman in the corner, richly jewelled, who sat with her pretty eyes watching and her lips compressed. What had she thought of it? She had said very little.

It is an unusual thing for a mixed gathering of this sort to argue about the Trinity. Simply because a tired bishop had fallen into their party. It was not fair to him to pretend that the atmosphere was a liberal and inquiring one, when the young man who had sat still and dormant by the table was in reality a keen and bitter Irish Roman Catholic. Then the question, a question begging question, was put quite suddenly, without preparation or prelude, by surprise. "Why, Bishop, was the Spermaticos Logos identified with the Second and not the Third Person of the Trinity?"

It was indiscreet, it was silly, to turn upon the speaker and affect an air of disengagement and modernity and to say: "Ah, that indeed is the unfortunate aspect of the whole affair."

Whereupon the fierce young man had exploded with: "To that, is it, that you Anglicans have come?"

The whole gathering had given itself up to the disputation, Lady Sunderbund, an actress, a dancer—though she, it is true, did not say very much—a novelist, a mechanical expert of some sort, a railway peer, geniuses, hairy and Celtic, people of no clearly definable position, but all quite unequal to the task of maintaining that air of reverent vagueness, that tenderness of touch, which is by all Anglican standards imperative in so deep, so mysterious, and, nowadays, in mixed society at least, so infrequent a discussion.

It was like animals breaking down a fence about some sacred spot. Within a couple of minutes the affair had become highly improper. They had raised their voices, they had spoken with the utmost familiarity of almost unspeakable things. There had been even attempts at epigram. Athanasian epigrams. Bent the novelist had doubted if originally there had been a Third Person in the Trinity at all. He suggested a reaction from a too Manichaean dualism at some date after the time of St. John's Gospel. He maintained obstinately that that Gospel was dualistic.

The unpleasant quality of the talk was far more manifest in the retrospect than it had been at the time. It had seemed then bold and strange, but not impossible; now in the cold darkness it seemed sacrilegious. And the bishop's share, which was indeed only the weak yielding of a tired man to an atmosphere he had misjudged, became a disgraceful display of levity and bad faith. They had baited him. Some one had said that nowadays every one was an Arian, knowingly or unknowingly. They had not concealed their conviction that the bishop did not really believe in the Creeds he uttered.

And that unfortunate first admission stuck terribly in his throat.

Oh! Why had he made it?

III

Sleep had gone.

The awakened sleeper groaned, sat up in the darkness, and felt gropingly in this unaccustomed bed and bedroom first for the edge of the bed and then for the electric light that was possibly on the little bedside table.

The searching hand touched something. A water bottle. The hand resumed its exploration. Here was something metallic and smooth, a stem. Either above or below there must be a switch....

The switch was found, grasped, and turned.

The darkness fled.

In a mirror the sleeper saw the reflection of his face and a corner of the bed in which he lay. The lamp had a tilted shade that threw a slanting bar of shadow across the field of reflection, lighting a right angled triangle very brightly and leaving the rest obscure. The bed was a very great one, a bed for the Anakim. It had a canopy with yellow silk curtains, surmounted by a gilded crown of carved wood. Between the curtains was a man's face, clean shaven, pale, with disordered brown hair and weary, pale blue eyes. He was clad in purple pyjamas, and the hand that now ran its fingers through the brown hair was long and lean and shapely.

Beside the bed was a convenient little table bearing the light, a water bottle and glass, a bunch of keys, a congested pocket book, a gold banded fountain pen, and a gold watch that indicated a quarter past three. On the lower edge of the picture in the mirror appeared the back of a gilt chair, over which a garment of peculiar construction had been carelessly thrown. It was in the form of that sleeveless cassock of purple, opening at the side, whose lower flap is called a bishop's apron; the corner of the frogged coat showed behind the chair back, and the sash lay crumpled on the floor. Black doeskin breeches, still warmly lined with their pants, lay where they had been thrust off at the corner of the bed, partly covering black hose and silver buckled shoes.

For a moment the tired gaze of the man in the bed rested upon these evidences of his episcopal dignity. Then he turned from them to the watch at the bedside.

He groaned helplessly.

IV

These country doctors were no good. There wasn't a physician in the diocese. He must go to London.

He looked into the weary eyes of his reflection and said, as one makes a reassuring promise, "London."

He was being worried. He was being intolerably worried, and he was ill and unable to sustain his positions. This doubt, this sudden discovery of controversial unsoundness, was only one aspect of his general neurasthenia. It had been creeping into his mind since the "Light Unden the Altar" controversy. Now suddenly it had leapt upon him from his own unwary lips.

The immediate trouble arose from his loyalty. He had followed the King's example; he had become a total abstainer and, in addition, on his own account he had ceased to smoke. And his digestion, which Princhester had first made sensitive, was deranged. He was suffering chemically, suffering one of those nameless sequences of maladjustments that still defy our ordinary medical science. It was afflicting him with a general malaise, it was affecting his energy, his temper, all the balance and comfort of his nerves. All day he was weary; all night he was wakeful. He was estranged from his body. He was distressed by a sense of detachment from the things about him, by a curious intimation of unreality in everything he experienced. And with that went this levity of conscience, a heaviness of soul and a levity of conscience, that could make him talk as though the Creeds did not matter—as though nothing mattered....

If only he could smoke!

He was persuaded that a couple of Egyptian cigarettes, or three at the outside, a day, would do wonders in restoring his nervous calm. That, and just a weak whisky and soda at lunch and dinner. Suppose now—!

His conscience, his sense of honour, deserted him. Latterly he had had several of these conscience blanks; it was only when they were over that he realized that they had occurred.

One might smoke up the chimney, he reflected. But he had no cigarettes! Perhaps if he were to slip downstairs....

Why had he given up smoking?

He groaned aloud. He and his reflection eyed one another in mutual despair.

There came before his memory the image of a boy's face, a swarthy little boy, grinning, grinning with a horrible knowingness and pointing his finger—an accusing finger. It had been the most exasperating, humiliating, and shameful incident in the bishop's career. It was the afternoon for his fortnightly address to the Shop girls' Church Association, and he had been seized with a panic fear, entirely irrational and unjustifiable, that he would not be able to deliver the address. The fear had arisen after lunch, had gripped his mind, and then as now had come the thought, "If only I could smoke!" And he had smoked. It seemed better to break a vow than fail the Association. He had fallen to the temptation with a completeness that now filled him with shame and horror. He had stalked Dunk, his valet butler, out of the dining room, had affected to need a book from the book case beyond the sideboard, had gone insincerely to the sideboard humming "From Greenland's icy mountains," and then, glancing over his shoulder, had stolen one of his own cigarettes, one of the fatter sort. With this and his bedroom matches he had gone off to the bottom of the garden among the laurels, looked everywhere except above the wall to be sure that he was alone, and at last lit up, only as he raised his eyes in gratitude for the first blissful inhalation to discover that dreadful little boy peeping at him from the crotch in the yew tree in the next garden. As though God had sent him to be a witness!

Their eyes had met. The bishop recalled with an agonized distinctness every moment, every error, of that shameful encounter. He had been too surprised to conceal the state of affairs from the pitiless scrutiny of those youthful eyes. He had instantly made as if to put the cigarette behind his back, and then as frankly dropped it....

His soul would not be more naked at the resurrection. The little boy had stared, realized the state of affairs slowly but surely, pointed his finger....

Never had two human beings understood each other more completely.

A dirty little boy! Capable no doubt of a thousand kindred scoundrelisms.

It seemed ages before the conscience stricken bishop could tear himself from the spot and walk back, with such a pretence of dignity as he could muster, to the house.

And instead of the discourse he had prepared for the Shop girls' Church Association, he had preached on temptation and falling, and how he knew they had all fallen, and how he understood and could sympathize with the bitterness of a secret shame, a moving but unsuitable discourse that had already been subjected to misconstruction and severe reproof in the local press of Princhester.

But the haunting thing in the bishop's memory was the face and gesture of the little boy. That grubby little finger stabbed him to the heart.

"Oh, God!" he groaned. "The meanness of it! How did I bring myself—?"

He turned out the light convulsively, and rolled over in the bed, making a sort of cocoon of himself. He bored his head into the pillow and groaned, and then struggled impatiently to throw the bed clothes off himself. Then he sat up and talked aloud.

"I must go to Brighton Pomfrey," he said. "And get a medical dispensation. If I do not smoke—"

He paused for a long time.

Then his voice sounded again in the darkness, speaking quietly, speaking with a note almost of satisfaction.

"I shall go mad. I must smoke or I shall go mad."

For a long time he sat up in the great bed with his arms about his knees.

V

Fearful things came to him; things at once dreadfully blasphemous and entirely weak minded.

The triangle and the eye became almost visible upon the black background of night. They were very angry. They were spinning round and round faster and faster. Because he was a bishop and because really he did not believe fully and completely in the Trinity. At one and the same time he did not believe in the Trinity and was terrified by the anger of the Trinity at his unbelief.... He was afraid. He was aghast.... And oh! he was weary....

He rubbed his eyes.

"If I could have a cup of tea!" he said.

Then he perceived with surprise that he had not thought of praying. What should he say? To what could he pray?

He tried not to think of that whizzing Triangle, that seemed now to be nailed like a Catherine wheel to the very centre of his forehead, and yet at the same time to be at the apex of the universe. Against that—for protection against that—he was praying. It was by a great effort that at last he pronounced the words:

"Lighten our darkness, we beseech Thee, O Lord ...."

Presently he had turned up his light, and was prowling about the room. The clear inky dinginess that comes before the raw dawn of a spring morning, found his white face at the window, looking out upon the great terrace and the park.

CHAPTER THE SECOND

THE WEAR AND TEAR OF EPISCOPACY

I

It was only in the last few years that the bishop had experienced these nervous and mental crises. He was a belated doubter. Whatever questionings had marked his intellectual adolescence had either been very slight or had been too adequately answered to leave any serious scars upon his convictions.

And even now he felt that he was afflicted physically rather than mentally, that some protective padding of nerve sheath or brain case had worn thin and weak, and left him a prey to strange disturbances, rather than that any new process of thought was eating into his mind. These doubts in his mind were still not really doubts; they were rather alien and, for the first time, uncontrolled movements of his intelligence. He had had a sheltered upbringing; he was the well connected son of a comfortable rectory, the only son and sole survivor of a family of three; he had been carefully instructed and he had been a willing learner; it had been easy and natural to take many things for granted. It had been very easy and pleasant for him to take the world as he found it and God as he found Him. Indeed for all his years up to manhood he had been able to take life exactly as in his infancy he took his carefully warmed and prepared bottle—unquestioningly and beneficially.

And indeed that has been the way with most bishops since bishops began.

It is a busy continuous process that turns boys into bishops, and it will stand few jars or discords. The student of ecclesiastical biography will find that an early vocation has in every age been almost universal among them; few are there among these lives that do not display the incipient bishop from the tenderest years. Bishop How of Wakefield composed hymns before he was eleven, and Archbishop Benson when scarcely older possessed a little oratory in which he conducted services and—a pleasant touch of the more secular boy—which he protected from a too inquisitive sister by means of a booby trap. It is rare that those marked for episcopal dignities go so far into the outer world as Archbishop Lang of York, who began as a barrister. This early predestination has always been the common episcopal experience. Archbishop Benson's early attempts at religious services remind one both of St. Thomas a Becket, the "boy bishop," and those early ceremonies of St. Athanasius which were observed and inquired upon by the good bishop Alexander. (For though still a tender infant, St. Athanasius with perfect correctness and validity was baptizing a number of his innocent playmates, and the bishop who "had paused to contemplate the sports of the child remained to confirm the zeal of the missionary.") And as with the bishop of the past, so with the bishop of the future; the Rev. H. J. Campbell, in his story of his soul's pilgrimage, has given us a pleasant picture of himself as a child stealing out into the woods to build himself a little altar.

Such minds as these, settled as it were from the outset, are either incapable of real scepticism or become sceptical only after catastrophic changes. They understand the sceptical mind with difficulty, and their beliefs are regarded by the sceptical mind with incredulity. They have determined their forms of belief before their years of discretion, and once those forms are determined they are not very easily changed. Within the shell it has adopted the intelligence may be active and lively enough, may indeed be extraordinarily active and lively, but only within the shell.

There is an entire difference in the mental quality of those who are converts to a faith and those who are brought up in it. The former know it from outside as well as from within. They know not only that it is, but also that it is not. The latter have a confidence in their creed that is one with their apprehension of sky or air or gravitation. It is a primary mental structure, and they not only do not doubt but they doubt the good faith of those who do. They think that the Atheist and Agnostic really believe but are impelled by a mysterious obstinacy to deny. So it had been with the Bishop of Princhester; not of cunning or design but in simple good faith he had accepted all the inherited assurances of his native rectory, and held by Church, Crown, Empire, decorum, respectability, solvency—and compulsory Greek at the Little Go—as his father had done before him. If in his undergraduate days he had said a thing or two in the modern vein, affected the socialism of William Morris and learnt some Swinburne by heart, it was out of a conscious wildness. He did not wish to be a prig. He had taken a far more genuine interest in the artistry of ritual.

Through all the time of his incumbency of the church of the Holy Innocents, St. John's Wood, and of his career as the bishop suffragan of Pinner, he had never faltered from his profound confidence in those standards of his home. He had been kind, popular, and endlessly active. His undergraduate socialism had expanded simply and sincerely into a theory of administrative philanthropy. He knew the Webbs. He was as successful with working class audiences as with fashionable congregations. His home life with Lady Ella (she was the daughter of the fifth Earl of Birkenholme) and his five little girls was simple, beautiful, and happy as few homes are in these days of confusion. Until he became Bishop of Princhester—he followed Hood, the first bishop, as the reign of his Majesty King Edward the Peacemaker drew to its close—no anticipation of his coming distress fell across his path.

II

He came to Princhester an innocent and trustful man. The home life at the old rectory of Otteringham was still his standard of truth and reality. London had not disillusioned him. It was a strange waste of people, it made him feel like a missionary in infidel parts, but it was a kindly waste. It was neither antagonistic nor malicious. He had always felt there that if he searched his Londoner to the bottom, he would find the completest recognition of the old rectory and all its data and implications.

But Princhester was different.

Princhester made one think that recently there had been a second and much more serious Fall.

Princhester was industrial and unashamed. It was a countryside savagely invaded by forges and mine shafts and gaunt black things. It was scarred and impeded and discoloured. Even before that invasion, when the heather was not in flower it must have been a black country. Its people were dour uncandid individuals, who slanted their heads and knitted their brows to look at you. Occasionally one saw woods brown and blistered by the gases from chemical works. Here and there remained old rectories, closely reminiscent of the dear old home at Otteringham, jostled and elbowed and overshadowed by horrible iron cylinders belching smoke and flame. The fine old abbey church of Princhester, which was the cathedral of the new diocese, looked when first he saw it like a lady Abbess who had taken to drink and slept in a coal truck. She minced apologetically upon the market place; the parvenu Town Hall patronized and protected her as if she were a poor relation....

The old aristocracy of the countryside was unpicturesquely decayed. The branch of the Walshinghams, Lady Ella's cousins, who lived near Pringle, was poor, proud and ignoble. And extremely unpopular. The rich people of the country were self made and inclined to nonconformity, the working people were not strictly speaking a "poor," they were highly paid, badly housed, and deeply resentful. They went in vast droves to football matches, and did not care a rap if it rained. The prevailing wind was sarcastic. To come here from London was to come from atmospheric blue greys to ashen greys, from smoke and soft smut to grime and black grimness.

The bishop had been charmed by the historical associations of Princhester when first the see was put before his mind. His realization of his diocese was a profound shock.

Only one hint had he had of what was coming. He had met during his season of congratulations Lord Gatling dining unusually at the Athenaeum. Lord Gatling and he did not talk frequently, but on this occasion the great racing peer came over to him. "You will feel like a cherub in a stokehole," Lord Gatling had said....

"They used to heave lumps of slag at old Hood's gaiters," said Lord Gatling.

"In London a bishop's a lord and a lark and nobody minds him," said Lord Gatling, "but Princhester is different. It isn't used to bishops.... Well,—I hope you'll get to like 'em."

III

Trouble began with a fearful row about the position of the bishop's palace. Hood had always evaded this question, and a number of strong willed self made men of wealth and influence, full of local patriotism and that competitive spirit which has made England what it is, already intensely irritated by Hood's prevarications, were resolved to pin his successor to an immediate decision. Of this the new bishop was unaware. Mindful of a bishop's constant need to travel, he was disposed to seek a home within easy reach of Pringle Junction, from which nearly every point in the diocese could be simply and easily reached. This fell in with Lady Ella's liking for the rare rural quiet of the Kibe valley and the neighbourhood of her cousins the Walshinghams. Unhappily it did not fall in with the inflexible resolution of each and every one of the six leading towns of the see to put up, own, obtrude, boast, and swagger about the biggest and showiest thing in episcopal palaces in all industrial England, and the new bishop had already taken a short lease and gone some way towards the acquisition of Ganford House, two miles from Pringle, before he realized the strength and fury of these local ambitions.

At first the magnates and influences seemed to be fighting only among themselves, and he was so ill advised as to broach the Ganford House project as a compromise that would glorify no one unfairly, and leave the erection of an episcopal palace for some future date when he perhaps would have the good fortune to have passed to "where beyond these voices there is peace," forgetting altogether among other oversights the importance of architects and builders in local affairs. His proposal seemed for a time to concentrate the rich passions of the whole countryside upon himself and his wife.

Because they did not leave Lady Ella alone. The Walshinghams were already unpopular in their county on account of a poverty and shyness that made them seem "stuck up" to successful captains of industry only too ready with the hand of friendship, the iron grip indeed of friendship, consciously hospitable and eager for admission and endorsements. And Princhester in particular was under the sway of that enterprising weekly, The White Blackbird, which was illustrated by, which indeed monopolized the gifts of, that brilliant young caricaturist "The Snicker."

It had seemed natural for Lady Ella to acquiesce in the proposals of the leading Princhester photographer. She had always helped where she could in her husband's public work, and she had been popular upon her own merits in Wealdstone. The portrait was abominable enough in itself; it dwelt on her chin, doubled her age, and denied her gentleness, but it was a mere starting point for the subtle extravagance of The Snicker's poisonous gift.... The thing came upon the bishop suddenly from the book stall at Pringle Junction.

He kept it carefully from Lady Ella.... It was only later that he found that a copy of The White Blackbird had been sent to her, and that she was keeping the horror from him. It was in her vein that she should reproach herself for being a vulnerable side to him.

Even when the bishop capitulated in favour of Princhester, that decision only opened a fresh trouble for him. Princhester wanted the palace to be a palace; it wanted to combine all the best points of Lambeth and Fulham with the marble splendours of a good modern bank. The bishop's architectural tastes, on the other hand, were rationalistic. He was all for building a useful palace in undertones, with a green slate roof and long horizontal lines. What he wanted more than anything else was a quite remote wing with a lot of bright little bedrooms and a sitting room and so on, complete in itself, examination hall and everything, with a long intricate connecting passage and several doors, to prevent the ordination candidates straying all over the place and getting into the talk and the tea. But the diocese wanted a proud archway—and turrets, and did not care a rap if the ordination candidates slept about on the carpets in the bishop's bedroom. Ordination candidates were quite outside the sphere of its imagination.

And he disappointed Princhester with his equipage. Princhester had a feeling that it deserved more for coming over to the church from nonconformity as it was doing. It wanted a bishop in a mitre and a gilt coach. It wanted a pastoral crook. It wanted something to go with its mace and its mayor. And (obsessed by The Snicker) it wanted less of Lady Ella. The cruelty and unreason of these attacks upon his wife distressed the bishop beyond measure, and baffled him hopelessly. He could not see any means of checking them nor of defending or justifying her against them.

The palace was awaiting its tenant, but the controversies and bitternesses were still swinging and swaying and developing when King George was being crowned. Close upon that event came a wave of social discontent, the great railway strike, a curious sense of social and political instability, and the first beginnings of the bishop's ill health.

IV

There came a day of exceptional fatigue and significance.

The industrial trouble was a very real distress to the bishop. He had a firm belief that it is a function of the church to act as mediator between employer and employed. It was a common saying of his that the aim of socialism—the right sort of socialism—was to Christianize employment. Regardless of suspicion on either hand, regardless of very distinct hints that he should "mind his own business," he exerted himself in a search for methods of reconciliation. He sought out every one who seemed likely to be influential on either side, and did his utmost to discover the conditions of a settlement. As far as possible and with the help of a not very efficient chaplain he tried to combine such interviews with his more normal visiting.

At times, and this was particularly the case on this day, he seemed to be discovering nothing but the incurable perversity and militancy of human nature. It was a day under an east wind, when a steely blue sky full of colourless light filled a stiff necked world with whitish high lights and inky shadows. These bright harsh days of barometric high pressure in England rouse and thwart every expectation of the happiness of spring. And as the bishop drove through the afternoon in a hired fly along a rutted road of slag between fields that were bitterly wired against the Sunday trespasser, he fell into a despondent meditation upon the political and social outlook.

His thoughts were of a sort not uncommon in those days. The world was strangely restless. Since the passing of Victoria the Great there had been an accumulating uneasiness in the national life. It was as if some compact and dignified paper weight had been lifted from people's ideas, and as if at once they had begun to blow about anyhow. Not that Queen Victoria had really been a paper weight or any weight at all, but it happened that she died as an epoch closed, an epoch of tremendous stabilities. Her son, already elderly, had followed as the selvedge follows the piece, he had passed and left the new age stripped bare. In nearly every department of economic and social life now there was upheaval, and it was an upheaval very different in character from the radicalism and liberalism of the Victorian days. There were not only doubt and denial, but now there were also impatience and unreason. People argued less and acted quicker. There was a pride in rebellion for its own sake, an indiscipline and disposition to sporadic violence that made it extremely hard to negotiate any reconciliations or compromises. Behind every extremist it seemed stood a further extremist prepared to go one better....

The bishop had spent most of the morning with one of the big employers, a tall dark man, lean and nervous, and obviously tired and worried by the struggle. He did not conceal his opinion that the church was meddling with matters quite outside its sphere. Never had it been conveyed to the bishop before how remote a rich and established Englishman could consider the church from reality.

"You've got no hold on them," he said. "It isn't your sphere."

And again: "They'll listen to you—if you speak well. But they don't believe you know anything about it, and they don't trust your good intentions. They won't mind a bit what you say unless you drop something they can use against us."

The bishop tried a few phrases. He thought there might be something in co operation, in profit sharing, in some more permanent relationship between the business and the employee.

"There isn't," said the employer compactly. "It's just the malice of being inferior against the man in control. It's just the spirit of insubordination and boredom with duty. This trouble's as old as the Devil."

"But that is exactly the business of the church," said the bishop brightly, "to reconcile men to their duty."

"By chanting the Athanasian creed at 'em, I suppose," said the big employer, betraying the sneer he had been hiding hitherto.

"This thing is a fight," said the big employer, carrying on before the bishop could reply. "Religion had better get out of the streets until this thing is over. The men won't listen to reason. They don't mean to. They're bit by Syndicalism. They're setting out, I tell you, to be unreasonable and impossible. It isn't an argument; it's a fight. They don't want to make friends with the employer. They want to make an end to the employer. Whatever we give them they'll take and press us for more. Directly we make terms with the leaders the men go behind it.... It's a raid on the whole system. They don't mean to work the system—anyhow. I'm the capitalist, and the capitalist has to go. I'm to be bundled out of my works, and some—some "—he seemed to be rejecting unsuitable words—"confounded politician put in. Much good it would do them. But before that happens I'm going to fight. You would."

The bishop walked to the window and stood staring at the brilliant spring bulbs in the big employer's garden, and at a long vista of newly mown lawn under great shapely trees just budding into green.

"I can't admit," he said, "that these troubles lie outside the sphere of the church."

The employer came and stood beside him. He felt he was being a little hard on the bishop, but he could not see any way of making things easier.

"One doesn't want Sacred Things," he tried, "in a scrap like this.

"We've got to mend things or end things," continued the big employer. "Nothing goes on for ever. Things can't last as they are going on now...."

Then he went on abruptly to something that for a time he had been keeping back.

"Of course just at present the church may do a confounded lot of harm. Some of you clerical gentlemen are rather too fond of talking socialism and even preaching socialism. Don't think I want to be overcritical. I admit there's no end of things to be said for a proper sort of socialism, Ruskin, and all that. We're all Socialists nowadays. Ideals—excellent. But—it gets misunderstood. It gives the men a sense of moral support. It makes them fancy that they are It. Encourages them to forget duties and set up preposterous claims. Class war and all that sort of thing. You gentlemen of the clergy don't quite realize that socialism may begin with Ruskin and end with Karl Marx. And that from the Class War to the Commune is just one step."

V

From this conversation the bishop had made his way to the vicarage of Mogham Banks. The vicar of Mogham Banks was a sacerdotal socialist of the most advanced type, with the reputation of being closely in touch with the labour extremists. He was a man addicted to banners, prohibited ornaments, special services at unusual hours, and processions in the streets. His taste in chasubles was loud, he gardened in a cassock and, it was said, he slept in his biretta; he certainly slept in a hair shirt, and he littered his church with flowers, candles, side altars, confessional boxes, requests for prayers for the departed, and the like. There had already been two Kensitite demonstrations at his services, and altogether he was a source of considerable anxiety to the bishop. The bishop did his best not to know too exactly what was going on at Mogham Banks. Sooner or later he felt he would be forced to do something—and the longer he could put that off the better. But the Rev. Morrice Deans had promised to get together three or four prominent labour leaders for tea and a frank talk, and the opportunity was one not to be missed. So the bishop, after a hasty and not too digestible lunch in the refreshment room at Pringle, was now in a fly that smelt of straw and suggested infectious hospital patients, on his way through the industry scarred countryside to this second conversation.

The countryside had never seemed so scarred to him as it did that day.

It was probably the bright hard spring sunshine that emphasized the contrast between that dear England of hedges and homes and the south west wind in which his imagination lived, and the crude presences of a mechanical age. Never before had the cuttings and heapings, the smashing down of trees, the obtrusion of corrugated iron and tar, the belchings of smoke and the haste, seemed so harsh and disregardful of all the bishop's world. Across the fields a line of gaunt iron standards, abominably designed, carried an electric cable to some unknown end. The curve of the hill made them seem a little out of the straight, as if they hurried and bent forward furtively.

"Where are they going?" asked the bishop, leaning forward to look out of the window of the fly, and then: "Where is it all going?"

And presently the road was under repair, and was being done at a great pace with a huge steam roller, mechanically smashed granite, and kettles of stinking stuff, asphalt or something of that sort, that looked and smelt like Milton's hell. Beyond, a gaunt hoarding advertised extensively the Princhester Music Hall, a mean beastly place that corrupted boys and girls; and also it clamoured of tyres and potted meats....

The afternoon's conference gave him no reassuring answer to his question, "Where is it all going?"

The afternoon's conference did no more than intensify the new and strange sense of alienation from the world that the morning's talk had evoked.

The three labour extremists that Morrice Deans had assembled obviously liked the bishop and found him picturesque, and were not above a certain snobbish gratification at the purple trimmed company they were in, but it was clear that they regarded his intervention in the great dispute as if it were a feeble waving from the bank across the waters of a great river.

"There's an incurable misunderstanding between the modern employer and the modern employed," the chief labour spokesman said, speaking in a broad accent that completely hid from him and the bishop and every one the fact that he was by far the best read man of the party. "Disraeli called them the Two Nations, but that was long ago. Now it's a case of two species. Machinery has made them into different species. The employer lives away from his work people, marries a wife foreign, out of a county family or suchlike, trains his children from their very birth in a different manner. Why, the growth curve is different for the two species. They haven't even a common speech between them. One looks east and the other looks west. How can you expect them to agree? Of course they won't agree. We've got to fight it out. They say we're their slaves for ever. Have you ever read Lady Bell's 'At the Works'? A well intentioned woman, but she gives the whole thing away. We say, No! It's our sort and not your sort. We'll do without you. We'll get a little more education and then we'll do without you. We're pressing for all we can get, and when we've got that we'll take breath and press for more. We're the Morlocks. Coming up. It isn't our fault that we've differentiated."

"But you haven't understood the drift of Christianity," said the bishop. "It's just to assert that men are One community and not two."

"There's not much of that in the Creeds," said a second labour leader who was a rationalist. "There's not much of that in the services of the church."

The vicar spoke before his bishop, and indeed he had plenty of time to speak before his bishop. "Because you will not set yourselves to understand the symbolism of her ritual," he said.

"If the church chooses to speak in riddles," said the rationalist.

"Symbols," said Morrice Deans, "need not be riddles," and for a time the talk eddied about this minor issue and the chief labour spokesman and the bishop looked at one another. The vicar instanced and explained certain apparently insignificant observances, his antagonist was contemptuously polite to these explanations. "That's all very pratty," he said....

The bishop wished that fine points of ceremonial might have been left out of the discussion.

Something much bigger than that was laying hold of his intelligence, the realization of a world extravagantly out of hand. The sky, the wind, the telegraph poles, had been jabbing in the harsh lesson of these men's voices, that the church, as people say, "wasn't in it." And that at the same time the church held the one remedy for all this ugliness and contention in its teaching of the universal fatherhood of God and the universal brotherhood of men. Only for some reason he hadn't the phrases and he hadn't the voice to assert this over their wrangling and their stiff resolution. He wanted to think the whole business out thoroughly, for the moment he had nothing to say, and there was the labour leader opposite waiting smilingly to hear what he had to say so soon as the bout between the vicar and the rationalist was over.

VI

That morning in the long galleries of the bishop's imagination a fresh painting had been added. It was a big wall painting rather in the manner of Puvis de Chavannes. And the central figure had been the bishop of Princhester himself. He had been standing upon the steps of the great door of the cathedral that looks upon the marketplace where the tram lines meet, and he had been dressed very magnificently and rather after the older use. He had been wearing a tunicle and dalmatic under a chasuble, a pectoral cross, purple gloves, sandals and buskins, a mitre and his presentation ring. In his hand he had borne his pastoral staff. And the clustering pillars and arches of the great doorway were painted with a loving flat particularity that omitted nothing but the sooty tinge of the later discolourations.

On his right hand had stood a group of employers very richly dressed in the fashion of the fifteenth century, and on the left a rather more numerous group of less decorative artisans. With them their wives and children had been shown, all greatly impressed by the canonicals. Every one had been extremely respectful.

He had been reconciling the people and blessing them and calling them his "sheep" and his "little children."

But all this was so different.

Neither party resembled sheep or little children in the least degree. .

The labour leader became impatient with the ritualistic controversy; he set his tea cup aside out of danger and leant across the corner of the table to the bishop and spoke in a sawing undertone. "You see," he said, "the church does not talk our language. I doubt if it understands our language. I doubt if we understand clearly where we are ourselves. These things have to be fought out and hammered out. It's a big dusty dirty noisy job. It may be a bloody job before it's through. You can't suddenly call a halt in the middle of the scrap and have a sort of millennium just because you want it....

"Of course if the church had a plan," he said, "if it had a proposal to make, if it had anything more than a few pious palliatives to suggest, that might be different. But has it?"

The bishop had a bankrupt feeling. On the spur of the moment he could say no more than: "It offers its mediation."

VII

Full as he was with the preoccupation of these things and so a little slow and inattentive in his movements, the bishop had his usual luck at Pringle Junction and just missed the 7.27 for Princhester. He might perhaps have got it by running through the subway and pushing past people, but bishops must not run through subways and push past people. His mind swore at the mischance, even if his lips refrained.

He was hungry and, tired; he would not get to the palace now until long after nine; dinner would be over and Lady Ella would naturally suppose he had dined early with the Rev. Morrice Deans. Very probably there would be nothing ready for him at all.

He tried to think he was exercising self control, but indeed all his sub conscious self was busy in a manner that would not have disgraced Tertullian with the eternal welfare of those city fathers whose obstinacy had fixed the palace at Princhester. He walked up and down the platform, gripping his hands very tightly behind him, and maintaining a serene upcast countenance by a steadfast effort. It seemed a small matter to him that the placards of the local evening papers should proclaim "Lloyd George's Reconciliation Meeting at Wombash Broken up by Suffragettes." For a year now he had observed a strict rule against buying the products of the local press, and he saw no reason for varying this protective regulation.

His mind was full of angry helplessness.

Was he to blame, was the church to blame, for its powerlessness in these social disputes? Could an abler man with a readier eloquence have done more?

He envied the cleverness of Cardinal Manning. Manning would have got right into the front of this affair. He would have accumulated credit for his church and himself....

But would he have done much?...

The bishop wandered along the platform to its end, and stood contemplating the convergent ways that gather together beyond the station and plunge into the hillside and the wilderness of sidings and trucks, signal boxes, huts, coal pits, electric standards, goods sheds, turntables, and engine houses, that ends in a bluish bricked up cliff against the hill. A train rushed with a roar and clatter into the throat of the great tunnel and was immediately silenced; its rear lights twinkled and vanished, and then out of that huge black throat came wisps of white steam and curled slowly upward like lazy snakes until they caught the slanting sunshine. For the first time the day betrayed a softness and touched this scene of black energy to gold. All late afternoons are beautiful, whatever the day has been—if only there is a gleam of sun. And now a kind of mechanical greatness took the place of mere black disorder in the bishop's perception of his see. It was harsh, it was vast and strong, it was no lamb he had to rule but a dragon. Would it ever be given to him to overcome his dragon, to lead it home, and bless it?

He stood at the very end of the platform, with his gaitered legs wide apart and his hands folded behind him, staring beyond all visible things.

Should he do something very bold and striking? Should he invite both men and masters to the cathedral, and preach tremendous sermons to them upon these living issues?

Short sermons, of course.

But stating the church's attitude with a new and convincing vigour.

He had a vision of the great aisle strangely full and alive and astir. The organ notes still echoed in the fretted vaulting, as the preacher made his way from the chancel to the pulpit. The congregation was tense with expectation, and for some reason his mind dwelt for a long time upon the figure of the preacher ascending the steps of the pulpit. Outside the day was dark and stormy, so that the stained glass windows looked absolutely dead. For a little while the preacher prayed. Then in the attentive silence the tenor of the preacher would begin, a thin jet of sound, a ray of light in the darkness, speaking to all these men as they had never been spoken to before....

Surely so one might call a halt to all these harsh conflicts. So one might lay hands afresh upon these stubborn minds, one might win them round to look at Christ the Master and Servant....

That, he thought, would be a good phrase: "Christ the Master and Servant."....

"Members of one Body," that should be his text.... At last it was finished. The big congregation, which had kept so still, sighed and stirred. The task of reconciliation was as good as done. "And now to God the Father, God the Son, and God the Holy Ghost...."

Outside the day had become suddenly bright, the threatening storm had drifted away, and great shafts of coloured light from the pictured windows were smiting like arrows amidst his hearers....

This idea of a great sermon upon capital and labour did so powerfully grip the bishop's imagination that he came near to losing the 8.27 train also.

He discovered it when it was already in the station. He had to walk down the platform very quickly. He did not run, but his gaiters, he felt, twinkled more than a bishop's should.

VIII

Directly he met his wife he realized that he had to hear something important and unpleasant.

She stood waiting for him in the inner hall, looking very grave and still. The light fell upon her pale face and her dark hair and her long white silken dress, making her seem more delicate and unworldly than usual and making the bishop feel grimy and sordid.

"I must have a wash," he said, though before he had thought of nothing but food. "I have had nothing to eat since tea time—and that was mostly talk."

Lady Ella considered. "There are cold things.... You shall have a tray in the study. Not in the dining room. Eleanor is there. I want to tell you something. But go upstairs first and wash your poor tired face."

"Nothing serious, I hope?" he asked, struck by an unusual quality in her voice.

"I will tell you," she evaded, and after a moment of mutual scrutiny he went past her upstairs.

Since they had come to Princhester Lady Ella had changed very markedly. She seemed to her husband to have gained in dignity; she was stiller and more restrained; a certain faint arrogance, a touch of the "ruling class" manner had dwindled almost to the vanishing point. There had been a time when she had inclined to an authoritative hauteur, when she had seemed likely to develop into one of those aggressive and interfering old ladies who play so overwhelming a part in British public affairs. She had been known to initiate adverse judgments, to exercise the snub, to cut and humiliate. Princhester had done much to purge her of such tendencies. Princhester had made her think abundantly, and had put a new and subtler quality into her beauty. It had taken away the least little disposition to rustle as she moved, and it had softened her voice.

Now, when presently she stood in the study, she showed a new circumspection in her treatment of her husband. She surveyed the tray before him.

"You ought not to drink that Burgundy," she said. "I can see you are dog tired. It was uncorked yesterday, and anyhow it is not very digestible. This cold meat is bad enough. You ought to have one of those quarter bottles of champagne you got for my last convalescence. There's more than a dozen left over."

The bishop felt that this was a pretty return of his own kindly thoughts "after many days," and soon Dunk, his valet butler, was pouring out the precious and refreshing glassful....

"And now, dear?" said the bishop, feeling already much better.

Lady Ella had come round to the marble fireplace. The mantel piece was a handsome work by a Princhester artist in the Gill style—with contemplative ascetics as supporters.

"I am worried about Eleanor," said Lady Ella.

"She is in the dining room now," she said, "having some dinner. She came in about a quarter past eight, half way through dinner."

"Where had she been?" asked the bishop.

"Her dress was torn—in two places. Her wrist had been twisted and a little sprained."

"My dear!"

"Her face—Grubby! And she had been crying."

"But, my dear, what had happened to her? You don't mean—?"

Husband and wife stared at one another aghast. Neither of them said the horrid word that flamed between them.

"Merciful heaven!" said the bishop, and assumed an attitude of despair.

"I didn't know she knew any of them. But it seems it is the second Walshingham girl—Phoebe. It's impossible to trace a girl's thoughts and friends. She persuaded her to go."

"But did she understand?"

"That's the serious thing," said Lady Ella.

She seemed to consider whether he could bear the blow.

"She understands all sorts of things. She argues.... I am quite unable to argue with her."

"About this vote business?"

"About all sorts of things. Things I didn't imagine she had heard of. I knew she had been reading books. But I never imagined that she could have understood...."

The bishop laid down his knife and fork.

"One may read in books, one may even talk of things, without fully understanding," he said.

Lady Ella tried to entertain this comforting thought. "It isn't like that," she said at last. "She talks like a grown up person. This—this escapade is just an accident. But things have gone further than that. She seems to think—that she is not being educated properly here, that she ought to go to a College. As if we were keeping things from her...."

The bishop reconsidered his plate.

"But what things?" he said.

"She says we get all round her," said Lady Ella, and left the implications of that phrase to unfold.

IX

For a time the bishop said very little.

Lady Ella had found it necessary to make her first announcement standing behind him upon the hearthrug, but now she sat upon the arm of the great armchair as close to him as possible, and spoke in a more familiar tone.

The thing, she said, had come to her as a complete surprise. Everything had seemed so safe. Eleanor had been thoughtful, it was true, but it had never occurred to her mother that she had really been thinking—about such things as she had been thinking about. She had ranged in the library, and displayed a disposition to read the weekly papers and the monthly reviews. But never a sign of discontent.

"But I don't understand," said the bishop. "Why is she discontented? What is there that she wants different?"

"Exactly," said Lady Ella.

"She has got this idea that life here is secluded in some way," she expanded. "She used words like 'secluded' and 'artificial' and—what was it?—'cloistered.' And she said—"

Lady Ella paused with an effect of exact retrospection.

"'Out there,' she said, 'things are alive. Real things are happening.' It is almost as if she did not fully believe—"

Lady Ella paused again.

The bishop sat with his arm over the back of his chair, and his face downcast.

"The ferment of youth," he said at last. "The ferment of youth. Who has given her these ideas?"

Lady Ella did not know. She could have thought a school like St. Aubyns would have been safe, but nowadays nothing was safe. It was clear the girls who went there talked as girls a generation ago did not talk. Their people at home encouraged them to talk and profess opinions about everything. It seemed that Phoebe Walshingham and Lady Kitty Kingdom were the leaders in these premature mental excursions. Phoebe aired religious doubts.

"But little Phoebe!" said the bishop.

"Kitty," said Lady Ella, "has written a novel."

"Already!"

"With elopements in it—and all sorts of things. She's had it typed. You'd think Mary Crosshampton would know better than to let her daughter go flourishing the family imagination about in that way."

"Eleanor told you?"

"By way of showing that they think of—things in general."

The bishop reflected. "She wants to go to College."

"They want to go in a set."

"I wonder if college can be much worse than school.... She's eighteen—? But I will talk to her...."

X

All our children are changelings. They are perpetually fresh strangers. Every day they vanish and a new person masquerades as yesterday's child until some unexpected development betrays the cheat.

The bishop had still to learn this perennial newness of the young. He learnt it in half an hour at the end of a fatiguing day.

He went into the dining room. He went in as carelessly as possible and smoking a cigarette. He had an honourable dread of being portentous in his family; almost ostentatiously he laid the bishop aside. Eleanor had finished her meal, and was sitting in the arm chair by the fire with one hand holding her sprained wrist.

"Well," he said, and strolled to the hearthrug. He had had an odd idea that he would find her still dirty, torn, and tearful, as her mother had described her, a little girl in a scrape. But she had changed into her best white evening frock and put up her hair, and became in the firelight more of a lady, a very young lady but still a lady, than she had ever been to him before. She was dark like her mother, but not of the same willowy type; she had more of her father's sturdy build, and she had developed her shoulders at hockey and tennis. The firelight brought out the gracious reposeful lines of a body that ripened in adolescence. And though there was a vibration of resolution in her voice she spoke like one who is under her own control.

"Mother has told you that I have disgraced myself," she began.

"No," said the bishop, weighing it. "No. But you seem to have been indiscreet, little Norah."

"I got excited," she said. "They began turning out the other women—roughly. I was indignant."

"You didn't go to interrupt?" he asked.

She considered. "No," she said. "But I went."

He liked her disposition to get it right. "On that side," he assisted.

"It isn't the same thing as really meaning, Daddy," she said.

"And then things happened?"

"Yes," she said to the fire.

A pause followed. If they had been in a law court, her barrister would have said, "That is my case, my lord." The bishop prepared to open the next stage in the proceedings.

"I think, Norah, you shouldn't have been there at all," he said.

"Mother says that."

"A man in my position is apt to be judged by his family. You commit more than yourself when you commit an indiscretion. Apart from that, it wasn't the place for a girl to be at. You are not a child now. We give you freedom—more freedom than most girls get—because we think you will use it wisely. You knew—enough to know that there was likely to be trouble."

The girl looked into the fire and spoke very carefully. "I don't think that I oughtn't to know the things that are going on."

The bishop studied her face for an instant. It struck him that they had reached something very fundamental as between parent and child. His modernity showed itself in the temperance of his reply.

"Don't you think, my dear, that on the whole your mother and I, who have lived longer and know more, are more likely to know when it is best that you should begin to know—this or that?"

The girl knitted her brows and seemed to be reading her answer out of the depths of the coals. She was on the verge of speaking, altered her mind and tried a different beginning.

"I think that every one must do their thinking—his thinking—for—oneself," she said awkwardly.

"You mean you can't trust—?"

"It isn't trusting. But one knows best for oneself when one is hungry."

"And you find yourself hungry?"

"I want to find out for myself what all this trouble about votes and things means."

"And we starve you—intellectually?"

"You know I don't think that. But you are busy...."

"Aren't you being perhaps a little impatient, Eleanor? After all—you are barely eighteen.... We have given you all sorts of liberties."

Her silence admitted it. "But still," she said after a long pause, "there are other girls, younger than I am, in these things. They talk about—oh, all sorts of things. Freely...."

"You've been awfully good to me," she said irrelevantly. "And of course this meeting was all pure accident."

Father and daughter remained silent for awhile, seeking a better grip.

"What exactly do you want, Eleanor?" he asked.

She looked up at him. "Generally?" she asked.

"Your mother has the impression that you are discontented."

"Discontented is a horrid word."

"Well—unsatisfied."

She remained still for a time. She felt the moment had come to make her demand.

"I would like to go to Newnham or Somerville—and work. I feel—so horribly ignorant. Of all sorts of things. If I were a son I should go—"

"Ye—es," said the bishop and reflected.

He had gone rather far in the direction of the Woman Suffrage people; he had advocated equality of standard in all sorts of matters, and the memory of these utterances hampered him.

"You could read here," he tried.

"If I were a son, you wouldn't say that."

His reply was vague. "But in this home," he said, "we have a certain atmosphere."

He left her to imply her differences in sensibility and response from the hardier male.

Her hesitation marked the full gravity of her reply. "It's just that," she said. "One feels—" She considered it further. "As if we were living in a kind of magic world—not really real. Out there—" she glanced over her shoulder at the drawn blind that hid the night. "One meets with different sorts of minds and different—atmospheres. All this is very beautiful. I've had the most wonderful home. But there's a sort of feeling as though it couldn't really go on, as though all these strikes and doubts and questionings—"

She stopped short at questionings, for the thing was said.

The bishop took her meaning gallantly and honestly.

"The church of Christ, little Norah, is built upon a rock."

She made no answer. She moved her head very slightly so that he could not see her face, and remained sitting rather stiffly and awkwardly with her eyes upon the fire.

Her silence was the third and greatest blow the bishop received that day....

It seemed very long indeed before either of them spoke. At last he said: "We must talk about these things again, Norah, when we are less tired and have more time.... You have been reading books.... When Caxton set up his printing press he thrust a new power between church and disciple and father and child.... And I am tired. We must talk it over a little later."

The girl stood up. She took her father's hands. "Dear, dear Daddy," she said, "I am so sorry to be a bother. I am so sorry I went to that meeting.... You look tired out."

"We must talk—properly," said the bishop, patting one hand, then discovering from her wincing face that it was the sprained one. "Your poor wrist," he said.

"It's so hard to talk, but I want to talk to you, Daddy. It isn't that I have hidden things...."

She kissed him, and the bishop had the odd fancy that she kissed him as though she was sorry for him....

It occurred to him that really there could be no time like the present for discussing these "questionings" of hers, and then his fatigue and shyness had the better of him again.

XI

The papers got hold of Eleanor's share in the suffragette disturbance. The White Blackbird said things about her.

It did not attack her. It did worse. It admired her ...impudently.

It spoke of her once as "Norah," and once as "the Scrope Flapper."

Its headline proclaimed: "Plucky Flappers Hold Up L. G."

CHAPTER THE THIRD

INSOMNIA

I

The night after his conversation with Eleanor was the first night of the bishop's insomnia. It was the definite beginning of a new phase in his life.

Doctors explain to us that the immediate cause of insomnia is always some poisoned or depleted state of the body, and no doubt the fatigues and hasty meals of the day had left the bishop in a state of unprecedented chemical disorder, with his nerves irritated by strange compounds and unsoothed by familiar lubricants. But chemical disorders follow mental disturbances, and the core and essence of his trouble was an intellectual distress. For the first time in his life he was really in doubt, about himself, about his way of living, about all his persuasions. It was a general doubt. It was not a specific suspicion upon this point or that. It was a feeling of detachment and unreality at once extraordinarily vague and extraordinarily oppressive. It was as if he discovered himself flimsy and transparent in a world of minatory solidity and opacity. It was as if he found himself made not of flesh and blood but of tissue paper.

But this intellectual insecurity extended into his physical sensations. It affected his feeling in his skin, as if it were not absolutely his own skin.

And as he lay there, a weak phantom mentally and bodily, an endless succession and recurrence of anxieties for which he could find no reassurance besieged him.

Chief of this was his distress for Eleanor.

She was the central figure in this new sense of illusion in familiar and trusted things. It was not only that the world of his existence which had seemed to be the whole universe had become diaphanous and betrayed vast and uncontrollable realities beyond it, but his daughter had as it were suddenly opened a door in this glassy sphere of insecurity that had been his abiding refuge, a door upon the stormy rebel outer world, and she stood there, young, ignorant, confident, adventurous, ready to step out.

"Could it be possible that she did not believe?"

He saw her very vividly as he had seen her in the dining room, slender and upright, half child, half woman, so fragile and so fearless. And the door she opened thus carelessly gave upon a stormy background like one of the stormy backgrounds that were popular behind portrait Dianas in eighteenth century paintings. Did she believe that all he had taught her, all the life he led was—what was her phrase?—a kind of magic world, not really real?

He groaned and turned over and repeated the words: "A kind of magic world—not really real!"

The wind blew through the door she opened, and scattered everything in the room. And still she held the door open.

He was astonished at himself. He started up in swift indignation. Had he not taught the child? Had he not brought her up in an atmosphere of faith? What right had she to turn upon him in this matter? It was—indeed it was—a sort of insolence, a lack of reverence....

It was strange he had not perceived this at the time.

But indeed at the first mention of "questionings" he ought to have thundered. He saw that quite clearly now. He ought to have cried out and said, "On your knees, my Norah, and ask pardon of God!"

Because after all faith is an emotional thing....

He began to think very rapidly and copiously of things he ought to have said to Eleanor. And now the eloquence of reverie was upon him. In a little time he was also addressing the tea party at Morrice Deans'. Upon them too he ought to have thundered. And he knew now also all that he should have said to the recalcitrant employer. Thunder also. Thunder is surely the privilege of the higher clergy—under Jove.

But why hadn't he thundered?

He gesticulated in the darkness, thrust out a clutching hand.

There are situations that must be gripped—gripped firmly. And without delay. In the middle ages there had been grip enough in a purple glove.

II

From these belated seizures of the day's lost opportunities the bishop passed to such a pessimistic estimate of the church as had never entered his mind before.

It was as if he had fallen suddenly out of a spiritual balloon into a world of bleak realism. He found himself asking unprecedented and devastating questions, questions that implied the most fundamental shiftings of opinion. Why was the church such a failure? Why had it no grip upon either masters or men amidst this vigorous life of modern industrialism, and why had it no grip upon the questioning young? It was a tolerated thing, he felt, just as sometimes he had felt that the Crown was a tolerated thing. He too was a tolerated thing; a curious survival....

This was not as things should be. He struggled to recover a proper attitude. But he remained enormously dissatisfied....

The church was no Levite to pass by on the other side away from the struggles and wrongs of the social conflict. It had no right when the children asked for the bread of life to offer them Gothic stone....

He began to make interminable weak plans for fulfilling his duty to his diocese and his daughter.

What could he do to revivify his clergy? He wished he had more personal magnetism, he wished he had a darker and a larger presence. He wished he had not been saddled with Whippham's rather futile son as his chaplain. He wished he had a dean instead of being his own dean. With an unsympathetic rector. He wished he had it in him to make some resounding appeal. He might of course preach a series of thumping addresses and sermons, rather on the lines of "Fors Clavigera," to masters and men, in the Cathedral. Only it was so difficult to get either masters or men into the Cathedral.

Well, if the people will not come to the bishop the bishop must go out to the people. Should he go outside the Cathedral—to the place where the trains met?

Interweaving with such thoughts the problem of Eleanor rose again into his consciousness.

Weren't there books she ought to read? Weren't there books she ought to be made to read? And books—and friends—that ought to be imperatively forbidden? Imperatively!

But how to define the forbidden?

He began to compose an address on Modern Literature (so called).

It became acrimonious.

Before dawn the birds began to sing.

His mind had seemed to be a little tranquillized, there had been a distinct feeling of subsidence sleepwards, when first one and then another little creature roused itself and the bishop to greet the gathering daylight.

It became a little clamour, a misty sea of sound in which individuality appeared and disappeared. For a time a distant cuckoo was very perceptible, like a landmark looming up over a fog, like the cuckoo in the Pastoral Symphony.

The bishop tried not to heed these sounds, but they were by their very nature insistent sounds. He lay disregarding them acutely.

Presently he pulled the coverlet over his ears.

A little later he sat up in bed.

Again in a slight detail he marked his strange and novel detachment from the world of his upbringing. His hallucination of disillusionment had spread from himself and his church and his faith to the whole animate creation. He knew that these were the voices of "our feathered songsters," that this was "a joyous chorus" greeting the day. He knew that a wakeful bishop ought to bless these happy creatures, and join with them by reciting Ken's morning hymn. He made an effort that was more than half habit, to repeat and he repeated with a scowling face and the voice of a schoolmaster:

"Awake my soul, and with the sun Thy daily stage of duty run...."

He got no further. He stopped short, sat still, thinking what utterly detestable things singing birds were. A. blackbird had gripped his attention. Never had he heard such vain repetitions. He struggled against the dark mood of criticism. "He prayeth best who loveth best—"

No, he did not love the birds. It was useless to pretend. Whatever one may say about other birds a cuckoo is a low detestable cad of a bird.

Then the bishop began to be particularly tormented by a bird that made a short, insistent, wheezing sound at regular intervals of perhaps twenty seconds. If a bird could have whooping cough, that, he thought, was the sort of whoop it would have. But even if it had whooping cough he could not pity it. He hung in its intervals waiting for the return of the wheeze.

And then that blackbird reasserted itself. It had a rich boastful note; it seemed proud of its noisy reiteration of simple self assertion. For some obscure reason the phrase "oleographic sounds" drifted into the bishop's thoughts. This bird produced the peculiar and irrational impression that it had recently made a considerable sum of money by shrewd industrialism. It was, he thought grimly, a genuine Princhester blackbird.

This wickedly uncharitable reference to his diocese ran all unchallenged through the bishop's mind. And others no less wicked followed it.

Once during his summer holidays in Florence he and Lady Ella had subscribed to an association for the protection of song birds. He recalled this now with a mild wonder. It seemed to him that perhaps after all it was as well to let fruit growers and Italians deal with singing birds in their own way. Perhaps after all they had a wisdom....

He passed his hands over his face. The world after all is not made entirely for singing birds; there is such a thing as proportion. Singing birds may become a luxury, an indulgence, an excess.

Did the birds eat the fruit in Paradise?

Perhaps there they worked for some collective musical effect, had some sort of conductor in the place of this—hullabaloo....

He decided to walk about the room for a time and then remake his bed....

The sunrise found the bishop with his head and shoulders out of the window trying to see that blackbird. He just wanted to look at it. He was persuaded it was a quite exceptional blackbird.

Again came that oppressive sense of the futility of the contemporary church, but this time it came in the most grotesque form. For hanging half out of the casement he was suddenly reminded of St. Francis of Assisi, and how at his rebuke the wheeling swallow stilled their cries.

But it was all so different then.

III

It was only after he had passed four similar nights, with intervening days of lassitude and afternoon siestas, that the bishop realized that he was in the grip of insomnia.

He did not go at once to a doctor, but he told his trouble to every one he met and received much tentative advice. He had meant to have his talk with Eleanor on the morning next after their conversation in the dining room, but his bodily and spiritual anaemia prevented him.

The fifth night was the beginning of the Whitsuntide Ember week, and he wore a red cassock and had a distracting and rather interesting day welcoming his ordination candidates. They had a good effect upon him; we spiritualize ourselves when we seek to spiritualize others, and he went to bed in a happier frame of mind than he had done since the day of the shock. He woke in the night, but he woke much more himself than he had been since the trouble began. He repeated that verse of Ken's:

"When in the night I sleepless lie,
My soul with heavenly thoughts supply;
Let no ill dreams disturb my rest,
No powers of darkness me molest."

Almost immediately after these there floated into his mind, as if it were a message, the dear familiar words:

"He giveth his Beloved sleep."

These words irradiated and soothed him quite miraculously, the clouds of doubt seemed to dissolve and vanish and leave him safe and calm under a clear sky; he knew those words were a promise, and very speedily he fell asleep and slept until he was called.

But the next day was a troubled one. Whippham had muddled his timetable and crowded his afternoon; the strike of the transport workers had begun, and the ugly noises they made at the tramway depot, where they were booing some one, penetrated into the palace. He had to snatch a meal between services, and the sense of hurry invaded his afternoon lectures to the candidates. He hated hurry in Ember week. His ideal was one of quiet serenity, of grave things said slowly, of still, kneeling figures, of a sort of dark cool spiritual germination. But what sort of dark cool spiritual germination is possible with an ass like Whippham about?

In the fresh courage of the morning the bishop had arranged for that talk with Eleanor he had already deferred too long, and this had proved less satisfactory than he had intended it to be.

The bishop's experience with the ordination candidates was following the usual course. Before they came there was something bordering upon distaste for the coming invasion; then always there was an effect of surprise at the youth and faith of the neophytes and a real response of the spirit to the occasion. Throughout the first twenty four hours they were all simply neophytes, without individuality to break up their uniformity of self devotion. Then afterwards they began to develop little personal traits, and scarcely ever were these pleasing traits. Always one or two of them would begin haunting the bishop, giving way to an appetite for special words, special recognitions. He knew the expression of that craving on their faces. He knew the way laying movements in room and passage that presently began.

This time in particular there was a freckled underbred young man who handed in what was evidently a carefully prepared memorandum upon what he called "my positions." Apparently he had a muddle of doubts about the early fathers and the dates of the earlier authentic copies of the gospels, things of no conceivable significance.

The bishop glanced through this bale of papers—it had of course no index and no synopsis, and some of the pages were not numbered—handed it over to Whippham, and when he proved, as usual, a broken reed, the bishop had the brilliant idea of referring the young man to Canon Bliss (of Pringle), "who has a special knowledge quite beyond my own in this field."

But he knew from the young man's eye even as he said this that it was not going to put him off for more than a day or so.

The immediate result of glancing over these papers was, however, to enhance in the bishop's mind a growing disposition to minimize the importance of all dated and explicit evidences and arguments for orthodox beliefs, and to resort to vague symbolic and liberal interpretations, and it was in this state that he came to his talk with Eleanor.

He did not give her much time to develop her objections. He met her half way and stated them for her, and overwhelmed her with sympathy and understanding. She had been "too literal." "Too literal" was his keynote. He was a little astonished at the liberality of his own views. He had been getting along now for some years without looking into his own opinions too closely and he was by no means prepared to discover how far he had come to meet his daughter's scepticisms. But he did meet them. He met them so thoroughly that he almost conveyed that hers was a needlessly conservative and oldfashioned attitude.

Occasionally he felt he was being a little evasive, but she did not seem to notice it. As she took his drift, her relief and happiness were manifest. And he had never noticed before how clear and pretty her eyes were; they were the most honest eyes he had ever seen. She looked at him very steadily as he explained, and lit up at his points. She brightened wonderfully as she realized that after all they were not apart, they had not differed; simply they had misunderstood....

And before he knew where he was, and in a mere parenthetical declaration of liberality, he surprised himself by conceding her demand for Newnham even before she had repeated it. It helped his case wonderfully.

"Call in every exterior witness you can. The church will welcome them.... No, I want you to go, my dear...."

But his mind was stirred again to its depths by this discussion. And in particular he was surprised and a little puzzled by this Newnham concession and the necessity of making his new attitude clear to Lady Ella....

It was with a sense of fatality that he found himself awake again that night, like some one lying drowned and still and yet perfectly conscious at the bottom of deep cold water.

He repeated, "He giveth his Beloved sleep," but all the conviction had gone out of the words.

IV

Neither the bishop's insomnia nor his incertitudes about himself and his faith developed in a simple and orderly manner. There were periods of sustained suffering and periods of recovery; it was not for a year or so that he regarded these troubles as more than acute incidental interruptions of his general tranquillity or realized that he was passing into a new phase of life and into a new quality of thought. He told every one of the insomnia and no one of his doubts; these he betrayed only by an increasing tendency towards vagueness, symbolism, poetry and toleration. Eleanor seemed satisfied with his exposition; she did not press for further enlightenment. She continued all her outward conformities except that after a time she ceased to communicate; and in September she went away to Newnham. Her doubts had not visibly affected Clementina or her other sisters, and the bishop made no further attempts to explore the spiritual life of his family below the surface of its formal acquiescence.

As a matter of fact his own spiritual wrestlings were almost exclusively nocturnal. During his spells of insomnia he led a curiously double existence. In the daytime he was largely the self he had always been, able, assured, ecclesiastical, except that he was a little jaded and irritable or sleepy instead of being quick and bright; he believed in God and the church and the Royal Family and himself securely; in the wakeful night time he experienced a different and novel self, a bare minded self, bleakly fearless at its best, shamelessly weak at its worst, critical, sceptical, joyless, anxious. The anxiety was quite the worst element of all. Something sat by his pillow asking grey questions: "What are you doing? Where are you going? Is it really well with the children? Is it really well with the church? Is it really well with the country? Are you indeed doing anything at all? Are you anything more than an actor wearing a costume in an archaic play? The people turn their backs on you."

He would twist over on his pillow. He would whisper hymns and prayers that had the quality of charms.

"He giveth his Beloved sleep"; that answered many times, and many times it failed.

The labour troubles of 1912 eased off as the year wore on, and the bitterness of the local press over the palace abated very considerably. Indeed there was something like a watery gleam of popularity when he brought down his consistent friend, the dear old Princess Christiana of Hoch and Unter, black bonnet, deafness, and all, to open a new wing of the children's hospital. The Princhester conservative paper took the occasion to inform the diocese that he was a fluent German scholar and consequently a persona grata with the royal aunts, and that the Princess Christiana was merely just one of a number of royalties now practically at the beck and call of Princhester. It was not true, but it was very effective locally, and seemed to justify a little the hauteur of which Lady Ella was so unjustly suspected. Yet it involved a possibility of disappointments in the future.

He went to Brighton Pomfrey too upon the score of his general health, and Brighton Pomfrey revised his general regimen, discouraged indiscreet fasting, and suggested a complete abstinence from red wine except white port, if indeed that can be called a red wine, and a moderate use of Egyptian cigarettes.

But 1913 was a strenuous year. The labour troubles revived, the suffragette movement increased greatly in violence and aggressiveness, and there sprang up no less than three ecclesiastical scandals in the diocese. First, the Kensitites set themselves firmly to make presentations and prosecutions against Morrice Deans, who was reserving the sacrament, wearing, they said, "Babylonish garments," going beyond all reason in the matter of infant confession, and generally brightening up Mogham Banks; next, a popular preacher in Wombash, published a book under the exasperating title, "The Light Under the Altar," in which he showed himself as something between an Arian and a Pantheist, and treated the dogma of the Trinity with as little respect as one would show to an intrusive cat; while thirdly, an obscure but overworked missioner of a tin mission church in the new working class district at Pringle, being discovered in some sort of polygamous relationship, had seen fit to publish in pamphlet form a scandalous admission and defence, a pamphlet entitled "Marriage True and False," taking the public needlessly into his completest confidence and quoting the affairs of Abraham and Hosea, reviving many points that are better forgotten about Luther, and appealing also to such uncanonical authorities as Milton, Plato, and John Humphrey Noyes. This abnormal concurrence of indiscipline was extremely unlucky for the bishop. It plunged him into strenuous controversy upon three fronts, so to speak, and involved a great number of personal encounters far too vivid for his mental serenity.

The Pringle polygamist was the most moving as Morrice Deans was the most exacting and troublesome and the Wombash Pantheist the most insidiously destructive figure in these three toilsome disputes. The Pringle man's soul had apparently missed the normal distribution of fig leaves; he was an illiterate, open eyed, hard voiced, freckled, rational minded creature, with large expository hands, who had come by a side way into the church because he was an indefatigable worker, and he insisted upon telling the bishop with an irrepressible candour and completeness just exactly what was the matter with his intimate life. The bishop very earnestly did not want these details, and did his utmost to avoid the controversial questions that the honest man pressed respectfully but obstinately upon him.

"Even St. Paul, my lord, admitted that it is better to marry than burn," said the Pringle misdemeanant, "and here was I, my lord, married and still burning!" and, "I think you would find, my lord, considering all Charlotte's peculiarities, that the situation was really much more trying than the absolute celibacy St. Paul had in view."...

The bishop listened to these arguments as little as possible, and did not answer them at all. But afterwards the offender came and wept and said he was ruined and heartbroken and unfairly treated because he wasn't a gentleman, and that was distressing. It was so exactly true—and so inevitable. He had been deprived, rather on account of his voice and apologetics than of his offence, and public opinion was solidly with the sentence. He made a gallant effort to found what he called a Labour Church in Pringle, and after some financial misunderstandings departed with his unambiguous menage to join the advanced movement on the Clyde.

The Morrice Deans enquiry however demanded an amount of erudition that greatly fatigued the bishop. He had a very fair general knowledge of vestments, but he had never really cared for anything but the poetry of ornaments, and he had to work strenuously to master the legal side of the question. Whippham, his chaplain, was worse than useless as a helper. The bishop wanted to end the matter as quickly, quietly, and favourably to Morrice Deans as possible; he thought Morrice Deans a thoroughly good man in his parish, and he believed that the substitution of a low churchman would mean a very complete collapse of church influence in Mogham Banks, where people were now thoroughly accustomed to a highly ornate service. But Morrice Deans was intractable and his pursuers indefatigable, and on several occasions the bishop sat far into the night devising compromises and equivocations that should make the Kensitites think that Morrice Deans wasn't wearing vestments when he was, and that should make Morrice Deans think he was wearing vestments when he wasn't. And it was Whippham who first suggested green tea as a substitute for coffee, which gave the bishop indigestion, as his stimulant for these nocturnal bouts.

Now green tea is the most lucid of poisons.

And while all this extra activity about Morrice Deans, these vigils and crammings and writings down, were using all and more energy than the bishop could well spare, he was also doing his quiet utmost to keep "The Light under the Altar" ease from coming to a head.

This man he hated.

And he dreaded him as well as hated him. Chasters, the author of "The Light under the Altar," was a man who not only reasoned closely but indelicately. There was a demonstrating, jeering, air about his preaching and writing, and everything he said and did was saturated by the spirit of challenge. He did not so much imitate as exaggerate the style of Matthew Arnold. And whatever was done publicly against him would have to be done very publicly because his book had got him a London reputation.

From the bishop's point of view Chasters was one of nature's ignoblemen. He seemed to have subscribed to the Thirty Nine Articles and passed all the tests and taken all the pledges that stand on the way to ordination, chiefly for the pleasure of attacking them more successfully from the rear; he had been given the living of Wombash by a cousin, and filled it very largely because it was not only more piquant but more remunerative and respectable to be a rationalist lecturer in a surplice. And in a hard kind of ultra Protestant way his social and parochial work was not badly done. But his sermons were terrible. "He takes a text," said one informant, "and he goes on firstly, secondly, thirdly, fourthly, like somebody tearing the petals from a flower. 'Finally,' he says, and throws the bare stalk into the dustbin."

The bishop avoided "The Light under the Altar" for nearly a year. It was only when a second book was announced with the winning title of "The Core of Truth in Christianity" that he perceived he must take action. He sat up late one night with a marked copy, a very indignantly marked copy, of the former work that an elderly colonel, a Wombash parishioner, an orthodox Layman of the most virulent type, had sent him. He perceived that he had to deal with a dialectician of exceptional ability, who had concentrated a quite considerable weight of scholarship upon the task of explaining away every scrap of spiritual significance in the Eucharist. From Chasters the bishop was driven by reference to the works of Legge and Frazer, and for the first time he began to measure the dimensions and power of the modern criticism of church doctrine and observance. Green tea should have lit his way to refutation; instead it lit up the whole inquiry with a light of melancholy confirmation. Neither by night nor by day could the bishop find a proper method of opening a counter attack upon Chasters, who was indisputably an intellectually abler man and a very ruthless beast indeed to assail, and meanwhile the demand that action should be taken increased.

The literature of church history and the controversies arising out of doctrinal development became the employment of the bishop's leisure and a commanding preoccupation. He would have liked to discuss with some one else the network of perplexities in which he was entangling himself, and more particularly with Canon Bliss, but his own positions were becoming so insecure that he feared to betray them by argument. He had grown up with a kind of intellectual modesty. Some things he had never yet talked about; it made his mind blench to think of talking about them. And his great aching gaps of wakefulness began now, thanks to the green tea, to be interspersed with theological dreams and visions of an extravagant vividness. He would see Frazer's sacrificial kings butchered picturesquely and terribly amidst strange and grotesque rituals; he would survey long and elaborate processions and ceremonials in which the most remarkable symbols were borne high in the sight of all men; he would cower before a gigantic and threatening Heaven. These green tea dreams and visions were not so much phases of sleep as an intensification and vivid furnishing forth of insomnia. It added greatly to his disturbance that—exceeding the instructions of Brighton Pomfrey—he had now experimented ignorantly and planlessly with one or two narcotics and sleeping mixtures that friends and acquaintances had mentioned in his hearing. For the first time in his life he became secretive from his wife. He knew he ought not to take these things, he knew they were physically and morally evil, but a tormenting craving drove him to them. Subtly and insensibly his character was being undermined by the growing nervous trouble.

He astonished himself by the cunning and the hypocritical dignity he could display in procuring these drugs. He arranged to have a tea making set in his bedroom, and secretly substituted green tea, for which he developed a powerful craving, in the place of the delicate China tea Lady Ella procured him.

V

These doctrinal and physical anxieties and distresses were at their worst in the spring and early summer of 1914. That was a time of great mental and moral disturbance. There was premonition in the air of those days. It was like the uneasiness sensitive people experience before a thunderstorm. The moral atmosphere was sullen and close. The whole world seemed irritable and mischievous. The suffragettes became extraordinarily malignant; the democratic movement went rotten with sabotage and with a cant of being "rebels"; the reactionary Tories and a crew of noisy old peeresses set themselves to create incurable confusion again in the healing wounds of Ireland, and feuds and frantic folly broke out at every point of the social and political edifice. And then a bomb burst at Sarajevo that silenced all this tumult. The unstable polity of Europe heeled over like a ship that founders.

Through the swiftest, tensest week in history Europe capsized into war.

VI

The first effect of the war upon the mind of the bishop, as upon most imaginative minds, was to steady and exalt it. Trivialities and exasperations seemed swept out of existence. Men lifted up their eyes from disputes that had seemed incurable and wrangling that promised to be interminable, and discovered a plain and tragic issue that involved every one in a common call for devotion. For a great number of men and women who had been born and bred in security, the August and September of 1914 were the supremely heroic period of their lives. Myriads of souls were born again to ideas of service and sacrifice in those tremendous days.

Black and evil thing as the war was, it was at any rate a great thing; it did this much for countless minds that for the first time they realized the epic quality of history and their own relationship to the destinies of the race. The flimsy roof under which we had been living our lives of comedy fell and shattered the floor under our feet; we saw the stars above and the abyss below. We perceived that life was insecure and adventurous, part of one vast adventure in space and time....

Presently the smoke and dust of battle hid the great distances again, but they could not altogether destroy the memories of this revelation.

For the first two months the bishop's attention was so detached from his immediate surroundings and employments, so absorbed by great events, that his history if it were told in detail would differ scarcely at all from the histories of most comparatively unemployed minds during those first dramatic days, the days when the Germans made their great rush upon Paris and it seemed that France was down, France and the whole fabric of liberal civilization. He emerged from these stunning apprehensions after the Battle of the Marne, to find himself busy upon a score of dispersed and disconnected war jobs, and trying to get all the new appearances and forces and urgencies of the war into relations with himself. One thing became very vivid indeed, that he wasn't being used in any real and effective way in the war. There was a mighty going to and fro upon Red Cross work and various war committees, a vast preparation for wounded men and for the succour of dislocated families; a preparation, that proved to be needless, for catastrophic unemployment. The war problem and the puzzle of German psychology ousted for a time all other intellectual interests; like every one else the bishop swam deep in Nietzsche, Bernhardi, Houston Stewart Chamberlain, and the like; he preached several sermons upon German materialism and the astonishing decay of the German character. He also read every newspaper he could lay his hands on—like any secular man. He signed an address to the Russian Orthodox church, beginning "Brethren," and he revised his impressions of the Filioque controversy. The idea of a reunion of the two great state churches of Russia and England had always attracted him. But hitherto it had been a thing quite out of scale, visionary, utopian. Now in this strange time of altered perspectives it seemed the most practicable of suggestions. The mayor and corporation and a detachment of the special reserve in uniform came to a great intercession service, and in the palace there were two conferences of local influential people, people of the most various types, people who had never met tolerantly before, expressing now opinions of unprecedented breadth and liberality.

All this sort of thing was fresh and exciting at first, and then it began to fall into a routine and became habitual, and as it became habitual he found that old sense of detachment and futility was creeping back again. One day he realized that indeed the whole flood and tumult of the war would be going on almost exactly as it was going on now if there had been neither cathedral nor bishop in Princhester. It came to him that if archbishops were rolled into patriarchs and patriarchs into archbishops, it would matter scarcely more in the world process that was afoot than if two men shook hands while their house was afire. At times all of us have inappropriate thoughts. The unfortunate thought that struck the bishop as a bullet might strike a man in an exposed trench, as he was hurrying through the cloisters to a special service and address upon that doubly glorious day in our English history, the day of St. Crispin, was of Diogenes rolling his tub.

It was a poisonous thought.

It arose perhaps out of an article in a weekly paper at which he had glanced after lunch, an article written by one of those sceptical spirits who find all too abundant expression in our periodical literature. The writer boldly charged the "Christian churches" with absolute ineffectiveness. This war, he declared, was above all other wars a war of ideas, of material organization against rational freedom, of violence against law; it was a war more copiously discussed than any war had ever been before, the air was thick with apologetics. And what was the voice of the church amidst these elemental issues? Bishops and divines who were patriots one heard discordantly enough, but where were the bishops and divines who spoke for the Prince of Peace? Where was the blessing of the church, where was the veto of the church? When it came to that one discovered only a broad preoccupied back busied in supplementing the Army Medical Corps with Red Cross activities, good work in its way—except that the canonicals seemed superfluous. Who indeed looked to the church for any voice at all? And so to Diogenes.

The bishop's mind went hunting for an answer to that indictment. And came back and came back to the image of Diogenes.

It was with that image dangling like a barbed arrow from his mind that the bishop went into the pulpit to preach upon St. Crispin's day, and looked down upon a thin and scattered congregation in which the elderly, the childless, and the unoccupied predominated.

That night insomnia resumed its sway.

Of course the church ought to be controlling this great storm, the greatest storm of war that had ever stirred mankind. It ought to be standing fearlessly between the combatants like a figure in a wall painting, with the cross of Christ uplifted and the restored memory of Christendom softening the eyes of the armed nations. "Put down those weapons and listen to me," so the church should speak in irresistible tones, in a voice of silver trumpets.

Instead it kept a long way from the fighting, tucked up its vestments, and was rolling its local tubs quite briskly.

VII

And then came the aggravation of all these distresses by an abrupt abandonment of smoking and alcohol. Alcoholic relaxation, a necessary mitigation of the unreality of peacetime politics, becomes a grave danger in war, and it was with an understandable desire to forward the interests of his realm that the King decided to set his statesmen an example—which unhappily was not very widely followed—by abstaining from alcohol during the continuance of the struggle. It did however swing over the Bishop of Princhester to an immediate and complete abandonment of both drink and tobacco. At that time he was finding comfort for his nerves in Manila cheroots, and a particularly big and heavy type of Egyptian cigarette with a considerable amount of opium, and his disorganized system seized upon this sudden change as a grievance, and set all his jangling being crying aloud for one cigarette—just one cigarette.

The cheroots, it seemed, he could better spare, but a cigarette became his symbol for his lost steadiness and ease.

It brought him low.

The reader has already been told the lamentable incident of the stolen cigarette and the small boy, and how the bishop, tormented by that shameful memory, cried aloud in the night.

The bishop rolled his tub, and is there any tub rolling in the world more busy and exacting than a bishop's? He rolled in it spite of ill health and insomnia, and all the while he was tormented by the enormous background of the world war, by his ineffective realization of vast national needs, by his passionate desire, for himself and his church, not to be ineffective.

The distressful alternation between nights of lucid doubt and days of dull acquiescence was resumed with an intensification of its contrasts. The brief phase of hope that followed the turn of the fighting upon the Maine, the hope that after all the war would end swiftly, dramatically, and justly, and everything be as it had been before—but pleasanter, gave place to a phase that bordered upon despair. The fall of Antwerp and the doubts and uncertainties of the Flanders situation weighed terribly upon the bishop. He was haunted for a time by nightmares of Zeppelins presently raining fire upon London. These visions became Apocalyptic. The Zeppelins came to England with the new year, and with the close of the year came the struggle for Ypres that was so near to being a collapse of the allied defensive. The events of the early spring, the bloody failure of British generalship at Neuve Chapelle, the naval disaster in the Dardanelles, the sinking of the Falaba, the Russian defeat in the Masurian Lakes, all deepened the bishop's impression of the immensity of the nation's difficulties and of his own unhelpfulness. He was ashamed that the church should hold back its curates from enlistment while the French priests were wearing their uniforms in the trenches; the expedition of the Bishop of London to hold open air services at the front seemed merely to accentuate the tub rolling. It was rolling the tub just where it was most in the way.

What was wrong? What was wanting?

The Westminster Gazette, The Spectator, and several other of the most trusted organs of public opinion were intermittently discussing the same question. Their discussions implied at once the extreme need that was felt for religion by all sorts of representative people, and the universal conviction that the church was in some way muddling and masking her revelation. "What is wrong with the Churches?" was, for example, the general heading of The Westminster Gazette's correspondence.

One day the bishop skimmed a brief incisive utterance by Sir Harry Johnston that pierced to the marrow of his own shrinking convictions. Sir Harry is one of those people who seem to write as well as speak in a quick tenor. "Instead of propounding plainly and without the acereted mythology of Asia Minor, Greece and Rome, the pure Gospel of Christ.... they present it overloaded with unbelievable myths (such as, among a thousand others, that Massacre of the Innocents which never took place).... bore their listeners by a Tibetan repetition of creeds that have ceased to be credible.... Mutually contradictory propositions.... Prayers and litanies composed in Byzantine and mediaeval times.... the want of actuality, the curious silliness which has, ever since the destruction of Jerusalem, hung about the exposition of Christianity.... But if the Bishops continue to fuss about the trappings of religion.... the maintenance of codes compiled by people who lived sixteen hundred or two thousand five hundred years ago.... the increasingly educated and practical minded working classes will not come to church, weekday or Sunday."

The bishop held the paper in his hand, and with a mind that he felt to be terribly open, asked himself how true that sharp indictment might be, and, granting its general truth, what was the duty of the church, that is to say of the bishops, for as Cyprian says, ecelesia est in episcopo. We say the creeds; how far may we unsay them?

So far he had taken no open action against Chasters. Suppose now he were to side with Chasters and let the whole diocese, the church of Princhester, drift as far as it chose under his inaction towards an extreme modernism, risking a conflict with, and if necessary fighting, the archbishop.... It was but for a moment that his mind swung to this possibility and then recoiled. The Laymen, that band of bigots, would fight. He could not contemplate litigation and wrangling about the teaching of the church. Besides, what were the "trappings of religion" and what the essentials? What after all was "the pure gospel of Christ" of which this writer wrote so glibly? He put the paper down and took a New Testament from his desk and opened it haphazard. He felt a curious wish that he could read it for the first time. It was over familiar. Everything latterly in his theology and beliefs had become over familiar. It had all become mechanical and dead and unmeaning to his tired mind....

Whippham came with a reminder of more tub rolling, and the bishop's speculations were broken off.

CHAPTER THE FOURTH

THE SYMPATHY OF LADY SUNDERBUND

I

That night when he cried aloud at the memory of his furtive cigarette, the bishop was staying with a rich man named Garstein Fellows. These Garstein Fellows people were steel people with a financial side to them; young Garstein Fellows had his fingers in various chemical businesses, and the real life of the firm was in various minor partners called Hartstein and Blumenhart and so forth, who had acquired a considerable amount of ungentlemanly science and energy in Germany and German Switzerland. But the Fellows element was good old Princhester stuff. There had been a Fellows firm in Princhester in 1819. They were not people the bishop liked and it was not a house the bishop liked staying at, but it had become part of his policy to visit and keep in touch with as many of the local plutocracy as he could, to give and take with them, in order to make the presence of the church a reality to them. It had been not least among the negligences and evasions of the sainted but indolent Hood that he had invariably refused overnight hospitality whenever it was possible for him to get back to his home. The morning was his working time. His books and hymns had profited at the cost of missing many a generous after dinner subscription, and at the expense of social unity. From the outset Scrope had set himself to alter this. A certain lack of enthusiasm on Lady Ella's part had merely provoked him to greater effort on his own. His ideal of what was needed with the people was something rather jolly and familiar, something like a very good and successful French or Irish priest, something that came easily and readily into their homes and laid a friendly hand on their shoulders. The less he liked these rich people naturally the more familiar his resolution to be successfully intimate made him. He put down the names and brief characteristics of their sons and daughters in a little note book and consulted it before every visit so as to get his most casual enquiries right. And he invited himself to the Garstein Fellows house on this occasion by telegram.

"A special mission and some business in Wombash may I have a scrap of supper and a bed?"

Now Mrs. Garstein Fellows was a thoroughly London woman; she was one of the banking Grunenbaums, the fair tall sort, and she had a very decided tendency to smartness. She had a little party in the house, a sort of long week end party, that made her hesitate for a minute or so before she framed a reply to the bishop's request.

It was the intention of Mrs. Garstein Fellows to succeed very conspicuously in the British world, and the British world she felt was a complicated one; it is really not one world but several, and if you would surely succeed you must keep your peace with all the systems and be a source of satisfaction to all of them. So at least Mrs. Garstein Fellows saw it, and her method was to classify her acquaintances according to their systems, to keep them in their proper bundles, and to give every one the treatment he or she was accustomed to receive. And since all things British are now changing and passing away, it may not be uninteresting to record the classification Mrs. Garstein Fellows adopted. First she set apart as most precious and desirable, and requiring the most careful treatment, the "court dowdies "—for so it was that the dignity and quiet good taste that radiated from Buckingham Palace impressed her restless, shallow mind—the sort of people who prefer pair horse carriages to automobiles, have quiet friendships in the highest quarters, quietly do not know any one else, busy themselves with charities, dress richly rather than impressively, and have either little water colour accomplishments or none at all, and no other relations with "art." At the skirts of this crowning British world Mrs. Garstein Fellows tugged industriously and expensively. She did not keep a carriage and pair and an old family coachman because that, she felt, would be considered pushing and presumptuous; she had the sense to stick to her common unpretending 80 h.p. Daimler; but she wore a special sort of blackish hat bonnet for such occasions as brought her near the centre of honour, which she got from a little good shop known only to very few outside the inner ring, which hat bonnet she was always careful to sit on for a few minutes before wearing. And it was to this first and highest and best section of her social scheme that she considered that bishops properly belonged. But some bishops, and in particular such a comparatively bright bishop as the Bishop of Princhester, she also thought of as being just as comfortably accommodated in her second system, the "serious liberal lot," which was more fatiguing and less boring, which talked of books and things, visited the Bells, went to all first nights when Granville Barker was the producer, and knew and valued people in the grey and earnest plains between the Cecils and the Sidney Webbs. And thirdly there were the smart intellectual lot, again not very well marked off, and on the whole practicable to bishops, of whom fewer particulars are needed because theirs is a perennial species, and then finally there was that fourth world which was paradoxically at once very brilliant and a little shady, which had its Night Club side, and seemed to set no limit to its eccentricities. It seemed at times to be aiming to shock and yet it had its standards, but here it was that the dancers and actresses and forgiven divorcees came in—and the bishops as a rule, a rule hitherto always respected, didn't. This was the ultimate world of Mrs. Garstein Fellows; she had no use for merely sporting people and the merely correct smart and the duller county families, sets that led nowhere, and it was from her fourth system of the Glittering Doubtfuls that this party which made her hesitate over the bishop's telegram, was derived.

She ran over their names as she sat considering her reply.

What was there for a bishop to object to? There was that admirable American widow, Lady Sunderbund. She was enormously rich, she was enthusiastic. She was really on probation for higher levels; it was her decolletage delayed her. If only she kept off theosophy and the Keltic renascence and her disposition to profess wild intellectual passions, there would be no harm in her. Provided she didn't come down to dinner in anything too fantastically scanty—but a word in season was possible. No! there was no harm in Lady Sunderbund. Then there were Ridgeway Kelso and this dark excitable Catholic friend of his, Paidraig O'Gorman. Mrs. Garstein Fellows saw no harm in them. Then one had to consider Lord Gatling and Lizzie Barusetter. But nothing showed, nothing was likely to show even if there was anything. And besides, wasn't there a Church and Stage Guild?

Except for those people there seemed little reason for alarm. Mrs. Garstein Fellows did not know that Professor Hoppart, who so amusingly combined a professorship of political economy with the writing of music hall lyrics, was a keen amateur theologian, nor that Bent, the sentimental novelist, had a similar passion. She did not know that her own eldest son, a dark, romantic looking youngster from Eton, had also come to the theological stage of development. She did however weigh the possibilities of too liberal opinions on what are called social questions on the part of Miss Sharsper, the novelist, and decided that if that lady was watched nothing so terrible could be said even in an undertone; and as for the Mariposa, the dancer, she had nothing but Spanish and bad French, she looked all right, and it wasn't very likely she would go out of her way to startle an Anglican bishop. Simply she needn't dance. Besides which even if a man does get a glimpse of a little something—it isn't as if it was a woman.

But of course if the party mustn't annoy the bishop, the bishop must do his duty by the party. There must be the usual purple and the silver buckles.

She wired back:

"A little party but it won't put you out send your man with your change."

II

In making that promise Mrs. Garstein Fellows reckoned without the morbid sensibility of the bishop's disorganized nervous system and the unsuspected theological stirrings beneath the apparent worldliness of Hoppart and Bent.

The trouble began in the drawing room after dinner. Out of deference to the bishop's abstinence the men did not remain to smoke, but came in to find the Mariposa and Lady Sunderbund smoking cigarettes, which these ladies continued to do a little defiantly. They had hoped to finish them before the bishop came up. The night was chilly, and a cheerful wood fire cracking and banging on the fireplace emphasized the ordinary heating. Mrs. Garstein Fellows, who had not expected so prompt an appearance of the men, had arranged her chairs in a semicircle for a little womanly gossip, and before she could intervene she found her party, with the exception of Lord Gatling, who had drifted just a little too noticeably with Miss Barnsetter into a window, sitting round with a conscious air, that was perhaps just a trifle too apparent, of being "good."

And Mr. Bent plunged boldly into general conversation.

"Are you reading anything now, Mrs. Garstein Fellows?" he asked. "I'm an interested party."

She was standing at the side of the fireplace. She bit her lip and looked at the cornice and meditated with a girlish expression. "Yes," she said. "I am reading again. I didn't think I should but I am."

"For a time," said Hoppart, "I read nothing but the papers. I bought from a dozen to twenty a day."

"That is wearing off," said the bishop.

"The first thing I began to read again," said Mrs. Garstein Fellows, "—I'm not saying it for your sake, Bishop—was the Bible."

"I went to the Bible," said Bent as if he was surprised.

"I've heard that before," said Ridgeway Kelso, in that slightly explosive manner of his. "All sorts of people who don't usually read the Bible—"

"But Mr. Kelso!" protested their hostess with raised eyebrows.

"I was thinking of Bent. But anyhow there's been a great wave of seriousness, a sudden turning to religion and religious things. I don't know if it comes your way, Bishop...."

"I've had no rows of penitents yet."

"We may be coming," said Hoppart.

He turned sideways to face the bishop. "I think we should be coming if—if it wasn't for old entangled difficulties. I don't know if you will mind my saying it to you, but...."

The bishop returned his frank glance. "I'd like to know above all things," he said. "If Mrs. Garstein Fellow will permit us. It's my business to know."

"We all want to know," said Lady Sunderbund, speaking from the low chair on the other side of the fireplace. There was a vibration in her voice and a sudden gleam of enthusiasm in her face. "Why shouldn't people talk se'iously sometimes?"

"Well, take my own case," said Hoppart. "In the last few weeks, I've been reading not only in the Bible but in the Fathers. I've read most of Athanasius, most of Eusebius, and—I'll confess it—Gibbon. I find all my old wonder come back. Why are we pinned to—to the amount of creed we are pinned to? Why for instance must you insist on the Trinity?"

"Yes," said the Eton boy explosively, and flushed darkly to find he had spoken.

"Here is a time when men ask for God," said Hoppart. "And you give them three!" cried Bent rather cheaply. "I confess I find the way encumbered by these Alexandrian elaborations," Hoppart completed.

"Need it be?" whispered Lady Sunderbund very softly.

"Well," said the bishop, and leant back in his armchair and knitted his brow at the fire. "I do not think," he said, "that men coming to God think very much of the nature of God. Nevertheless," he spoke slowly and patted the arm of his chair, "nevertheless the church insists that certain vitally important truths have to be conveyed, certain mortal errors are best guarded against, by these symbols."

"You admit they are symbols."

"So the church has always called them."

Hoppart showed by a little movement and grimace that he thought the bishop quibbled.

"In every sense of the word," the bishop hastened to explain, "the creeds are symbolical. It is clear they seek to express ineffable things by at least an extended use of familiar words. I suppose we are all agreed nowadays that when we speak of the Father and of the Son we mean something only in a very remote and exalted way parallel with—with biological fatherhood and sonship."

Lady Sunderbund nodded eagerly. "Yes," she said, "oh, yes," and held up an expectant face for more.

"Our utmost words, our most elaborately phrased creeds, can at the best be no better than the shadow of something unseen thrown upon the screen of experience."

He raised his rather weary eyes to Hoppart as if he would know what else needed explanation. He was gratified by Lady Sunderbund's approval, but he affected not to see or hear it. But it was Bent who spoke.

He spoke in the most casual way. He made the thing seem the most incidental of observations.

"What puzzles me," he said, "is why the early Christians identified the Spermaticos Logos of the Stoics with the second and not with the third person of the Trinity."

To which the bishop, rising artlessly to the bait, replied, "Ah! that indeed is the unfortunate aspect of the whole affair."

And then the Irish Catholic came down on him....

III

How the bishop awakened in the night after this dispute has been told already in the opening section of this story. To that night of discomfort we now return after this comprehensive digression. He awoke from nightmares of eyes and triangles to bottomless remorse and perplexity. For the first time he fully measured the vast distances he had travelled from the beliefs and attitudes of his early training, since his coming to Princhester. Travelled—or rather slipped and fallen down the long slopes of doubt.

That clear inky dimness that comes before dawn found his white face at the window looking out upon the great terrace and the park.

IV

After a bout of mental distress and sleeplessness the bishop would sometimes wake in the morning not so much exhausted as in a state of thin mental and bodily activity. This was more particularly so if the night had produced anything in the nature of a purpose. So it was on this occasion. The day was clear before him; at least it could be cleared by sending three telegrams; his man could go back to Princhester and so leave him perfectly free to go to Brighton Pomfrey in London and secure that friendly dispensation to smoke again which seemed the only alternative to a serious mental breakdown. He would take his bag, stay the night in London, smoke, sleep well, and return the next morning. Dunk, his valet butler, found him already bathed and ready for a cup of tea and a Bradshaw at half past seven. He went on dressing although the good train for London did not start until 10.45.

Mrs. Garstein Fellows was by nature and principle a late riser; the breakfast room showed small promise yet of the repast, though the table was set and bright with silver and fresh flowers, and a wood fire popped and spurted to greet and encourage the March sunshine. But standing in the doorway that led to the promise and daffodils and crocuses of Mrs. Garstein Fellows' garden stood Lady Sunderbund, almost with an effect of waiting, and she greeted the bishop very cheerfully, doubted the immediate appearance of any one else, and led him in the most natural manner into the new but already very pleasant shrubbery.

In some indefinable special way the bishop had been aware of Lady Sunderbund's presence since first he had met her, but it was only now that he could observe her with any particularity. She was tall like his own Lady Ella but not calm and quiet; she was electric, her eyes, her smiles, her complexion had as it were an established brightness that exceeded the common lustre of things. This morning she was dressed in grey that was nevertheless not grey but had an effect of colour, and there was a thread of black along the lines of her body and a gleam of gold. She carried her head back with less dignity than pride; there was a little frozen movement in her dark hair as if it flamed up out of her head. There were silver ornaments in her hair. She spoke with a pretty little weakness of the r's that had probably been acquired abroad. And she lost no time in telling him, she was eager to tell him, that she had been waylaying him. "I did so want to talk to you some maw," she said. "I was shy last night and they we' all so noisy and eaga'. I p'ayed that you might come down early.

"It's an oppo'tunity I've longed for," she said.

She did her very pretty best to convey what it was had been troubling her. 'iligion bad been worrying her for years. Life was—oh—just ornaments and games and so wea'isome, so wea'isome, unless it was 'iligious. And she couldn't get it 'iligious.

The bishop nodded his head gravely.

"You unde'stand?" she pressed.

"I understand too well—the attempt to get hold—and keep hold."

"I knew you would!" she cried.

She went on with an impulsive rapidity. O'thodoxy had always 'ipelled her,—always. She had felt herself confronted by the most insurmountable difficulties, and yet whenever she had gone away from Christianity—she had gone away from Christianity, to the Theosophists and the Christian Scientists—she had felt she was only "st'aying fu'tha." And then suddenly when he was speaking last night, she had felt he knew. It was so wonderful to hear the "k'eed was only a symbol."

"Symbol is the proper name for it," said the bishop. "It wasn't for centuries it was called the Creed."

Yes, and so what it really meant was something quite different from what it did mean.

The bishop felt that this sentence also was only a symbol, and nodded encouragingly—but gravely, warily.

And there she was, and the point was there were thousands and thousands and thousands of educated people like her who were dying to get through these old fashioned symbols to the true faith that lay behind them. That they knew lay behind them. She didn't know if he had read "The Light under the Altar"?

"He's vicar of Wombash—in my diocese," said the bishop with restraint.

"It's wonde'ful stuff," said Lady Sunderbund. "It's spi'tually cold, but it's intellectually wonde'ful. But we want that with spi'tuality. We want it so badly. If some one—"

She became daring. She bit her under lip and flashed her spirit at him.

"If you—" she said and paused.

"Could think aloud," said the bishop.

"Yes," she said, nodding rapidly, and became breathless to hear.

It would certainly be an astonishing end to the Chasters difficulty if the bishop went over to the heretic, the bishop reflected.

"My dear lady, I won't disguise," he began; "in fact I don't see how I could, that for some years I have been growing more and more discontented with some of our most fundamental formulae. But it's been very largely a shapeless discontent—hitherto. I don't think I've said a word to a single soul. No, not a word. You are the first person to whom I've ever made the admission that even my feelings are at times unorthodox."

She lit up marvellously at his words. "Go on," she whispered.

But she did not need to tell him to go on. Now that he had once broached the casket of his reserves he was only too glad of a listener. He talked as if they were intimate and loving friends, and so it seemed to both of them they were. It was a wonderful release from a long and painful solitude.

To certain types it is never quite clear what has happened to them until they tell it. So that now the bishop, punctuated very prettily by Lady Sunderbund, began to measure for the first time the extent of his departure from the old innate convictions of Otteringham Rectory. He said that it was strange to find doubt coming so late in life, but perhaps it was only in recent years that his faith had been put to any really severe tests. It had been sheltered and unchallenged.

"This fearful wa'," Lady Sunderbund interjected.

But Princhester had been a critical and trying change, and "The Light under the Altar" case had ploughed him deeply. It was curious that his doubts always seemed to have a double strand; there was a moral objection based on the church's practical futility and an intellectual strand subordinated to this which traced that futility largely to its unconvincing formulae.

"And yet you know," said the bishop, "I find I can't go with Chasters. He beats at the church; he treats her as though she were wrong. I feel like a son, growing up, who finds his mother isn't quite so clear spoken nor quite so energetic as she seemed to be once. She's right, I feel sure. I've never doubted her fundamental goodness."

"Yes," said Lady Sunderbund, very eagerly, "yes."

"And yet there's this futility.... You know, my dear lady, I don't know what to do. One feels on the one hand, that here is a cloud of witnesses, great men, sainted men, subtle men, figures permanently historical, before whom one can do nothing but bow down in the utmost humility, here is a great instrument and organization—what would the world be without the witness of the church?—and on the other hand here are our masses out of hand and hostile, our industrial leaders equally hostile; there is a failure to grip, and that failure to grip is so clearly traceable to the fact that our ideas are not modern ideas, that when we come to profess our faith we find nothing in our mouths but antiquated Alexandrian subtleties and phrases and ideas that may have been quite alive, quite significant, quite adequate in Asia Minor or Egypt, among men essentially orientals, fifteen hundred years ago, but which now—"

He expressed just what they came to now by a gesture.

She echoed his gesture.

"Probably I'm not alone among my brethren," he went on, and then: "But what is one to do?"

With her hands she acted her sense of his difficulty.

"One may be precipitate," he said. "There's a kind of loyalty and discipline that requires one to keep the ranks until one's course of action is perfectly clear. One owes so much to so many. One has to consider how one may affect—oh! people one has never seen."

He was lugging things now into speech that so far had been scarcely above the threshold of his conscious thought. He went on to discuss the entire position of the disbelieving cleric. He discovered a fine point.

"If there was something else, an alternative, another religion, another Church, to which one could go, the whole case would be different. But to go from the church to nothingness isn't to go from falsehood to truth. It's to go from truth, rather badly expressed, rather conservatively hidden by its protections, truth in an antiquated costume, to the blackest lie—in the world."

She took that point very brightly.

"One must hold fast to 'iligion," she said, and looked earnestly at him and gripped fiercely, pink thumbs out, with her beautiful hands held up.

That was it, exactly. He too was gripping. But while on the outside the Midianites of denial were prowling for these clinging souls, within the camp they were assailed by a meticulous orthodoxy that was only too eager to cast them forth. The bishop dwelt for a time upon the curious fierceness orthodoxy would sometimes display. Nowadays atheism can be civil, can be generous; it is orthodoxy that trails a scurrilous fringe.

"Who was that young man with a strong Irish accent—who contradicted me so suddenly?" he asked.

"The dark young man?"

"The noisy young man."

"That was Mist' Pat'ick O'Go'man. He is a Kelt and all that. Spells Pat'ick with eva so many letters. You know. They say he spends ouas and ouas lea'ning E'se. He wo'ies about it. They all t'y to lea'n E'se, and it wo'ies them and makes them hate England moa and moa."

"He is orthodox. He—is what I call orthodox to the ridiculous extent."

"'idiculous."

A deep toned gong proclaimed breakfast over a square mile or so of territory, and Lady Sunderbund turned about mechanically towards the house. But they continued their discussion.

She started indeed a new topic. "Shall we eva, do 'ou think, have a new 'iligion—t'ua and betta?"

That was a revolutionary idea to him.

He was still fending it off from him when a gap in the shrubs brought them within sight of the house and of Mrs. Garstein Fellows on the portico waving a handkerchief and crying "Break fast."

"I wish we could talk for houas," said Lady Sunderbund.

"I've been glad of this talk," said the bishop. "Very glad."

She lifted her soft abundant skirts and trotted briskly across the still dewy lawn towards the house door. The bishop followed gravely and slowly with his hands behind his back and an unusually peaceful expression upon his face. He was thinking how rare and precious a thing it is to find intelligent friendship in women. More particularly when they were dazzlingly charming and pretty. It was strange, but this was really his first woman friend. If, as he hoped, she became his friend.

Lady Sunderbund entered the breakfast room in a gusty abundance like Botticelli's Primavera, and kissed Mrs. Garstein Fellows good morning. She exhaled a glowing happiness. "He is wondyful," she panted. "He is most wondyful."

"Mr. Hidgeway Kelso?"

"No, the dee' bishop! I love him. Are those the little sausages I like? May I take th'ee? I've been up houas."

The dee' bishop appeared in the sunlit doorway.

V

The bishop felt more contentment in the London train than he had felt for many weeks. He had taken two decisive and relieving steps. One was that he had stated his case to another human being, and that a very charming and sympathetic human being, he was no longer a prey to a current of secret and concealed thoughts running counter to all the appearances of his outward life; and the other was that he was now within an hour or so of Brighton Pomfrey and a cigarette. He would lunch on the train, get to London about two, take a taxi at once to the wise old doctor, catch him over his coffee in a charitable and understanding mood, and perhaps be smoking a cigarette publicly and honourably and altogether satisfyingly before three.

So far as Brighton Pomfrey's door this program was fulfilled without a hitch. The day was fine and he had his taxi opened, and noted with a patriotic satisfaction as he rattled through the streets, the glare of the recruiting posters on every vacant piece of wall and the increasing number of men in khaki in the streets. But at the door he had a disappointment. Dr. Brighton Pomfrey was away at the front—of all places; he had gone for some weeks; would the bishop like to see Dr. Dale?

The bishop hesitated. He had never set eyes on this Dr. Dale.

Indeed, he had never heard of Dr. Dale.

Seeing his old friend Brighton Pomfrey and being gently and tactfully told to do exactly what he was longing to do was one thing; facing some strange doctor and going slowly and elaborately through the whole story of his illness, his vow and his breakdown, and perhaps having his reaction time tested and all sorts of stripping and soundings done, was quite another. He was within an ace of turning away.

If he had turned away his whole subsequent life would have been different. It was the very slightest thing in the world tipped the beam. It was the thought that, after all, whatever inconvenience and unpleasantness there might be in this interview, there was at the end of it a very reasonable prospect of a restored and legitimate cigarette.

CHAPTER THE FIFTH

THE FIRST VISION

I

Dr. Dale exceeded the bishop's worst apprehensions. He was a lean, lank, dark young man with long black hair and irregular, rather prolonged features; his chin was right over to the left; he looked constantly at the bishop's face with a distinctly sceptical grey eye; he could not have looked harder if he had been a photographer or a portrait painter. And his voice was harsh, and the bishop was particularly sensitive to voices.

He began by understanding far too much of the bishop's illness, and he insisted on various familiarities with the bishop's heart and tongue and eye and knee that ruffled the bishop's soul.

"Brighton Pomfrey talked of neurasthenia?" he asked. "That was his diagnosis," said the bishop. "Neurasthenia," said the young man as though he despised the word.

The bishop went on buttoning up his coat.

"You don't of course want to break your vows about drinking and smoking," said the young man with the very faintest suggestion of derision in his voice.

"Not if it can possibly be avoided," the bishop asserted. "Without a loss, that is, of practical efficiency," he added. "For I have much to do."

"I think that it is possible to keep your vow," said the young man, and the bishop could have sworn at him. "I think we can manage that all right."

II

The bishop sat at the table resting his arm upon it and awaiting the next development of this unsatisfactory interview. He was on the verge of asking as unpleasantly as possible when Brighton Pomfrey would return.

The young man stood upon Brighton Pomfrey's hearth rug and was evidently contemplating dissertations.

"Of course," he said, as though he discussed a problem with himself, "you must have some sort of comfort. You must get out of this state, one way or another."

The bishop nodded assent. He had faint hopes of this young man's ideas of comfort.

Dr. Dale reflected. Then he went off away from the question of comfort altogether. "You see, the trouble in such a case as this is peculiarly difficult to trace to its sources because it comes just upon the border line of bodily and mental things. You may take a drug or alter your regimen and it disturbs your thoughts, you may take an idea and it disturbs your health. It is easy enough to say, as some do, that all ideas have a physical substratum; it is almost as easy to say with the Christian Scientist that all bodily states are amenable to our ideas. The truth doesn't, I think, follow the border between those opposite opinions very exactly on either side. I can't, for instance, tell you to go home and pray against these uncertainties and despairs, because it is just these uncertainties and despairs that rob you of the power of efficient prayer."

He did not seem to expect anything from the bishop.

"I don't see that because a case brings one suddenly right up against the frontier of metaphysics, why a doctor should necessarily pull up short at that, why one shouldn't go on into either metaphysics or psychology if such an extension is necessary for the understanding of the case. At any rate if you'll permit it in this consultation...."

"Go on," said the bishop, holding on to that promise of comfort. "The best thing is to thrash out the case in your own way. And then come to what is practical."

"What is really the matter here—the matter with you that is—is a disorganization of your tests of reality. It's one of a group of states hitherto confused. Neurasthenia, that comprehensive phrase—well, it is one of the neurasthenias. Here, I confess, I begin to talk of work I am doing, work still to be published, finished first and then published.... But I go off from the idea that every living being lives in a state not differing essentially from a state of hallucination concerning the things about it. Truth, essential truth, is hidden. Always. Of course there must be a measure of truth in our working illusions, a working measure of truth, or the creature would smash itself up and end itself, but beyond that discretion of the fire and the pitfall lies a wide margin of error about which we may be deceived for years. So long as it doesn't matter, it doesn't matter. I don't know if I make myself clear."

"I follow you," said the bishop a little wearily, "I follow you. Phenomena and noumena and so on and so on. Kant and so forth. Pragmatism. Yes."

With a sigh.

"And all that," completed Dr. Dale in a voice that suggested mockery. "But you see we grow into a way of life, we settle down among habits and conventions, we say 'This is all right' and 'That is always so.' We get more and more settled into our life as a whole and more and more confident. Unless something happens to shake us out of our sphere of illusion. That may be some violent contradictory fact, some accident, or it may be some subtle change in one's health and nerves that makes us feel doubtful. Or a change of habits. Or, as I believe, some subtle quickening of the critical faculty. Then suddenly comes the feeling as though we were lost in a strange world, as though we had never really seen the world before."

He paused.

The bishop was reluctantly interested. "That does describe something—of the mental side," he admitted. "I never believe in concealing my own thoughts from an intelligent patient," said Dr. Dale, with a quiet offensiveness. "That sort of thing belongs to the dark ages of the 'pothecary's art. I will tell you exactly my guesses and suppositions about you. At the base of it all is a slight and subtle kidney trouble, due I suggest to your going to Princhester and drinking the local water—"

"But it's excellent water. They boast of it."

"By all the established tests. As a matter of fact many of our best drinking waters have all sorts of unspecified qualities. Burton water, for example, is radioactive by Beetham's standards up to the ninth degree. But that is by the way. My theory about your case is that this produced a change in your blood, that quickened your sensibilities and your critical faculties just at a time when a good many bothers—I don't of course know what they were, but I can, so to speak, see the marks all over you—came into your life."

The bishop nodded.

"You were uprooted. You moved from house to house, and failed to get that curled up safe feeling one has in a real home in any of them."

"If you saw the fireplaces and the general decoration of the new palace!" admitted the bishop. "I had practically no control."

"That confirms me," said Dr. Dale. "Insomnia followed, and increased the feeling of physical strangeness by increasing the bodily disturbance. I suspect an intellectual disturbance."

· He paused.

"There was," said the bishop.

"You were no longer at home anywhere. You were no longer at home in your diocese, in your palace, in your body, in your convictions. And then came the war. Quite apart from everything else the mind of the whole world is suffering profoundly from the shock of this war—much more than is generally admitted. One thing you did that you probably did not observe yourself doing, you drank rather more at your meals, you smoked a lot more. That was your natural and proper response to the shock."

"Ah!" said the bishop, and brightened up.

"It was remarked by Tolstoy, I think, that few intellectual men would really tolerate the world as it is if it were not for smoking and drinking. Even novelists have their moments of lucidity. Certainly these things soothe the restlessness in men's minds, deaden their sceptical sensibilities. And just at the time when you were getting most dislodged—you gave them up."

"And the sooner I go back to them the better," said the bishop brightly. "I quite see that."

"I wouldn't say that," said Dr. Dale....

III

"That," said Dr. Dale, "is just where my treatment of this case differs from the treatment of "—he spoke the name reluctantly as if he disliked the mere sound of it—"Dr. Brighton Pomfrey."

"Hitherto, of course," said the bishop, "I've been in his hands."

"He," said Dr. Dale, "would certainly set about trying to restore your old sphere of illusion, your old familiar sensations and ideas and confidences. He would in fact turn you back. He would restore all your habits. He would order you a rest. He would send you off to some holiday resort, fresh in fact but familiar in character, the High lands, North Italy, or Switzerland for example. He would forbid you newspapers and order you to botanize and prescribe tranquillizing reading; Trollope's novels, the Life of Gladstone, the works of Mr. A. C. Benson, memoirs and so on. You'd go somewhere where there was a good Anglican chaplain, and you'd take some of the services yourself. And we'd wash out the effects of the Princhester water with Contrexeville, and afterwards put you on Salutaris or Perrier. I don't know whether I shouldn't have inclined to some such treatment before the war began. Only—"

He paused.

"You think—?"

Dr. Dale's face betrayed a sudden sombre passion. "It won't do now," he said in a voice of quiet intensity. "It won't do now."

He remained darkly silent for so long that at last the bishop spoke. "Then what," he asked, "do you suggest?

"Suppose we don't try to go back," said Dr. Dale. "Suppose we go on and go through."

"Where?"

"To reality.

"I know it's doubtful, I know it's dangerous," he went on, "but I am convinced that now we can no longer keep men's minds and souls in these feathered nests, these spheres of illusion. Behind these veils there is either God or the Darkness.... Why should we not go on?"

The bishop was profoundly perplexed. He heard himself speaking. "It would be unworthy of my cloth," he was saying.

Dr. Dale completed the sentence: "to go back."

"Let me explain a little more," he said, "what I mean by 'going on.' I think that this loosening of the ties of association that bind a man to his everyday life and his everyday self is in nine cases out of ten a loosening of the ties that bind him to everyday sanity. One common form of this detachment is the form you have in those cases of people who are found wandering unaware of their names, unaware of their places of residence, lost altogether from themselves. They have not only lost their sense of identity with themselves, but all the circumstances of their lives have faded out of their minds like an idle story in a book that has been read and put aside. I have looked into hundreds of such cases. I don't think that loss of identity is a necessary thing; it's just another side of the general weakening of the grip upon reality, a kind of anaemia of the brain so that interest fades and fails. There is no reason why you should forget a story because you do not believe it—if your brain is strong enough to hold it. But if your brain is tired and weak, then so soon as you lose faith in your records, your mind is glad to let them go. When you see these lost identity people that is always your first impression, a tired brain that has let go."

The bishop felt extremely like letting go.

"But how does this apply to my case?"

"I come to that," said Dr. Dale, holding up a long large hand. "What if we treat this case of yours in a new way? What if we give you not narcotics but stimulants and tonics? What if we so touch the blood that we increase your sense of physical detachment while at the same time feeding up your senses to a new and more vivid apprehension of things about you?" He looked at his patient's hesitation and added: "You'd lose all that craving feeling, that you fancy at present is just the need of a smoke. The world might grow a trifle—transparent, but you'd keep real. Instead of drugging oneself back to the old contentment—"

"You'd drug me on to the new," said the bishop.

"But just one word more!" said Dr. Dale. "Hear why I would do this! It was easy and successful to rest and drug people back to their old states of mind when the world wasn't changing, wasn't spinning round in the wildest tornado of change that it has ever been in. But now—Where can I send you for a rest? Where can I send you to get you out of sight and hearing of the Catastrophe? Of course old Brighton Pomfrey would go on sending people away for rest and a nice little soothing change if the Day of Judgment was coming in the sky and the earth was opening and the sea was giving up its dead. He'd send 'em to the seaside. Such things as that wouldn't shake his faith in the Channel crossing. My idea is that it's not only right for you to go through with this, but that it's the only thing to do. If you go right on and right through with these doubts and intimations—"

He paused.

"You may die like a madman," he said, "but you won't die like a tame rabbit."

IV

The bishop sat reflecting. What fascinated and attracted him was the ending of all the cravings and uneasinesses and restlessness that had distressed his life for over four years; what deterred him was the personality of this gaunt young man with his long grey face, his excited manner, his shock of black hair. He wanted that tonic—with grave misgivings. "If you think this tonic is the wiser course," he began. "I'd give it you if you were my father," said Dr. Dale. "I've got everything for it," he added.

"You mean you can make it up—without a prescription."

"I can't give you a prescription. The essence of it—It's a distillate I have been trying. It isn't in the Pharmacopeia."

Again the bishop had a twinge of misgiving.

But in the end he succumbed. He didn't want to take the stuff, but also he did not want to go without his promised comfort.

Presently Dale had given him a little phial—and was holding up to the window a small medicine glass into which he was pouring very carefully twenty drops of the precious fluid. "Take it only," he said, "when you feel you must."

"It is the most golden of liquids," said the bishop, peering at it.

"When you want more I will make you more. Later of course, it will be possible to write a prescription. Now add the water—so.

"It becomes opalescent. How beautifully the light plays in it!

"Take it."

The bishop dismissed his last discretion and drank.

"Well?" said Dr. Dale.

"I am still here," said the bishop, smiling, and feeling a joyous tingling throughout his body. "It stirs me."

V

The bishop stood on the pavement outside Dr. Brighton Pomfrey's house. The massive door had closed behind him.

It had been an act of courage, of rashness if you will, to take this draught. He was acutely introspective, ready for anything, for the most disagreeable or the most bizarre sensations. He was asking himself, Were his feet steady? Was his head swimming?

His doubts glowed into assurance.

Suddenly he perceived that he was sure of God.

Not perhaps of the God of Nicaea, but what did these poor little quibblings and definitions of the theologians matter? He had been worrying about these definitions and quibblings for four long restless years. Now they were just failures to express—what surely every one knew—and no one would ever express exactly. Because here was God, and the kingdom of God was manifestly at hand. The visible world hung before him as a mist might hang before the rising sun. He stood proudly and masterfully facing a universe that had heretofore bullied him into doubt and apologetics, a universe that had hitherto been opaque and was now betrayed translucent.

That was the first effect of the new tonic, complete reassurance, complete courage. He turned to walk towards Mount Street and Berkeley Square as a sultan might turn to walk among his slaves.

But the tonic was only beginning.

Before he had gone a dozen steps he was aware that he seemed more solid and larger than the people about him. They had all a curious miniature effect, as though he was looking at them through the wrong end of an opera glass. The houses on either side of the street and the traffic shared this quality in an equal measure. It was as if he was looking at the world through apertures in a miniature cinematograph peep show. This surprised him and a little dashed his first glow of satisfaction.

He passed a man in khaki who, he fancied, looked at him with an odd expression. He observed the next passers by narrowly and suspiciously, a couple of smartish young men, a lady with a poodle, a grocer's boy with a basket, but none seemed to observe anything remarkable about him. Then he caught the eye of a taxi driver and became doubtful again.

He had a feeling that this tonic was still coming in like a tide. It seemed to be filling him and distending him, in spite of the fact that he was already full. After four years of flaccidity it was pleasant to be distended again, but already he felt more filled than he had ever been before. At present nothing was showing, but all his body seemed braced and uplifted. He must be careful not to become inflated in his bearing.

And yet it was difficult not to betray a little inflation. He was so filled with assurance that things were right with him and that God was there with him. After all it was not mere fancy; he was looking through the peepholes of his eyes at the world of illusion and appearance. The world that was so intent upon its immediate business, so regardless of eternal things, that had so dominated him but a little while ago, was after all a thing more mortal than himself.

Another man in khaki passed him.

For the first time he saw the war as something measurable, as something with a beginning and an end, as something less than the immortal spirit in man. He had been too much oppressed by it. He perceived all these people in the street were too much oppressed by it. He wanted to tell them as much, tell them that all was well with them, bid them be of good cheer. He wanted to bless them. He found his arm floating up towards gestures of benediction. Self control became increasingly difficult.

All the way down Berkeley Square the bishop was in full bodied struggle with himself. He was trying to control himself, trying to keep within bounds. He felt that he was stepping too high, that his feet were not properly reaching the ground, that he was walking upon cushions of air.

The feeling of largeness increased, and the feeling of transparency in things about him. He avoided collision with passers by—excessively. And he felt his attention was being drawn more and more to something that was going on beyond the veil of visible things. He was in Piccadilly now, but at the same time Piccadilly was very small and he was walking in the presence of God.

He had a feeling that God was there though he could not see him. And at the same time he was in this transitory world, with people going to and fro, men with umbrellas tucked dangerously under their arms, men in a hurry, policemen, young women rattling Red Cross collecting boxes, smart people, loafers. They distracted one from God.

He set out to cross the road just opposite Prince's, and jumping needlessly to give way to an omnibus had the narrowest escape from a taxicab.

He paused on the pavement edge to recover himself. The shock of his near escape had, as people say, pulled him together.

What was he to do? Manifestly this opalescent draught was overpowering him. He ought never to have taken it. He ought to have listened to the voice of his misgivings. It was clear that he was not in a fit state to walk about the streets. He was—what had been Dr. Dale's term?—losing his sense of reality. What was he to do? He was alarmed but not dismayed. His thoughts were as full bodied as the rest of his being, they came throbbing and bumping into his mind. What was he to do?

Brighton Pomfrey ought never to have left his practice in the hands of this wild eyed experimenter.

Strange that after a lifetime of discretion and men's respect one should be standing on the Piccadilly pavement—intoxicated!

It came into his head that he was not so very far from the Athenaeum, and surely there if anywhere a bishop may recover his sense of being—ordinary.

And behind everything, behind the tall buildings and the swarming people there was still the sense of a wide illuminated space, of a light of wonder and a Presence. But he must not give way to that again! He had already given way altogether too much. He repeated to himself in a whisper, "I am in Piccadilly."

If he kept tight hold upon himself he felt he might get to the Athenaeum before—before anything more happened.

He murmured directions to himself. "Keep along the pavement. Turn to the right at the Circus. Now down the hill. Easily down the hill. Don't float! Junior Army and Navy Stores. And the bookseller."

And presently he had a doubt of his name and began to repeat it.

"Edward Princhester. Edward Scrope, Lord Bishop of Princhester."

And all the while voices within him were asserting, "You are in the kingdom of Heaven. You are in the presence of God. Place and time are a texture of illusion and dreamland. Even now, you are with God."

VI

The porter of the Athenaeum saw him come in, looking well—flushed indeed—but queer in expression; his blue eyes were wide open and unusually vague and blue.

He wandered across towards the dining room, hesitated, went to look at the news, seemed in doubt whether he would not go into the smoking room, and then went very slowly upstairs, past the golden angel up to the great drawing room.

In the drawing room he found only Sir James Mounce, the man who knew the novels of Sir Walter Scott by heart and had the minutest and most unsparing knowledge of every detail in the life of that supreme giant of English literature. He had even, it was said, acquired a Scotch burr in the enthusiasm of his hero worship. It was usually sufficient only to turn an ear towards him for him to talk for an hour or so. He was now studying Bradshaw.

The bishop snatched at him desperately. He felt that if he went away there would be no hold left upon the ordinary things of life.

"Sir James," he said, "I was wondering the other day when was the exact date of the earliest public ascription of Waverley to Scott."

"Eh!" said Sir James, "but I'd like to talk that over with ye. Indeed I would. It would be depending very largely on what ye called 'public.' But—"

He explained something about an engagement in Birmingham that night, a train to catch. Reluctantly but relentlessly he abandoned the proffered ear. But he promised that the next time they met in the club he would go into the matter "exhausteevely."

The door closed upon him. The bishop was alone. He was flooded with the light of the world that is beyond this world. The things about him became very small and indistinct.

He would take himself into a quiet corner in the library of this doll's house, and sit his little body down in one of the miniature armchairs. Then if he was going to faint or if the trancelike feeling was to become altogether a trance—well, a bishop asleep in an armchair in the library of the Athenaeum is nothing to startle any one.

He thought of that convenient hidden room, the North Library, in which is the bust of Croker. There often one can be quite alone.... It was empty, and he went across to the window that looks out upon Pall Mall and sat down in the little uncomfortable easy chair by the desk with its back to the Benvenuto Cellini.

And as he sat down, something snapped—like the snapping of a lute string—in his brain.

VII

With a sigh of deep relief the bishop realized that this world had vanished.

He was in a golden light.

He perceived it as a place, but it was a place without buildings or trees or any very definite features. There was a cloudy suggestion of distant hills, and beneath his feet were little gem like flowers, and a feeling of divinity and infinite friendliness pervaded his being. His impressions grew more definite. His feet seemed to be bare. He was no longer a bishop nor clad as a bishop. That had gone with the rest of the world. He was seated on a slab of starry rock.

This he knew quite clearly was the place of God.

He was unable to disentangle thoughts from words. He seemed to be speaking in his mind.

"I have been very foolish and confused and perplexed. I have been like a creature caught among thorns."

"You served the purpose of God among those thorns." It seemed to him at first that the answer also was among his thoughts.

"I seemed so silly and so little. My wits were clay."

"Clay full of desires."

"Such desires!"

"Blind desires. That will presently come to the light."

"Shall we come to the light?"

"But here it is, and you see it!"

VIII

It became clearer in the mind of the bishop that a figure sat beside him, a figure of great strength and beauty, with a smiling face and kindly eyes. A strange thought and a strange courage came to the bishop.

"Tell me," he whispered, "are you God?"

"I am the Angel of God."

The bishop thought over that for some moments.

"I want," he said, "to know about God.

"I want," he said, with a deepening passion of the soul, "to know about God. Slowly through four long years I have been awakening to the need of God. Body and soul I am sick for the want of God and the knowledge of God. I did not know what was the matter with me, why my life had become so disordered and confused that my very appetites and habits are all astray. But I am perishing for God as a waterless man upon a raft perishes for drink, and there is nothing but madness if I touch the seas about me. Not only in my thoughts but in my under thoughts and in my nerves and bones and arteries I have need of God. You see I grew up in the delusion that I knew God, I did not know that I was unprovisioned and unprovided against the tests and strains and hardships of life. I thought that I was secure and safe. I was told that we men—who were apes not a quarter of a million years ago, who still have hair upon our arms and ape's teeth in our jaws—had come to the full and perfect knowledge of God. It was all put into a creed. Not a word of it was to be altered, not a sentence was to be doubted any more. They made me a teacher of this creed. They seemed to explain it to me. And when I came to look into it, when my need came and I turned to my creed, it was old and shrivelled up, it was the patched up speculations of vanished Greeks and Egyptians, it was a mummy of ancient disputes, old and dry, that fell to dust as I unwrapped it. And I was dressed up in the dress of old dead times and put before an altar of forgotten sacrifices, and I went through ceremonies as old as the first seedtime; and suddenly I knew clearly that God was not there, God was not in my

Creed, not in my cathedral, not in my ceremonies, nowhere in my life. And at the same time I knew, I knew as I had never known before, that certainly there was God."

He paused. "Tell me," said the friend at his side; "tell me."

"It was as if a child running beside its mother, looked up and saw that he had never seen her face before, that she was not his mother, and that the words he had seemed to understand were—now that he listened—words in an unknown tongue.

"You see, I am but a common sort of man, dear God; I have neither lived nor thought in any way greatly, I have gone from one day to the next day without looking very much farther than the end of the day, I have gone on as life has befallen; if no great trouble had come into my life, so I should have lived to the end of my days. But life which began for me easily and safely has become constantly more difficult and strange. I could have held my services and given my benedictions, I could have believed I believed in what I thought I believed.... But now I am lost and astray—crying out for God...."

IX

"Let us talk a little about your troubles," said the Angel. "Let us talk about God and this creed that worries you and this church of yours."

"I feel as though I had been struggling to this talk through all the years—since my doubts began."

"The story your Creed is trying to tell is much the same story that all religions try to tell. In your heart there is God, beyond the stars there is God. Is it the same God?"

"I don't know," said the bishop.

"Does any one know?"

"I thought I knew."

"Your creed is full of Levantine phrases and images, full of the patched contradictions of the human intelligence utterly puzzled. It is about those two Gods, the God beyond the stars and the God in your heart. It says that they are the same God, but different. It says that they have existed together for all time, and that one is the Son of the other. It has added a third Person—but we won't go into that."

The bishop was reminded suddenly of the dispute at Mrs. Garstein Fellows'. "We won't go into that," he agreed. "No!"

"Other religions have told the story in a different way. The Cathars and Gnostics did. They said that the God in your heart is a rebel against the God beyond the stars, that the Christ in your heart is like Prometheus—or Hiawatha—or any other of the sacrificial gods, a rebel. He arises out of man. He rebels against that high God of the stars and crystals and poisons and monsters and of the dead emptiness of space.... The Manicheans and the Persians made out our God to be fighting eternally against that Being of silence and darkness beyond the stars. The Buddhists made the Lord Buddha the leader of men out of the futility and confusion of material existence to the great peace beyond. But it is all one story really, the story of the two essential Beings, always the same story and the same perplexity cropping up under different names, the story of one being who stirs us, calls to us, and leads us, and of another who is above and outside and in and beneath all things, inaccessible and incomprehensible. All these religions are trying to tell something they do not clearly know—of a relationship between these two, that eludes them, that eludes the human mind, as water escapes from the hand. It is unity and opposition they have to declare at the same time; it is agreement and propitiation, it is infinity and effort."

"And the truth?" said the bishop in an eager whisper. "You can tell me the truth."

The Angel's answer was a gross familiarity. He thrust his hand through the bishop's hair and ruffled it affectionately, and rested for a moment holding the bishop's cranium in his great palm.

"But can this hold it?" he said....

"Not with this little box of brains," said the Angel. "You could as soon make a meal of the stars and pack them into your belly. You haven't the things to do it with inside this."

He gave the bishop's head a little shake and relinquished it.

He began to argue as an elder brother might.

"Isn't it enough for you to know something of the God that comes down to the human scale, who has been born on your planet and arisen out of Man, who is Man and God, your leader? He's more than enough to fill your mind and use up every faculty of your being. He is courage, he is adventure, he is the King, he fights for you and with you against death...."

"And he is not infinite? He is not the Creator?" asked the bishop.

"So far as you are concerned, no," said the Angel.

"So far as I am concerned?"

"What have you to do with creation?"

And at that question it seemed that a great hand swept carelessly across the blackness of the farther sky, and smeared it with stars and suns and shining nebulas as a brush might smear dry paint across a canvas.

The bishop stared in front of him. Then slowly he bowed his head, and covered his face with his hands.

"And I have been in orders," he murmured; "I have been teaching people the only orthodox and perfect truth about these things for seven and twenty years."

And suddenly he was back in his gaiters and his apron and his shovel hat, a little black figure exceedingly small in a very great space....

X

It was a very great space indeed because it was all space, and the roof was the ebony of limitless space from which the stars swung flaming, held by invisible ties, and the soil beneath his feet was a dust of atoms and the little beginnings of life. And long before the bishop bared his face again, he knew that he was to see his God.

He looked up slowly, fearing to be dazzled.

But he was not dazzled. He knew that he saw only the likeness and bodying forth of a being inconceivable, of One who is greater than the earth and stars and yet no greater than a man. He saw a being for ever young, for ever beginning, for ever triumphant. The quality and texture of this being was a warm and living light like the effulgence at sunrise; He was hope and courage like a sunlit morning in spring. He was adventure for ever, and His courage and adventure flowed into and submerged and possessed the being of the man who beheld him. And this presence of God stood over the bishop, and seemed to speak to him in a wordless speech.

He bade him surrender himself. He bade him come out upon the Adventure of Life, the great Adventure of the earth that will make the atoms our bond slaves and subdue the stars, that will build up the white fires of ecstasy to submerge pain for ever, that will overcome death. In Him the spirit of creation had become incarnate, had joined itself to men, summoning men to Him, having need of them, having need of them, having need of their service, even as great kings and generals and leaders need and use men. For a moment, for an endless age, the bishop bowed himself in the being and glory of God, felt the glow of the divine courage and confidence in his marrow, felt himself one with God.

For a timeless interval....

Never had the bishop had so intense a sense of reality. It seemed that never before had he known anything real. He knew certainly that God was his King and master, and that his unworthy service could be acceptable to God. His mind embraced that idea with an absolute conviction that was also absolute happiness.

XI

The thoughts and sensations of the bishop seemed to have lifted for a time clean away from the condition of time, and then through a vast orbit to be returning to that limitation.

He was aware presently that things were changing, that the light was losing its diviner rays, that in some indescribable manner the glory and the assurance diminished.

The onset of the new phase was by imperceptible degrees. From a glowing, serene, and static realization of God, everything relapsed towards change and activity. He was in time again and things were happening, it was as if the quicksands of time poured by him, and it was as if God was passing away from him. He fell swiftly down from the heaven of self forgetfulness to a grotesque, pathetic and earthly self consciousness.

He became acutely aware of his episcopal livery. And that God was passing away from him.

It was as if God was passing, and as if the bishop was unable to rise up and follow him.

Then it was as if God had passed, and as if the bishop was in headlong pursuit of him and in a great terror lest he should be left behind. And he was surely being left behind.

He discovered that in some unaccountable way his gaiters were loose; most of their buttons seemed to have flown off, and his episcopal sash had slipped down about his feet. He was sorely impeded. He kept snatching at these things as he ran, in clumsy attempts to get them off.

At last he had to stop altogether and kneel down and fumble with the last obstinate button.

"Oh God!" he cried, "God my captain! Wait for me! Be patient with me!"

And as he did so God turned back and reached out his hand. It was indeed as if he stood and smiled. He stood and smiled as a kind man might do; he dazzled and blinded his worshipper, and yet it was manifest that he had a hand a man might clasp.

Unspeakable love and joy irradiated the whole being of the bishop as he seized God's hand and clasped it desperately with both his own. It was as if his nerves and arteries and all his substance were inundated with golden light....

It was again as if he merged with God and became God....

CHAPTER THE SIXTH

EXEGETICAL

I

Without any sense of transition the bishop found himself seated in the little North Library of the Athenaeum club and staring at the bust of John Wilson Croker. He was sitting motionless and musing deeply. He was questioning with a cool and steady mind whether he had seen a vision or whether he had had a dream. If it had been a dream it had been an extraordinarily vivid and convincing dream. He still seemed to be in the presence of God, and it perplexed him not at all that he should also be in the presence of Croker. The feeling of mental rottenness and insecurity that had weakened his thought through the period of his illness, had gone. He was secure again within himself.

It did not seem to matter fundamentally whether it was an experience of things without or of things within him that had happened to him. It was clear to him that much that he had seen was at most expressive, that some was altogether symbolical. For example, there was that sudden absurd realization of his sash and gaiters, and his perception of them as encumbrances in his pursuit of God. But the setting and essential of the whole thing remained in his mind neither expressive nor symbolical, but as real and immediately perceived, and that was the presence and kingship of God. God was still with him and about him and over him and sustaining him. He was back again in his world and his ordinary life, in his clothing and his body and his club, but God had been made and remained altogether plain and manifest.

Whether an actual vision had made his conviction, or whether the conviction of his own subconscious mind had made the dream, seemed but a small matter beside the conviction that this was indeed the God he had desired and the God who must rule his life.

"The stuff? The stuff had little to do with it. It just cleared my head.... I have seen. I have seen really. I know."

II

For a long time as it seemed the bishop remained wrapped in clouds of luminous meditation. Dream or vision it did not matter; the essential thing was that he had made up his mind about God, he had found God. Moreover, he perceived that his theological perplexities had gone. God was higher and simpler and nearer than any theological God, than the God of the Three Creeds. Those creeds lay about in his mind now like garments flung aside, no trace nor suspicion of divinity sustained them any longer. And now—Now he would go out into the world.

The little Library of the Athenaeum has no visible door. He went to the book masked entrance in the corner, and felt among the bookshelves for the hidden latch. Then he paused, held by a curious thought. What exactly was the intention of that symbolical struggle with his sash and gaiters, and why had they impeded his pursuit of God?

To what particularly significant action was he going out?

The Three Creeds were like garments flung aside. But he was still wearing the uniform of a priest in the service of those three creeds.

After a long interval he walked into the big reading room. He ordered some tea and dry toast and butter, and sat down very thoughtfully in a corner. He was still sitting and thinking at half past eight.

It may seem strange to the reader that this bishop who had been doubting and criticizing the church and his system of beliefs for four long years had never before faced the possibility of a severance from his ecclesiastical dignity. But he had grown up in the church, his life had been so entirely clerical and Anglican, that the widest separation he had hitherto been able to imagine from this past had left him still a bishop, heretical perhaps, innovating in the broadening of beliefs and the liberalizing of practice, defensive even as Chasters was defensive, but still with the palace and his dignities, differing in opinion rather than in any tangible reality from his previous self. For a bishop, disbelief in the Church is a far profounder scepticism than mere disbelief in God. God is unseen, and in daily things unfelt; but the Church is with the predestined bishop always. His concept of the extremest possible departure from orthodoxy had been something that Chasters had phrased as "a restatement of Christ." It was a new idea, an idea that had come with an immense effect of severance and novelty, that God could be other than the God of the Creed, could present himself to the imagination as a figure totally unlike the white, gentle, and compromising Redeemer of an Anglican's thought. That the bishop should treat the whole teaching of the church and the church itself as wrong, was an idea so new that it fell upon him now like a thunderbolt out of a cloudless sky. But here, clear in his mind now, was a feeling, amounting to conviction, that it was the purpose and gesture of the true God that he should come right out of the church and all his professions.

And in the first glow of his vision he felt this gesture imperative. He must step right out.... Whither? how? And when?

To begin with it seemed to him that an immediate renunciation was demanded. But it was a momentous step. He wanted to think. And to go on thinking. Rather than to act precipitately. Although the imperative seemed absolute, some delaying and arresting instinct insisted that he must "think" If he went back to Princhester, the everyday duties of his position would confront him at once with an effect of a definite challenge. He decided to take one of the Reform club bedrooms for two or three days, and wire to Princhester that he was "unavoidably delayed in town," without further explanations. Then perhaps this inhibitory force would give way.

It did not, however, give way. His mind sat down for two days in a blank amazement at the course before him, and at the end of that time this reasonless and formless institution was as strong as ever. During that time, except for some incidental exchanges at his clubs, he talked to no one. At first he did not want to talk to any one. He remained mentally and practically active, with a still intensely vivid sense that God, the true God, stood watching him and waiting for him to follow. And to follow meant slipping right out of all the world he had ever known. To thrust his foot right over the edge of a cliff would scarcely have demanded more from the bishop's store of resolution. He stood on the very verge. The chief secretion of his mind was a shadowy experiment or so in explanation of why he did not follow.

III

Insensibly the extreme vividness of his sense of God's nearness decreased. But he still retained a persuasion of the reality of an immediate listener waiting, and of the need of satisfying him.

On the third day he found his mind still further changed. He no longer felt that God was in Pall Mall or St. James's Park, whither he resorted to walk and muse. He felt now that God was somewhere about the horizon....

He felt too no longer that he thought straight into the mind of God. He thought now of what he would presently say to God. He turned over and rehearsed phrases. With that came a desire to try them first on some other hearer. And from that to the attentive head of Lady Sunderbund, prettily bent towards him, was no great leap. She would understand, if any one could understand, the great change that had happened in his mind.

He found her address in the telephone book. She could be quite alone to him if he wouldn't mind "just me." It was, he said, exactly what he desired.

But when he got to her great airy flat overlooking Hyde Park, with its Omega Workshop furniture and its arresting decoration, he was not so sure whether this encounter was so exactly the thing he had desired as he had supposed.

The world had become opaque and real again as he walked up St. James's Street and past the Ritz. He had a feeling that he was taking an afternoon off from God. The adventurous modernity of the room in which he waited intensified that. One whole white wall was devoted to a small picture by Wyndham Lewis. It was like a picture of an earthquake in a city of aniline pink and grey and keen green cardboard, and he wished it had never existed.

He turned his back upon it and stared out of the window over the trees and greenery. The balcony was decorated with white and pink geraniums in pots painted black and gold, and the railings of the balcony were black and gold with crimson shape like squares wildly out of drawing.

Lady Sunderbund kept him waiting perhaps five minutes. Then she came sailing in to him.

She was dressed in a way and moved across the room in a way that was more reminiscent of Botticelli's Spring than ever—only with a kind of superadded stiffish polonaise of lace—and he did not want to be reminded of Botticelli's Spring or wonder why she had taken to stiff lace polonaises. He did not enquire whether he had met Lady Sunderbund to better advantage at Mrs. Garstein Fellows' or whether his memory had overrated her or whether anything had happened to his standard of taste, but his feeling now was decidedly one of disappointment, and all the talk and self examination he had promised himself seemed to wither and hide away within him. For a time he talked of her view, and then admired her room and its arrangement, which he thought really were quite unbecomingly flippant and undignified for a room. Then came the black tea things on their orange tray, and he searched in his mind for small talk to sustain their interview.

But he had already betrayed his disposition to "go on with our talk" in his telephone enquiry, and Lady Sunderbund, perceiving his shyness, began to make openings for him, at first just little hinting openings, and then larger and larger ones, until at last one got him.

"I'm so glad," she said, "to see you again. I'm so glad to go on with our talk. I've thought about it and thought about it."

She beamed at him happily.

"I've thought ova ev'y wo'd you said," she went on, when she had finished conveying her pretty bliss to him. "I've been so helped by thinking the k'eeds are symbols. And all you said. And I've felt time after time, you couldn't stay whe' you we'. That what you we' saying to me, would have to be said 'ight out."

That brought him in. He could not very well evade that opening without incivility. After all he had asked to see her, and it was a foolish thing to let little decorative accidentals put him off his friendly purpose. A woman may have flower pots painted gold with black checkers and still be deeply understanding. He determined to tell her what was in his mind. But he found something barred him from telling that he had had an actual vision of God. It was as if that had been a private and confidential meeting. It wasn't, he felt, for him either to boast a privilege or tell others of things that God had not chosen to show them.

"Since I saw you," he said, "I have thought a great deal—of the subject of our conversation."

"I have been t'ying to think," she said in a confirmatory tone, as if she had co operated.

"My faith in God grows," he said.

She glowed. Her lips fell apart. She flamed attention.

"But it grows less like the faith of the church, less and less. I was born and trained in Anglicanism, and it is with a sort of astonishment I find myself passing now out of every sort of Catholicism— seeing it from the outside...."

"Just as one might see Buddhism," she supplied.

"And yet feeling nearer, infinitely nearer to God," he said.

"Yes," she panted; "yes."

"I thought if one went out, one went out just to doubt and darkness."

"And you don't?"

"No."

"You have gone at one step to a new 'iligion!"

He stared for a moment at the phrase.

"To religion," he said.

"It is so wondyful," she said, with her hands straight down upon the couch upon which she was sitting, and leaning forward at him, so as to seem almost as much out of drawing as a modern picture.

"It seems," he reflected; "—as if it were a natural thing."

She came back to earth very slowly. She turned to the tea things with hushed and solemn movements as though she administered a ceremony of peculiar significance. The bishop too rose slowly out of the profundity of his confession. "No sugar please," he said, arresting the lump in mid air.

It was only when they were embarked upon cups of tea and had a little refreshed themselves, that she carried the talk further.

"Does it mean that you must leave the church?" she asked.

"It seemed so at first," he said. "But now I do not know. I do not know what I ought to do."

She awaited his next thought.

"It is as if one had lived in a room all one's life and thought it the world—and then suddenly walked out through a door and discovered the sea and the mountains and stars. So it was with me and the Anglican Church. It seems so extraordinary now—and it would have seemed the most natural thing a year ago—to think that I ever believed that the Anglican Compromise was the final truth of religion, that nothing more until the end of the world could ever be known that Cosmo Gordon Lang did not know, that there could be no conception of God and his quality that Randall Davidson did not possess."

He paused.

"I did," he said.

"I did," she responded with round blue eyes of wonder.

"At the utmost the Church of England is a tabernacle on a road."

"A 'oad that goes whe'?" she rhetorized.

"Exactly," said the bishop, and put down his cup.

"You see, my dear Lady Sunderbund," he resumed, "I am exactly in the same position of that man at the door."

She quoted aptly and softly: "The wo'ld was all befo' them whe' to choose."

He was struck by the aptness of the words.

"I feel I have to come right out into the bare truth. What exactly then do I become? Do I lose my priestly function because I discover how great God is? But what am I to do?"

He opened a new layer of his thoughts to her.

"There is a saying," he remarked, "once a priest, always a priest. I cannot imagine myself as other than what I am."

"But o'thodox no maw," she said.

"Orthodox—self satisfied, no longer. A priest who seeks, an exploring priest."

"In a Chu'ch of P'og'ess and B'othe'hood," she carried him on.

"At any rate, in a progressive and learning church."

She flashed and glowed assent.

"I have been haunted," he said, "by those words spoken at Athens. 'Whom therefore ye ignorantly worship, Him declare I unto you.' That comes to me with an effect of—guidance is an old fashioned word—shall I say suggestion? To stand by the altar bearing strange names and ancient symbols, speaking plainly to all mankind of the one true God—!"

IV

He did not get much beyond this point at the time, though he remained talking with Lady Sunderbund for nearly an hour longer. The rest was merely a beating out of what had already been said. But insensibly she renewed her original charm, and as he became accustomed to her he forgot a certain artificiality in her manner and the extreme modernity of her costume and furniture. She was a wonderful listener; nobody else could have helped him to expression in quite the same way, and when he left her he felt that now he was capable of stating his case in a coherent and acceptable form to almost any intelligent hearer. He had a point of view now that was no longer embarrassed by the immediate golden presence of God; he was no longer dazzled nor ecstatic; his problem had diminished to the scale of any other great human problem, to the scale of political problems and problems of integrity and moral principle, problems about which there is no such urgency as there is about a house on fire, for example.

And now the desire for expression was running strong. He wanted to state his situation; if he did not state he would have to act; and as he walked back to the club dinner he turned over possible interlocutors in his thoughts. Lord Rampound sat with him at dinner, and he came near broaching the subject with him. But Lord Rampound that evening had that morbid running of bluish legal anecdotes which is so common an affliction with lawyers, and theology sinks and dies in that turbid stream.

But as he lay in bed that night he thought of his old friend and helper Bishop Likeman, and it was borne in upon him that he should consult him. And this he did next day.

Since the days when the bishop had been only plain Mr. Scrope, the youngest and most helpful of Likeman's historical band of curates, their friendship had continued. Likeman had been a second father to him; in particular his tact and helpfulness had shone during those days of doubt and anxiety when dear old Queen Victoria, God's representative on earth, had obstinately refused, at the eleventh hour, to make him a bishop. She had those pigheaded fits, and she was touchy about the bishops. She had liked Scrope on account of the excellence of his German pronunciation, but she had been irritated by newspaper paragraphs—nobody could ever find out who wrote them and nobody could ever find out who showed them to the old lady—anticipating his elevation. She had gone very red in the face and stiffened in the Guelphic manner whenever Scrope was mentioned, and so a rich harvest of spiritual life had remained untilled for some months. Likeman had brought her round.

It seemed arguable that Scrope owed some explanation to Likeman before he came to any open breach with the Establishment.

He found Likeman perceptibly older and more shrivelled on account of the war, but still as sweet and lucid and subtle as ever. His voice sounded more than ever like a kind old woman's.

He sat buried in his cushions—for "nowadays I must save every scrap of vitality"—and for a time contented himself with drawing out his visitor's story.

Of course, one does not talk to Likeman of visions or intuitions. "I am disturbed, I find myself getting out of touch;" that was the bishop's tone.

Occasionally Likeman nodded slowly, as a physician might do at the recital of familiar symptoms. "Yes," he said, "I have been through most of this.... A little different in the inessentials.... How clear you are!"

"You leave our stupid old Trinities—as I left them long ago," said old Likeman, with his lean hand feeling and clawing at the arm of his chair.

"But—!"

The old man raised his hand and dropped it. "You go away from it all—straight as a line. I did. You take the wings of the morning and fly to the uttermost parts of the earth. And there you find—"

He held up a lean finger, and inclined it to tick off each point.

"Fate—which is God the Father, the Power of the Heart, which is God the Son, and that Light which comes in upon us from the inaccessible Godhead, which is God the Holy Spirit."

"But I know of no God the Holy Spirit, and Fate is not God at all. I saw in my vision one sole God, uncrucified, militant—conquering and to conquer."

Old Likeman stared. "You saw!"

The Bishop of Princhester had not meant to go so far. But he stuck to his words. "As if I saw with my eyes. A God of light and courage."

"You have had visions, Scrope?"

"I seemed to see."

"No, you have just been dreaming dreams."

"But why should one not see?"

"See! The things of the spirit. These symbols as realities! These metaphors as men walking!"

"You talk like an agnostic."

"We are all agnostics. Our creeds are expressions of ourselves and our attitude and relationship to the unknown. The triune God is just the form of our need and disposition. I have always assumed that you took that for granted. Who has ever really seen or heard or felt God? God is neither of the senses nor of the mind; he is of the soul. You are realistic, you are materialistic...."

His voice expostulated.

The Bishop of Princhester reflected. The vision of God was far off among his memories now, and difficult to recall. But he said at last: "I believe there is a God and that he is as real a person as you or I. And he is not the theological God we set out before the world."

"Personification," said Likeman. "In the eighteenth century they used to draw beautiful female figures as Science and Mathematics. Young men have loved Science—and Freedom—as Pygmalion loved Galatea. Have it so if you will. Have a visible person for your Deity. But let me keep up my—spirituality."

"Your spirituality seems as thin as a mist. Do you really believe—anything?"

"Everything!" said Likeman emphatically, sitting up with a transitory vigour. "Everything we two have ever professed together. I believe that the creeds of my church do express all that can possibly be expressed in the relationship of—That"—he made a comprehensive gesture with a twist of his hand upon its wrist—"to the human soul. I believe that they express it as well as the human mind can express it. Where they seem to be contradictory or absurd, it is merely that the mystery is paradoxical. I believe that the story of the Fall and of the Redemption is a complete symbol, that to add to it or to subtract from it or to alter it is to diminish its truth; if it seems incredible at this point or that, then simply I admit my own mental defect. And I believe in our Church, Scrope, as the embodied truth of religion, the divine instrument in human affairs. I believe in the security of its tradition, in the complete and entire soundness of its teaching, in its essential authority and divinity."

He paused, and put his head a little on one side and smiled sweetly. "And now can you say I do not believe?"

"But the historical Christ, the man Jesus?"

"A life may be a metaphor. Why not? Yes, I believe it all. All."

The Bishop of Princhester was staggered by this complete acceptance. "I see you believe all you profess," he said, and remained for a moment or so rallying his forces.

"Your vision—if it was a vision—I put it to you, was just some single aspect of divinity," said Likeman. "We make a mistake in supposing that Heresy has no truth in it. Most heresies are only a disproportionate apprehension of some essential truth. Most heretics are men who have suddenly caught a glimpse through the veil of some particular verity.... They are dazzled by that aspect. All the rest has vanished.... They are obsessed. You are obsessed clearly by this discovery of the militancy of God. God the Son—as Hero. And you want to go out to the simple worship of that one aspect. You want to go out to a Dissenter's tent in the wilderness, instead of staying in the Great Temple of the Ages."

Was that true?

For some moments it sounded true.

The Bishop of Princhester sat frowning and looking at that. Very far away was the vision now of that golden Captain who bade him come. Then at a thought the bishop smiled.

"The Great Temple of the Ages," he repeated. "But do you remember the trouble we had when the little old Queen was so pigheaded?"

"Oh! I remember, I remember," said Likeman, smiling with unshaken confidence. "Why not?"

"For sixty years all we bishops in what you call the Great Temple of the Ages, were appointed and bullied and kept in our places by that pink irascible bit of dignity. I remember how at the time I didn't dare betray my boiling indignation even to you—I scarcely dared admit it to myself...."

He paused.

"It doesn't matter at all," and old Likeman waved it aside.

"Not at all," he confirmed, waving again.

"I spoke of the whole church of Christ on earth," he went on. "These things, these Victorias and Edwards and so on, are temporary accidents—just as the severance of an Anglican from a Roman communion and a Greek orthodox communion are temporary accidents. You will remark that wise men in all ages have been able to surmount the difficulty of these things. Why? Because they knew that in spite of all these splits and irregularities and defacements—like the cracks and crannies and lichens on a cathedral wall—the building held good, that it was shelter and security. There is no other shelter and security. And so I come to your problem. Suppose it is true that you have this incidental vision of the militant aspect of God, and he isn't, as you see him now that is,—he isn't like the Trinity, he isn't like the Creed, he doesn't seem to be related to the Church, then comes the question, are you going out for that? And whither do you go if you do go out? The Church remains. We alter doctrines not by changing the words but by shifting the accent. We can under accentuate below the threshold of consciousness."

"But can we?"

"We do. Where's Hell now? Eighty years ago it warmed the whole Church. It was—as some atheist or other put it the other day—the central heating of the soul. But never mind that point now. Consider the essential question, the question of breaking with the church. Ask yourself, whither would you go? To become an oddity! A Dissenter. A Negative. Self emasculated. The spirit that denies. You would just go out. You would just cease to serve Religion. That would be all. You wouldn't do anything. The Church would go on; everything else would go on. Only you would be lost in the outer wilderness.

"But then—"

Old Likeman leant forward and pointed a bony finger. "Stay in the Church and modify it. Bring this new light of yours to the altar."

There was a little pause.

"No man," the bishop thought aloud, "putteth new wine into old bottles."

Old Likeman began to speak and had a fit of coughing. "Some of these texts—whuff, whuff—like a conjuror's hat—whuff—make 'em—fit anything."

A man servant appeared and handed a silver box of lozenges into which the old bishop dipped with a trembling hand.

"Tricks of that sort," he said, "won't do, Scrope—among professionals.

"And besides," he was inspired; "true religion is old wine—as old as the soul.

"You are a bishop in the Church of Christ on Earth," he summed it up. "And you want to become a detached and wandering Ancient Mariner from your shipwreck of faith with something to explain—that nobody wants to hear. You are going out I suppose you have means?"

The old man awaited the answer to his abrupt enquiry with a handful of lozenges.

"No," said the Bishop of Princhester, "practically—I haven't."

"My dear boy!" it was as if they were once more rector and curate. "My dear brother! do you know what the value of an ex bishop is in the ordinary labour market?"

"I have never thought of that."

"Evidently. You have a wife and children?"

"Five daughters."

"And your wife married you—I remember, she married you soon after you got that living in St. John's Wood. I suppose she took it for granted that you were fixed in an ecclesiastical career. That was implicit in the transaction."

"I haven't looked very much at that side of the matter yet," said the Bishop of Princhester.

"It shouldn't be a decisive factor," said Bishop Likeman, "not decisive. But it will weigh. It should weigh...."

The old man opened out fresh aspects of the case. His argument was for delay, for deliberation. He went on to a wider set of considerations. A man who has held the position of a bishop for some years is, he held, no longer a free man in matters of opinion. He has become an official part of a great edifice which supports the faith of multitudes of simple and dependant believers. He has no right to indulge recklessly in intellectual and moral integrities. He may understand, but how is the flock to understand? He may get his own soul clear, but what will happen to them? He will just break away their supports, astonish them, puzzle them, distress them, deprive them of confidence, convince them of nothing.

"Intellectual egotism may be as grave a sin," said Bishop Likeman, "as physical selfishness.

"Assuming even that you are absolutely right," said Bishop Likeman, "aren't you still rather in the position of a man who insists upon Swedish exercises and a strengthening dietary on a raft?"

"I think you have made out a case for delay," said his hearer.

"Three months."

The Bishop of Princhester conceded three months.

"Including every sort of service. Because, after all, even supposing it is damnable to repeat prayers and creeds you do not believe in, and administer sacraments you think superstition, nobody can be damned but yourself. On the other hand if you express doubts that are not yet perfectly digested— you experiment with the souls of others...."

V

The bishop found much to ponder in his old friend's counsels. They were discursive and many fronted, and whenever he seemed to be penetrating or defeating the particular considerations under examination the others in the background had a way of appearing invincible. He had a strong persuasion that Likeman was wrong—and unanswerable. And the true God now was no more than the memory of a very vividly realized idea. It was clear to the bishop that he was no longer a churchman or in the generally accepted sense of the word a Christian, and that he was bound to come out of the church. But all sense of urgency had gone. It was a matter demanding deliberation and very great consideration for others.

He took no more of Dale's stuff because he felt bodily sound and slept well. And he was now a little shy of this potent fluid. He went down to Princhester the next day, for his compromise of an interval of three months made it seem possible to face his episcopal routine again. It was only when he was back in his own palace that the full weight of his domestic responsibilities in the discussion of the course he had to take, became apparent.

Lady Ella met him with affection and solicitude.

"I was tired and mentally fagged," he said. "A day or so in London had an effect of change."

She agreed that he looked much better, and remained for a moment or so scrutinizing him with the faint anxiety of one resolved to be completely helpful.

He regarded her with a renewed sense of her grace and dignity and kindliness. She was wearing a grey dress of soft silky material, touched with blue and covered with what seemed to him very rich and beautiful lace; her hair flowed back very graciously from her broad brow, and about her wrist and neck were delicate lines of gold. She seemed tremendously at home and right just where she was, in that big hospitable room, cultured but Anglican, without pretensions or novelties, with a glow of bound books, with the grand piano that Miriam, his third daughter, was beginning to play so well, with the tea equipage of shining silver and fine porcelain.

He sat down contentedly in the low armchair beside her.

It wasn't a setting that one would rashly destroy....

And that evening at dinner this sense of his home as a complex of finely adjusted things not to be rashly disturbed was still more in the mind of the bishop. At dinner he had all his domesticities about him. It was the family time, from eight until ten, at which latter hour he would usually go back from the drawing room to his study. He surveyed the table. Eleanor was at home for a few days, looking a little thin and bright but very keen and happy. She had taken a first in the first part of the Moral Science Tripos, and she was working hard now for part two. Clementina was to go back to Newnham with her next September. She aspired to history. Miriam's bent was musical. She and Phoebe and Daphne and Clementina were under the care of skilful Mademoiselle Lafarge, most tactful of Protestant French women, Protestant and yet not too Protestant, one of those rare French Protestants in whom a touch of Bergson and the Pasteur Monod

"scarce suspected, animates the whole."

And also they had lessons, so high are our modern standards of education, from Mr. Blent, a brilliant young mathematician in orders, who sat now next to Lady Ella. Mr. Whippham, the chaplain, was at the bishop's right hand, ready for any chance of making arrangements to clear off the small arrears of duty the little holiday in London had accumulated. The bishop surveyed all these bright young people between himself and the calm beauty of his wife. He spoke first to one and then another upon the things that interested them. It rejoiced his heart to be able to give them education and opportunity, it pleased him to see them in clothes that he knew were none the less expensive because of their complete simplicity. Miriam and Mr. Blent wrangled pleasantly about Debussy, and old Dunk waited as though in orders of some rare and special sort that qualified him for this service.

All these people, the bishop reflected, counted upon him that this would go on....

Eleanor was answering some question of her mother's. They were so oddly alike and so curiously different, and both in their several ways so fine. Eleanor was dark like his own mother. Perhaps she did a little lack Lady Ella's fine reserves; she could express more, she could feel more acutely, she might easily be very unhappy or very happy....

All these people counted on him. It was indeed acutely true, as Likeman had said, that any sudden breach with his position would be a breach of faith—so far as they were concerned.

And just then his eye fell upon the epergne, a very old and beautiful piece of silver, that graced the dinner table. It had been given him, together with an episcopal ring, by his curates and choristers at the Church of the Holy Innocents, when he became bishop of Pinner. When they gave it him, had any one of them dreamt that some day he might be moved to strike an ungracious blow at the mother church that had reared them all?

It was his custom to join the family in the drawing room after dinner. To night he was a little delayed by Whippham, with some trivialities about next month's confirmations in Pringle and Princhester. When he came in he found Miriam playing, and playing very beautifully one of those later sonatas of Beethoven, he could never remember whether it was Of. 109 or Of. 111, but he knew that he liked it very much; it was solemn and sombre with phases of indescribable sweetness—while Clementina, Daphne and Mademoiselle Lafarge went on with their war knitting and Phoebe and Mr. Blent bent their brows over chess. Eleanor was reading the evening paper. Lady Ella sat on a high chair by the coffee things, and he stood in the doorway surveying the peaceful scene for a moment or so, before he went across the room and sat down on the couch close to her.

"You look tired," she whispered softly.

"Worries."

"That Chasters case?"

"Things developing out of that. I must tell you later." It would be, he felt, a good way of breaking the matter to her.

"Is the Chasters case coming on again, Daddy?" asked Eleanor.

He nodded.

"It's a pity," she said.

"What?

"That he can't be left alone."

"It's Sir Reginald Phipps. The Church would be much more tolerant if it wasn't for the House of Laymen. But they—they feel they must do something."

He seized the opportunity of the music ceasing to get away from the subject. "Miriam dear," he asked, raising his voice; "is that 109 or 111? I can never tell."

"That is always 111, Daddy," said Miriam. "It's the other one is 109." And then evidently feeling that she had been pert: "Would you like me to play you 109, Daddy?"

"I should love it, my dear." And he leant back and prepared to listen in such a thorough way that Eleanor would have no chance of discussing the Chasters' heresies. But this was interrupted by the consummation of the coffee, and Mr. Blent, breaking a long silence with "Mate in three, if I'm not mistaken," leapt to his feet to be of service. Eleanor, with the rough seriousness of youth, would not leave the Chasters case alone.

"But need you take action against Mr. Chasters?" she asked at once.

"It's a very complicated subject, my dear," he said.

"His arguments?"

"The practical considerations."

"But what are practical considerations in such a case?"

"That's a post graduate subject, Norah," her father said with a smile and a sigh.

"But," began Eleanor, gathering fresh forces.

"Daddy is tired," Lady Ella intervened, patting him on the head.

"Oh, terribly!—of that," he said, and so escaped Eleanor for the evening.

But he knew that before very long he would have to tell his wife of the changes that hung over their lives; it would be shabby to let the avalanche fall without giving the longest possible warning; and before they parted that night he took her hands in his and said: "There is much I have to tell you, dear. Things change, the whole world changes. The church must not live in a dream....

"No," she whispered. "I hope you will sleep to night," and held up her grave sweet face to be kissed.

VI

But he did not sleep perfectly that night.

He did not sleep indeed very badly, but he lay for some time thinking, thinking not onward but as if he pressed his mind against very strong barriers that had closed again. His vision of God which had filled the heavens, had become now gem like, a minute, hard, clear cut conviction in his mind that he had to disentangle himself from the enormous complications of symbolism and statement and organization and misunderstanding in the church and achieve again a simple and living worship of a simple and living God. Likeman had puzzled and silenced him, only upon reflection to convince him that amidst such intricacies of explanation the spirit cannot live. Creeds may be symbolical, but symbols must not prevaricate. A church that can symbolize everything and anything means nothing.

It followed from this that he ought to leave the church. But there came the other side of this perplexing situation. His feelings as he lay in his bed were exactly like those one has in a dream when one wishes to run or leap or shout and one can achieve no movement, no sound. He could not conceive how he could possibly leave the church.

His wife became as it were the representative of all that held him helpless. She and he had never kept secret from one another any plan of action, any motive, that affected the other. It was clear to him that any movement towards the disavowal of doctrinal Christianity and the renunciation of his see must be first discussed with her. He must tell her before he told the world.

And he could not imagine his telling her except as an incredibly shattering act.

So he left things from day to day, and went about his episcopal routines. He preached and delivered addresses in such phrases as he knew people expected, and wondered profoundly why it was that it should be impossible for him to discuss theological points with Lady Ella. And one afternoon he went for a walk with Eleanor along the banks of the Prin, and found himself, in response to certain openings of hers, talking to her in almost exactly the same terms as Likeman had used to him.

Then suddenly the problem of this theological eclaircissement was complicated in an unexpected fashion.

He had just been taking his Every Second Thursday Talk with Diocesan Men Helpers. He had been trying to be plain and simple upon the needless narrowness of enthusiastic laymen. He was still in the Bishop Andrews cap and purple cassock he affected on these occasions; the Men Helpers loved purple; and he was disentangling himself from two or three resolute bores—for our loyal laymen can be at times quite superlative bores—when Miriam came to him.

"Mummy says, 'Come to the drawing room if you can.' There is a Lady Sunderbund who seems particularly to want to see you."

He hesitated for a moment, and then decided that this was a conversation he ought to control.

He found Lady Sunderbund looking very tall and radiantly beautiful in a sheathlike dress of bright crimson trimmed with snow white fur and a white fur toque. She held out a long white gloved hand to him and cried in a tone of comradeship and profound understanding: "I've come, Bishop!"

"You've come to see me?" he said without any sincerity in his polite pleasure.

"I've come to P'inchesta to stay!" she cried with a bright triumphant rising note.

She evidently considered Lady Ella a mere conversational stop gap, to be dropped now that the real business could be commenced. She turned her pretty profile to that lady, and obliged the bishop with a compact summary of all that had preceded his arrival. "I have been telling Lady Ella," she said, "I've taken a house, fu'nitua and all! Hea. In P'inchesta! I've made up my mind to sit unda you—as they say in Clapham. I've come 'ight down he' fo' good. I've taken a little house—oh! a sweet little house that will be all over 'oses next month. I'm living f'om 'oom to 'oom and having the othas done up. It's in that little quiet st'eet behind you' ga'den wall. And he' I am!"

"Is it the old doctor's house?" asked Lady Ella.

"Was it an old docta?" cried Lady Sunderbund. "How delightful! And now I shall be a patient!"

She concentrated upon the bishop.

"Oh, I've been thinking all the time of all the things you told me. Ova and ova. It's all so wondyful and so—so like a G'ate Daw opening. New light. As if it was all just beginning."

She clasped her hands.

The bishop felt that there were a great number of points to this situation, and that it was extremely difficult to grasp them all at once. But one that seemed of supreme importance to his whirling intelligence was that Lady Ella should not know that he had gone to relieve his soul by talking to Lady Sunderbund in London. It had never occurred to him at the time that there was any shadow of disloyalty to Lady Ella in his going to Lady Sunderbund, but now he realized that this was a thing that would annoy Lady Ella extremely. The conversation had in the first place to be kept away from that. And in the second place it had to be kept away from the abrupt exploitation of the new theological developments.

He felt that something of the general tension would be relieved if they could all three be got to sit down.

"I've been talking for just upon two hours," he said to Lady Ella. "It's good to see the water boiling for tea."

He put a chair for Lady Sunderbund to the right of Lady Ella, got her into it by infusing an ecclesiastical insistence into his manner, and then went and sat upon the music stool on his wife's left, so as to establish a screen of tea things and cakes and so forth against her more intimate enthusiasm. Meanwhile he began to see his way clearer and to develop his line.

"Well, Lady Sunderbund," he said, "I can assure you that I think you will be no small addition to the church life of Princhester. But I warn you this is a hard working and exacting diocese. We shall take your money, all we can get of it, we shall take your time, we shall work you hard."

"Wo'k me hard!" cried Lady Sunderbund with passion.

"We will, we will," said the bishop in a tone that ignored her passionate note.

"I am sure Lady Sunderbund will be a great help to us," said Lady Ella. "We want brightening. There's a dinginess...."

Lady Sunderbund beamed an acknowledgment. "I shall exact a 'eturn," she said. "I don't mind wo'king, but I shall wo'k like the poo' students in the Middle Ages did, to get my teaching. I've got my own soul to save as well as help saving othas. Since oua last talk—"

She found the bishop handing her bread and butter. For a time the bishop fought a delaying action with the tea things, while he sought eagerly and vainly in his mind for some good practical topic in which he could entangle and suppress Lady Sunderbund's enthusiasms. From this she broke away by turning suddenly to Lady Ella.

"Youa husband's views," she said, "we'e a 'eal 'evelation to me. It was like not being blind—all at once."

Lady Ella was always pleased to hear her husband praised. Her colour brightened a little. "They seem very ordinary views," she said modestly.

"You share them?" cried Lady Sunderbund.

"But of course," said Lady Ella.

"Wondyful!" cried Lady Sunderbund.

"Tell me, Lady Sunderbund," said the bishop, "are you going to alter the outer appearance of the old doctor's house?" And found that at last he had discovered the saving topic.

"Ha'dly at all," she said. "I shall just have it pointed white and do the doa—I'm not su' how I shall do the doa. Whetha I shall do the doa gold or a vehy, vehy 'itch blue."

For a time she and Lady Ella, to whom these ideas were novel, discussed the animation of grey and sombre towns by house painting. In such matter Lady Sunderbund had a Russian mind. "I can't bea' g'ey," she said. "Not in my su'oundings, not in my k'eed, nowhe'e." She turned to the bishop. "If I had my way I would paint you' cathed'al inside and out."

"They used to be painted," said the bishop. "I don't know if you have seen Ely. There the old painting has been largely restored...."

From that to the end there was no real danger, and at last the bishop found himself alone with his wife again.

"Remarkable person," he said tentatively. "I never met any one whose faults were more visible. I met her at Wimbush House."

He glanced at his watch.

"What did she mean," asked Lady Ella abruptly, "by talking of your new views? And about revelations?"

"She probably misunderstood something I said at the Garstein Fellows'," he said. "She has rather a leaping mind."

He turned to the window, looked at his nails, and appeared to be suddenly reminded of duties elsewhere....

It was chiefly manifest to him that the difficulties in explaining the changes of his outlook to Lady Ella had now increased enormously.

VII

A day or so after Lady Sunderbund's arrival in Princhester the bishop had a letter from Likeman. The old man was manifestly in doubt about the effect of their recent conversation.

"My dear Scrope," it began. "I find myself thinking continually about our interview and the difficulties you laid bare so frankly to me. We touched upon many things in that talk, and I find myself full of afterthoughts, and not perfectly sure either quite of what I said or of what I failed to say. I feel that in many ways I was not perhaps so clear and convincing as the justice of my case should have made me, and you are one of my own particular little company, you were one of the best workers in that band of good workers, your life and your career are very much my concern. I know you will forgive me if I still mingle something of the paternal with my fraternal admonitions. I watched you closely. I have still my old diaries of the St. Matthew's days, and I have been looking at them to remind me of what you once were. It was my custom to note my early impressions of all the men who worked with me, because I have a firm belief in the soundness of first impressions and the considerable risk one runs of having them obscured by the accidents and habituations of constant intercourse. I found that quite early in your days at St. Matthew's I wrote against your name 'enthusiastic, but a saving delicacy.' After all our life long friendship I would not write anything truer. I would say of you to day, 'This man might have been a revivalist, if he were not a gentleman.' There is the enthusiast, there is the revivalist, in you. It seems to me that the stresses and questions of this great crisis in the world's history have brought it nearer to the surface than I had ever expected it to come.

"I quite understand and I sympathize with your impatience with the church at the present time; we present a spectacle of pompous insignificance hard to bear with. We are doing very little, and we are giving ourselves preposterous airs. There seems to be an opinion abroad that in some quasi automatic way the country is going to collapse after the war into the arms of the church and the High Tories; a possibility I don't accept for a moment. Why should it? These forcible feeble reactionaries are much more likely to explode a revolution that will disestablish us. And I quite understand your theological difficulties—quite. The creeds, if their entire symbolism is for a moment forgotten, if they are taken as opaque statements of fact, are inconsistent, incredible. So incredible that no one believes them; not even the most devout. The utmost they do is to avert their minds—reverentially. Credo quia impossibile. That is offensive to a Western mind. I can quite understand the disposition to cry out at such things, 'This is not the Church of God!'—to run out from it—

"You have some dream, I suspect, of a dramatic dissidence.

"Now, my dear Brother and erstwhile pupil, I ask you not to do this thing. Wait, I implore you. Give me—and some others, a little time. I have your promise for three months, but even after that, I ask you to wait. Let the reform come from within the church. The church is something more than either its creeds, its clergy, or its laymen. Look at your cathedral rising out of and dominating Princhester. It stands not simply for Athanasius; it stands but incidentally for Athanasius; it stands for all religion. Within that fabric—let me be as frank here as in our private conversation—doctrine has altered again and again. To day two distinct religions worship there side by side; one that fades and one that grows brighter. There is the old quasi materialistic belief of the barbarians, the belief in such things, for example, as that Christ the physical Son of God descended into hell and stayed there, seeing the sights I suppose like any tourist and being treated with diplomatic civilities for three terrestrial days; and on the other hand there is the truly spiritual belief that you and I share, which is absolutely intolerant of such grotesque ideas. My argument to you is that the new faith, the clearer vision, gains ground; that the only thing that can prevent or delay the church from being altogether possessed by what you call and I admit is, the true God, is that such men as yourself, as the light breaks upon you, should be hasty and leave the church. You see my point of view, do you not? It is not one that has been assumed for our discussion; it is one I came to long years ago, that I was already feeling my way to in my St. Matthew's Lenton sermons.

"A word for your private ear. I am working. I cannot tell you fully because I am not working alone. But there are movements afoot in which I hope very shortly to be able to ask you to share. That much at least I may say at this stage. Obscure but very powerful influences are at work for the liberalizing of the church, for release from many narrow limitations, for the establishment of a modus vivendi with the nonconformist and dissentient bodies in Britain and America, and with the churches of the East. But of that no more now.

"And in conclusion, my dear Scrope, let me insist again upon the eternal persistence of the essential Religious Fact:"

(Greek Letters Here)

(Rev. i. 18. "Fear not. I am the First and Last thing, the Living thing.")

And these promises which, even if we are not to take them as promises in the exact sense in which, let us say, the payment of five sovereigns is promised by a five pound note, are yet assertions of practically inevitable veracity:

(Greek Letters Here)

(Phil. i. 6. "He who began... will perfect." Eph. v. 14. "He will illuminate.")

The old man had written his Greek tags in shakily resolute capitals. It was his custom always to quote the Greek Testament in his letters, never the English version. It is a practice not uncommon with the more scholarly of our bishops. It is as if some eminent scientific man were to insist upon writing H_2O instead of "water," and "sodium chloride" instead of "table salt" in his private correspondence. Or upon hanging up a stuffed crocodile in his hall to give the place tone. The Bishop of Princhester construed these brief dicta without serious exertion, he found them very congenial texts, but there were insuperable difficulties in the problem why Likeman should suppose they had the slightest weight upon his side of their discussion. The more he thought the less they seemed to be on Likeman's side, until at last they began to take on a complexion entirely opposed to the old man's insidious arguments, until indeed they began to bear the extraordinary interpretation of a special message, unwittingly delivered.

VIII

The bishop was still thinking over this communication when he was interrupted by Lady Ella. She came with a letter in her hand to ask him whether she might send five and twenty pounds to a poor cousin of his, a teacher in a girls' school, who had been incapacitated from work by a dislocation of the cartilage of her knee. If she could go to that unorthodox but successful practitioner, Mr. Barker, the bone setter, she was convinced she could be restored to efficiency. But she had no ready money. The bishop agreed without hesitation. His only doubt was the certainty of the cure, but upon that point Lady Ella was convinced; there had been a great experience in the Walshingham family.

"It is pleasant to be able to do things like this," said Lady Ella, standing over him when this matter was settled.

"Yes," the bishop agreed; "it is pleasant to be in a position to do things like this...."

CHAPTER THE SEVENTH

THE SECOND VISION

I

A month later found the bishop's original state of perplexity and insomnia returned and intensified. He had done none of all the things that had seemed so manifestly needing to be done after his vision in the Athenaeum. All the relief and benefit of his experience in London had vanished out of his life. He was afraid of Dr. Dale's drug; he knew certainly that it would precipitate matters; and all his instincts in the state of moral enfeeblement to which he had relapsed, were to temporize.

Although he had said nothing further about his changed beliefs to Lady Ella, yet he perceived clearly that a shadow had fallen between them. She had a wife's extreme sensitiveness to fine shades of expression and bearing, and manifestly she knew that something was different. Meanwhile Lady Sunderbund had become a frequent worshipper in the cathedral, she was a figure as conspicuous in sombre Princhester as a bird of paradise would have been; common people stood outside her very very rich blue door on the chance of seeing her; she never missed an opportunity of hearing the bishop preach or speak, she wrote him several long and thoughtful letters with which he did not bother Lady Ella, she communicated persistently, and manifestly intended to become a very active worker in diocesan affairs.

It was inevitable that she and the bishop should meet and talk occasionally in the cathedral precincts, and it was inevitable that he should contrast the flexibility of her rapid and very responsive mind with a certain defensiveness, a stoniness, in the intellectual bearing of Lady Ella.

If it had been Lady Sunderbund he had had to explain to, instead of Lady Ella, he could have explained a dozen times a day.

And since his mind was rehearsing explanations it was not unnatural they should overflow into this eagerly receptive channel, and that the less he told Lady Ella the fuller became his spiritual confidences to Lady Sunderbund.

She was clever in realizing that they were confidences and treating them as such, more particularly when it chanced that she and Lady Ella and the bishop found themselves in the same conversation.

She made great friends with Miriam, and initiated her by a whole collection of pretty costume plates into the mysteries of the "Ussian Ballet" and the works of Mousso'gski and "Imsky Ko'zakof."

The bishop liked a certain religiosity in the texture of Moussorgski's music, but failed to see the "significance "—of many of the costumes.

II

It was on a Sunday night—the fourth Sunday after Easter—that the supreme crisis of the bishop's life began. He had had a feeling all day of extreme dulness and stupidity; he felt his ministrations unreal, his ceremonies absurd and undignified. In the night he became bleakly and painfully awake. His mind occupied itself at first chiefly with the tortuousness and weakness of his own character. Every day he perceived that the difficulty of telling Lady Ella of the change in his faith became more mountainous. And every day he procrastinated. If he had told her naturally and simply on the evening of his return from London—before anything material intervened—everything would have been different, everything would have been simpler....

He groaned and rolled over in his bed.

There came upon him the acutest remorse and misery. For he saw that amidst these petty immediacies he had lost touch with God. The last month became incredible. He had seen God. He had touched God's hand. God had been given to him, and he had neglected the gift. He was still lost amidst the darkness and loneliness, the chaotic ends and mean shifts, of an Erastian world. For a month now and more, after a vision of God so vivid and real and reassuring that surely no saint nor prophet had ever had a better, he had made no more than vague responsive movements; he had allowed himself to be persuaded into an unreasonable and cowardly delay, and the fetters of association and usage and minor interests were as unbroken as they had been before ever the vision shone. Was it credible that there had ever been such a vision in a life so entirely dictated by immediacy and instinct as his? We are all creatures of the dark stream, we swim in needs and bodily impulses and small vanities; if ever and again a bubble of spiritual imaginativeness glows out of us, it breaks and leaves us where we were.

"Louse that I am!" he cried.

He still believed in God, without a shadow of doubt; he believed in the God that he had seen, the high courage, the golden intention, the light that had for a moment touched him. But what had he to do with God, he, the loiterer, the little thing?

He was little, he was funny. His prevarications with his wife, for example, were comic. There was no other word for him but "funny."

He rolled back again and lay staring.

"Who will deliver me from the body of this death?" What right has a little bishop in a purple stock and doeskin breeches, who hangs back in his palace from the very call of God, to a phrase so fine and tragic as "the body of this death?"

He was the most unreal thing in the universe. He was a base insect giving himself airs. What advantage has a bishop over the Praying Mantis, that cricket which apes the attitude of piety? Does he matter more—to God?

"To the God of the Universe, who can tell? To the God of man,—yes."

He sat up in bed struck by his own answer, and full of an indescribable hunger for God and an indescribable sense of his complete want of courage to make the one simple appeal that would satisfy that hunger. He tried to pray. "O God!" he cried, "forgive me! Take me!" It seemed to him that he was not really praying but only making believe to pray. It seemed to him that he was not really existing but only seeming to exist. He seemed to himself to be one with figures on a china plate, with figures painted on walls, with the flimsy imagined lives of men in stories of forgotten times. "O God!" he said, "O God," acting a gesture, mimicking appeal.

"Anaemic," he said, and was given an idea.

He got out of bed, he took his keys from the night table at the bed head and went to his bureau.

He stood with Dale's tonic in his hand. He remained for some time holding it, and feeling a curious indisposition to go on with the thing in his mind.

He turned at last with an effort. He carried the little phial to his bedside, and into the tumbler of his water bottle he let the drops fall, drop by drop, until he had counted twenty. Then holding it to the bulb of his reading lamp he added the water and stood watching the slow pearly eddies in the mixture mingle into an opalescent uniformity. He replaced the water bottle and stood with the glass in his hand. But he did not drink.

He was afraid.

He knew that he had only to drink and this world of confusion would grow transparent, would roll back and reveal the great simplicities behind. And he was afraid.

He was afraid of that greatness. He was afraid of the great imperatives that he knew would at once take hold of his life. He wanted to muddle on for just a little longer. He wanted to stay just where he was, in his familiar prison house, with the key of escape in his hand. Before he took the last step into the very presence of truth, he would—think.

He put down the glass and lay down upon his bed....

III

He awoke in a mood of great depression out of a dream of wandering interminably in an endless building of innumerable pillars, pillars so vast and high that the ceiling was lost in darkness. By the scale of these pillars he felt himself scarcely larger than an ant. He was always alone in these wanderings, and always missing something that passed along distant passages, something desirable, something in the nature of a procession or of a ceremony, something of which he was in futile pursuit, of which he heard faint echoes, something luminous of which he seemed at times to see the last fading reflection, across vast halls and wildernesses of shining pavement and through Cyclopaean archways. At last there was neither sound nor gleam, but the utmost solitude, and a darkness and silence and the uttermost profundity of sorrow....

It was bright day. Dunk had just come into the room with his tea, and the tumbler of Dr. Dale's tonic stood untouched upon the night table. The bishop sat up in bed. He had missed his opportunity. To day was a busy day, he knew.

"No," he said, as Dunk hesitated whether to remove or leave the tumbler. "Leave that."

Dunk found room for it upon the tea tray, and vanished softly with the bishop's evening clothes.

The bishop remained motionless facing the day. There stood the draught of decision that he had lacked the decision even to touch.

From his bed he could just read the larger items that figured upon the engagement tablet which it was Whippham's business to fill over night and place upon his table. He had two confirmation services, first the big one in the cathedral and then a second one in the evening at Pringle, various committees and an interview with Chasters. He had not yet finished his addresses for these confirmation services....

The task seemed mountainous—overwhelming.

With a gesture of desperation he seized the tumblerful of tonic and drank it off at a gulp.

IV

For some moments nothing seemed to happen.

Then he began to feel stronger and less wretched, and then came a throbbing and tingling of artery and nerve.

He had a sense of adventure, a pleasant fear in the thing that he had done. He got out of bed, leaving his cup of tea untasted, and began to dress. He had the sensation of relief a prisoner may feel who suddenly tries his cell door and finds it open upon sunshine, the outside world and freedom.

He went on dressing although he was certain that in a few minutes the world of delusion about him would dissolve, and that he would find himself again in the great freedom of the place of God.

This time the transition came much sooner and much more rapidly. This time the phases and quality of the experience were different. He felt once again that luminous confusion between the world in which a human life is imprisoned and a circumambient and interpenetrating world, but this phase passed very rapidly; it did not spread out over nearly half an hour as it had done before, and almost immediately he seemed to plunge away from everything in this life altogether into that outer freedom he sought. And this time there was not even the elemental scenery of the former vision. He stood on nothing; there was nothing below and nothing above him. There was no sense of falling, no terror, but a feeling as though he floated released. There was no light, but as it were a clear darkness about him. Then it was manifest to him that he was not alone, but that with him was that same being that in his former vision had called himself the Angel of God. He knew this without knowing why he knew this, and either he spoke and was answered, or he thought and his thought answered him back. His state of mind on this occasion was altogether different from the first vision of God; before it had been spectacular, but now his perception was altogether super sensuous.

(And nevertheless and all the time it seemed that very faintly he was still in his room.)

It was he who was the first to speak. The great Angel whom he felt rather than saw seemed to be waiting for him to speak.

"I have come," he said, "because once more I desire to see God."

"But you have seen God."

"I saw God. God was light, God was truth. And I went back to my life, and God was hidden. God seemed to call me. He called. I heard him, I sought him and I touched his hand. When I went back to my life I was presently lost in perplexity. I could not tell why God had called me nor what I had to do."

"And why did you not come here before?"

"Doubt and fear. Brother, will you not lay your hand on mine?"

The figure in the darkness became distincter. But nothing touched the bishop's seeking hands.

"I want to see God and to understand him. I want reassurance. I want conviction. I want to understand all that God asks me to do. The world is full of conflict and confusion and the spirit of war. It is dark and dreadful now with suffering and bloodshed. I want to serve God who could save it, and I do not know how."

It seemed to the bishop that now he could distinguish dimly but surely the form and features of the great Angel to whom he talked. For a little while there was silence, and then the Angel spoke.

"It was necessary first," said the Angel, "that you should apprehend God and desire him. That was the purport of your first vision. Now, since you require it, I will tell you and show you certain things about him, things that it seems you need to know, things that all men need to know. Know then first that the time is at hand when God will come into the world and rule it, and when men will know what is required of them. This time is close at hand. In a little while God will be made manifest throughout the earth. Men will know him and know that he is King. To you this truth is to be shown—that you may tell it to others."

"This is no vision?" said the bishop, "no dream that will pass away?"

"Am I not here beside you?"

V

The bishop was anxious to be very clear. Things that had been shapelessly present in his mind now took form and found words for themselves.

"The God I saw in my vision—He is not yet manifest in the world?"

"He comes. He is in the world, but he is not yet manifested. He whom you saw in your vision will speedily be manifest in the world. To you this vision is given of the things that come. The world is already glowing with God. Mankind is like a smouldering fire that will presently, in quite a little time, burst out into flame.

"In your former vision I showed you God," said the Angel. "This time I will show you certain signs of the coming of God. And then you will understand the place you hold in the world and the task that is required of you."

VI

And as the Angel spoke he lifted up his hands with the palms upward, and there appeared above them a little round cloud, that grew denser until it had the likeness of a silver sphere. It was a mirror in the form of a ball, but a mirror not shining uniformly; it was discoloured with greyish patches that had a familiar shape. It circled slowly upon the Angel's hands. It seemed no greater than the compass of a human skull, and yet it was as great as the earth. Indeed it showed the whole earth. It was the earth. The hands of the Angel vanished out of sight, dissolved and vanished, and the spinning world hung free. All about the bishop the velvet darkness broke into glittering points that shaped out the constellations, and nearest to them, so near as to seem only a few million miles away in the great emptiness into which everything had resolved itself, shone the sun, a ball of red tongued fires. The Angel was but a voice now; the bishop and the Angel were somewhere aloof from and yet accessible to the circling silver sphere.

At the time all that happened seemed to happen quite naturally, as things happen in a dream. It was only later, when all this was a matter of memory, that the bishop realized how strange and incomprehensible his vision had been. The sphere was the earth with all its continents and seas, its ships and cities, its country sides and mountain ranges. It was so small that he could see it all at once, and so great and full that he could see everything in it. He could see great countries like little patches upon it, and at the same time he could see the faces of the men upon the highways, he could see the feelings in men's hearts and the thoughts in their minds. But it did not seem in any way wonderful to the bishop that so he should see those things, or that it was to him that these things were shown.

"This is the whole world," he said.

"This is the vision of the world," the Angel answered.

"It is very wonderful," said the bishop, and stood for a moment marvelling at the compass of his vision. For here was India, here was Samarkand, in the light of the late afternoon; and China and the swarming cities upon her silvery rivers sinking through twilight to the night and throwing a spray and tracery of lantern spots upon the dark; here was Russia under the noontide, and so great a battle of artillery raging on the Dunajec as no man had ever seen before; whole lines of trenches dissolved into clouds of dust and heaps of blood streaked earth; here close to the waiting streets of Constantinople were the hills of Gallipoli, the grave of British Imperialism, streaming to heaven with the dust and smoke of bursting shells and rifle fire and the smoke and flame of burning brushwood. In the sea of Marmora a big ship crowded with Turkish troops was sinking; and, purple under the clear water, he could see the shape of the British submarine which had torpedoed her and had submerged and was going away. Berlin prepared its frugal meals, still far from famine. He saw the war in Europe as if he saw it on a map, yet every human detail showed. Over hundreds of miles of trenches east and west of Germany he could see shells bursting and the men below dropping, and the stretcher bearers going back with the wounded. The roads to every front were crowded with reserves and munitions. For a moment a little group of men indifferent to all this struggle, who were landing amidst the Antarctic wilderness, held his attention; and then his eyes went westward to the dark rolling Atlantic across which, as the edge of the night was drawn like a curtain, more and still more ships became visible beating upon their courses eastward or westward under the overtaking day.

The wonder increased; the wonder of the single and infinitely multitudinous adventure of mankind.

"So God perhaps sees it," he whispered.

VII

"Look at this man," said the Angel, and the black shadow of a hand seemed to point.

It was a Chinaman sitting with two others in a little low room separated by translucent paper windows from a noisy street of shrill voiced people. The three had been talking of the ultimatum that Japan had sent that day to China, claiming a priority in many matters over European influences they were by no means sure whether it was a wrong or a benefit that had been done to their country. From that topic they had passed to the discussion of the war, and then of wars and national aggressions and the perpetual thrusting and quarrelling of mankind. The older man had said that so life would always be; it was the will of Heaven. The little, very yellow faced, emaciated man had agreed with him. But now this younger man, to whose thoughts the Angel had so particularly directed the bishop's attention, was speaking. He did not agree with his companion.

"War is not the will of Heaven," he said; "it is the blindness of men."

"Man changes," he said, "from day to day and from age to age. The science of the West has taught us that. Man changes and war changes and all things change. China has been the land of flowery peace, and she may yet give peace to all the world. She has put aside that puppet Emperor at Peking, she turns her face to the new learning of the West as a man lays aside his heavy robes, in order that her task may be achieved."

The older man spoke, his manner was more than a little incredulous, and yet not altogether contemptuous. "You believe that someday there will be no more war in the world, that a time will come when men will no longer plot and plan against the welfare of men?"

"Even that last," said the younger man. "Did any of us dream twenty five years ago that here in China we should live to see a republic? The age of the republics draws near, when men in every country of the world will look straight up to the rule of Right and the empire of Heaven."

("And God will be King of the World," said the Angel. "Is not that faith exactly the faith that is coming to you?")

The two other Chinamen questioned their companion, but without hostility.

"This war," said the Chinaman, "will end in a great harvesting of kings."

"But Japan—" the older man began.

The bishop would have liked to hear more of that conversation, but the dark hand of the Angel motioned him to another part of the world. "Listen to this," said the Angel.

He pointed the bishop to where the armies of Britain and Turkey lay in the heat of Mesopotamia. Along the sandy bank of a wide, slow flowing river rode two horsemen, an Englishman and a Turk. They were returning from the Turkish lines, whither the Englishman had been with a flag of truce. When Englishmen and Turks are thrown together they soon become friends, and in this case matters had been facilitated by the Englishman's command of the Turkish language. He was quite an exceptional Englishman. The Turk had just been remarking cheerfully that it wouldn't please the Germans if they were to discover how amiably he and his charge had got on. "It's a pity we ever ceased to be friends," he said.

"You Englishmen aren't like our Christians," he went on.

The Englishmen wanted to know why.

"You haven't priests in robes. You don't chant and worship crosses and pictures, and quarrel among yourselves."

"We worship the same God as you do," said the Englishman.

"Then why do we fight?"

"That's what we want to know."

"Why do you call yourselves Christians? And take part against us? All who worship the One God are brothers."

"They ought to be," said the Englishman, and thought. He was struck by what seemed to him an amazingly novel idea.

"If it weren't for religions all men would serve God together," he said. "And then there would be no wars—only now and then perhaps just a little honest fighting...."

"And see here," said the Angel. "Here close behind this frightful battle, where the German phalanx of guns pounds its way through the Russian hosts. Here is a young German talking to two wounded Russian prisoners, who have stopped to rest by the roadside. He is a German of East Prussia; he knows and thinks a little Russian. And they too are saying, all three of them, that the war is not God's will, but the confusion of mankind.

"Here," he said, and the shadow of his hand hovered over the burning ghats of Benares, where a Brahmin of the new persuasion watched the straight spires of funereal smoke ascend into the glow of the late afternoon, while he talked to an English painter, his friend, of the blind intolerance of race and caste and custom in India.

"Or here."

The Angel pointed to a group of people who had gathered upon a little beach at the head of a Norwegian fiord. There were three lads, an old man and two women, and they stood about the body of a drowned German sailor which had been washed up that day. For a time they had talked in whispers, but now suddenly the old man spoke aloud.

"This is the fourth that has come ashore," he said. "Poor drowned souls! Because men will not serve God."

"But folks go to church and pray enough," said one of the women.

"They do not serve God," said the old man. "They just pray to him as one nods to a beggar. They do not serve God who is their King. They set up their false kings and emperors, and so all Europe is covered with dead, and the seas wash up these dead to us. Why does the world suffer these things? Why did we Norwegians, who are a free spirited people, permit the Germans and the Swedes and the English to set up a king over us? Because we lack faith. Kings mean secret counsels, and secret counsels bring war. Sooner or later war will come to us also if we give the soul of our nation in trust to a king.... But things will not always be thus with men. God will not suffer them for ever. A day comes, and it is no distant day, when God himself will rule the earth, and when men will do, not what the king wishes nor what is expedient nor what is customary, but what is manifestly right."....

"But men are saying that now in a thousand places," said the Angel. "Here is something that goes a little beyond that."

His pointing hand went southward until they saw the Africanders riding down to Windhuk. Two men, Boer farmers both, rode side by side and talked of the German officer they brought prisoner with them. He had put sheep dip in the wells of drinking water; his life was fairly forfeit, and he was not to be killed. "We want no more hate in South Africa," they agreed. "Dutch and English and German must live here now side by side. Men cannot always be killing."

"And see his thoughts," said the Angel.

The German's mind was one amazement. He had been sure of being shot, he had meant to make a good end, fierce and scornful, a relentless fighter to the last; and these men who might have shot him like a man were going to spare him like a dog. His mind was a tumbled muddle of old and new ideas. He had been brought up in an atmosphere of the foulest and fiercest militarism; he had been trained to relentlessness, ruthlessness and so forth; war was war and the bitterer the better, frightfulness was your way to victory over every enemy. But these people had found a better way. Here were Dutch and English side by side; sixteen years ago they had been at war together and now they wore the same uniform and rode together, and laughed at him for a queer fellow because he was for spitting at them and defying them, and folding his arms and looking level at the executioners' rifles. There were to be no executioners' rifles.... If it was so with Dutch and English, why shouldn't it be so presently with French and Germans? Why someday shouldn't French, German, Dutch and English, Russian and Pole, ride together under this new star of mankind, the Southern Cross, to catch whatever last mischief maker was left to poison the wells of goodwill?

His mind resisted and struggled against these ideas. "Austere," he whispered. "The ennobling tests of war." A trooper rode up alongside, and offered him a drink of water

"Just a mouthful," he said apologetically. "We've had to go rather short."...

"There's another brain busy here with the same idea," the Angel interrupted. And the bishop found himself looking into the bedroom of a young German attache in Washington, sleepless in the small hours.

"Ach!" cried the young man, and sat up in bed and ran his hands through his fair hair.

He had been working late upon this detestable business of the Lusitania; the news of her sinking had come to hand two days before, and all America was aflame with it. It might mean war. His task had been to pour out explanations and justifications to the press; to show that it was an act of necessity, to pretend a conviction that the great ship was loaded with munitions, to fight down the hostility and anger that blazed across a continent. He had worked to his limit. He had taken cup after cup of coffee, and had come to bed worked out not two hours ago. Now here he was awake after a nightmare of drowning women and children, trying to comfort his soul by recalling his own arguments. Never once since the war began had he doubted the rightness of the German cause. It seemed only a proof of his nervous exhaustion that he could doubt it now. Germany was the best organized, most cultivated, scientific and liberal nation the earth had ever seen, it was for the good of mankind that she should be the dominant power in the world; his patriotism had had the passion of a mission. The English were indolent, the French decadent, the Russians barbaric, the Americans basely democratic; the rest of the world was the "White man's Burthen"; the clear destiny of mankind was subservience to the good Prussian eagle. Nevertheless—those wet draggled bodies that swirled down in the eddies of the sinking Titan—Ach! He wished it could have been otherwise. He nursed his knees and prayed that there need not be much more of these things before the spirit of the enemy was broken and the great Peace of Germany came upon the world.

And suddenly he stopped short in his prayer.

Suddenly out of the nothingness and darkness about him came the conviction that God did not listen to his prayers....

Was there any other way?

It was the most awful doubt he had ever had, for it smote at the training of all his life. "Could it be possible that after all our old German God is not the proper style and title of the true God? Is our old German God perhaps only the last of a long succession of bloodstained tribal effigies—and not God at all?"

For a long time it seemed that the bishop watched the thoughts that gathered in the young attache's mind. Until suddenly he broke into a quotation, into that last cry of the dying Goethe, for "Light. More Light!"...

"Leave him at that," said the Angel. "I want you to hear these two young women."

The hand came back to England and pointed to where Southend at the mouth of the Thames was all agog with the excitement of an overnight Zeppelin raid. People had got up hours before their usual time in order to look at the wrecked houses before they went up to their work in town. Everybody seemed abroad. Two nurses, not very well trained as nurses go nor very well educated women, were snatching a little sea air upon the front after an eventful night. They were too excited still to sleep. They were talking of the horror of the moment when they saw the nasty thing "up there," and felt helpless as it dropped its bombs. They had both hated it.

"There didn't ought to be such things," said one.

"They don't seem needed," said her companion.

"Men won't always go on like this—making wars and all such wickedness."

"It's 'ow to stop them?"

"Science is going to stop them."

"Science?"

"Yes, science. My young brother—oh, he's a clever one—he says such things! He says that it's science that they won't always go on like this. There's more sense coming into the world and more—my young brother says so. Says it stands to reason; it's Evolution. It's science that men are all brothers; you can prove it. It's science that there oughtn't to be war. Science is ending war now by making it horrible like this, and making it so that no one is safe. Showing it up. Only when nobody is safe will everybody want to set up peace, he says. He says it's proved there could easily be peace all over the world now if it wasn't for flags and kings and capitalists and priests. They still manage to keep safe and out of it. He says the world ought to be just one state. The World State, he says it ought to be."

("Under God," said the bishop, "under God.")

"He says science ought to be King of the whole world."

"Call it Science if you will," said the bishop. "God is wisdom."

"Out of the mouths of babes and elementary science students," said the Angel. "The very children in the board schools are turning against this narrowness and nonsense and mischief of nations and creeds and kings. You see it at a thousand points, at ten thousand points, look, the world is all flashing and flickering; it is like a spinthariscope; it is aquiver with the light that is coming to mankind. It is on the verge of blazing even now."

"Into a light."

"Into the one Kingdom of God. See here! See here! And here! This brave little French priest in a helmet of steel who is daring to think for the first time in his life; this gentle mannered emir from Morocco looking at the grave diggers on the battlefield; this mother who has lost her son...."

"You see they all turn in one direction, although none of them seem to dream yet that they are all turning in the same direction. They turn, every one, to the rule of righteousness, which is the rule of God. They turn to that communism of effort in the world which alone permits men to serve God in state and city and their economic lives.... They are all coming to the verge of the same salvation, the salvation of one human brotherhood under the rule of one Righteousness, one Divine will.... Is that the salvation your church offers?"

VIII

"And now that we have seen how religion grows and spreads in men's hearts, now that the fields are white with harvest, I want you to look also and see what the teachers of religion are doing," said the Angel.

He smiled. His presence became more definite, and the earthly globe about them and the sun and the stars grew less distinct and less immediately there. The silence invited the bishop to speak.

"In the light of this vision, I see my church plainly for the little thing it is," he said.

He wanted to be perfectly clear with the Angel and himself.

"This church of which I am a bishop is just a part of our poor human struggle, small and pitiful as one thinks of it here in the light of the advent of God's Kingdom, but very great, very great indeed, ancient and high and venerable, in comparison with me. But mostly it is human. It is most human. For my story is the church's story, and the church's story is mine. Here I could almost believe myself the church itself. The world saw a light, the nations that were sitting in darkness saw a great light. Even as I saw God. And then the church began to forget and lose itself among secondary things. As I have done.... It tried to express the truth and lost itself in a maze of theology. It tried to bring order into the world and sold its faith to Constantine. These men who had professed the Invisible King of the World, shirked his service. It is a most terrible disaster that Christianity has sold itself to emperors and kings. They forged a saying of the Master's that we should render unto Ceasar the things that are Ceasar's and unto God the things that are God's....

"Who is this Ceasar to set himself up to share mankind with God? Nothing that is Ceasar's can be any the less God's. But Constantine Caesar sat in the midst of the council, his guards were all about it, and the poor fanatics and trimmers and schemers disputed nervously with their eyes on him, disputed about homoousian and homoiousian, and grimaced and pretended to be very very fierce and exact to hide how much they were frightened and how little they knew, and because they did not dare to lay violent hands upon that usurper of the empire of the world....

"And from that day forth the Christian churches have been damned and lost. Kept churches. Lackey churches. Roman, Russian, Anglican; it matters not. My church indeed was twice sold, for it doubled the sin of Nicaea and gave itself over to Henry and Elizabeth while it shammed a dispute about the sacraments. No one cared really about transubstantiation any more than the earlier betrayers cared about consubstantiality; that dispute did but serve to mask the betrayal."

He turned to the listening Angel. "What can you show me of my church that I do not know? Why! we Anglican bishops get our sees as footmen get a job. For months Victoria, that old German Frau, delayed me—because of some tittle tattle.... The things we are! Snape, who afterwards became Bishop of Burnham, used to waylay the Prince Consort when he was riding in Hyde Park and give him, he boasts, 'a good loud cheer,' and then he would run very fast across the park so as to catch him as he came round, and do it again.... It is to that sort of thing we bearers of the light have sunken....

"I have always despised that poor toady," the bishop went on. "And yet here am I, and God has called me and shown me the light of his countenance, and for a month I have faltered. That is the mystery of the human heart, that it can and does sin against the light. What right have I, who have seen the light—and failed, what right have I—to despise any other human being? I seem to have been held back by a sort of paralysis.

"Men are so small, so small still, that they cannot keep hold of the vision of God. That is why I want to see God again.... But if it were not for this strange drug that seems for a little while to lift my mind above the confusion and personal entanglements of every day, I doubt if even now I could be here. I am here, passionate to hold this moment and keep the light. As this inspiration passes, I shall go back, I know, to my home and my place and my limitations. The littleness of men! The forgetfulness of men! I want to know what my chief duty is, to have it plain, in terms so plain that I can never forget.

"See in this world," he said, turning to the globe, "while Chinese merchants and Turkish troopers, school board boys and Norwegian fishermen, half trained nurses and Boer farmers are full of the spirit of God, see how the priests of the churches of Nicaea spend their time."

And now it was the bishop whose dark hands ran over the great silver globe, and it was the Angel who stood over him and listened, as a teacher might stand over a child who is learning a lesson. The bishop's hand rested for a second on a cardinal who was planning a political intrigue to produce a reaction in France, then for a moment on a Pomeranian pastor who was going out to his well tilled fields with his Sunday sermon, full of fierce hatred of England, still echoing in his head. Then he paused at a Mollah preaching the Jehad, in doubt whether he too wasn't a German pastor, and then at an Anglican clergyman still lying abed and thinking out a great mission of Repentance and Hope that should restore the authority of the established church—by incoherent missioning—without any definite sin indicated for repentance nor any clear hope for anything in particular arising out of such activities. The bishop's hand went seeking to and fro, but nowhere could he find any religious teacher, any religious body rousing itself to meet the new dawn of faith in the world. Some few men indeed seemed thoughtful, but within the limitation of their vows. Everywhere it was church and creed and nation and king and property and partisanship, and nowhere was it the True God that the priests and teachers were upholding. It was always the common unhampered man through whom the light of God was breaking; it was always the creed and the organization of the religious professionals that stood in the way to God....

"God is putting the priests aside," he cried, "and reaching out to common men. The churches do not serve God. They stand between man and God. They are like great barricades on the way to God."

The bishop's hand brushed over Archbishop Pontifex, who was just coming down to breakfast in his palace. This pompous old man was dressed in a purple garment that set off his tall figure very finely, and he was holding out his episcopal ring for his guests to kiss, that being the customary morning greeting of Archbishop Pontifex. The thought of that ring kissing had made much hard work at lower levels "worth while" to Archbishop Pontifex. And seventy miles away from him old Likeman breakfasted in bed on Benger's food, and searched his Greek Testament for tags to put to his letters. And here was the familiar palace at Princhester, and in an armchair in his bed room sat Bishop Scrope insensible and motionless, in a trance in which he was dreaming of the coming of God.

"I see my futility. I see my vanity. But what am I to do?" he said, turning to the darkness that now wrapped about the Angel again, fold upon fold. "The implications of yesterday bind me for the morrow. This is my world. This is what I am and what I am in. How can I save myself? How can I turn from these habits and customs and obligations to the service of the one true God? When I see myself, then I understand how it is with the others. All we priests and teachers are men caught in nets. I would serve God. Easily said! But how am I to serve God? How am I to help and forward His coming, to make myself part of His coming?"

He perceived that he was returning into himself, and that the vision of the sphere and of the starry spaces was fading into non existence.

He struggled against this return. He felt that his demand was still unanswered. His wife's face had suddenly come very close to him, and he realized she intervened between him and that solution.

What was she doing here?

IX

The great Angel seemed still to be near at hand, limitless space was all about him, and yet the bishop perceived that he was now sitting in the arm chair in his bedroom in the palace of Princhester. He was both there and not there. It seemed now as if he had two distinct yet kindred selves, and that the former watched the latter. The latter was now awakening to the things about him; the former marked his gestures and listened with an entire detachment to the words he was saying. These words he was saying to Lady Ella: "God is coming to rule the world, I tell you. We must leave the church."

Close to him sat Lady Ella, watching him with an expression in which dismay and resolution mingled. Upon the other side of him, upon a little occasional table, was a tray with breakfast things. He was no longer the watcher now, but the watched.

Lady Ella bent towards him as he spoke. She seemed to struggle with and dismiss his astonishing statement.

"Edward," she said, "you have been taking a drug." He looked round at his night table to see the little phial. It had gone. Then he saw that Lady Ella held it very firmly in her hand.

"Dunk came to me in great distress. He said you were insensible and breathing heavily. I came. I realized. I told him to say nothing to any one, but to fetch me a tray with your breakfast. I have kept all the other servants away and I have waited here by you.... Dunk I think is safe.... You have been muttering and moving your head from side to side...."

The bishop's mind was confused. He felt as though God must be standing just outside the room. "I have failed in my duty," he said. "But I am very near to God." He laid his hand on her arm. "You know, Ella, He is very close to us...."

She looked perplexed.

He sat up in his chair.

"For some months now," he said, "there have been new forces at work in my mind. I have been invaded by strange doubts and still stranger realizations. This old church of ours is an empty mask. God is not specially concerned in it."

"Edward!" she cried, "what are you saying?"

"I have been hesitating to tell you. But I see now I must tell you plainly. Our church is a cast hull. It is like the empty skin of a snake. God has gone out of it."

She rose to her feet. She was so horrified that she staggered backward, pushing her chair behind her. "But you are mad," she said.

He was astonished at her distress. He stood up also.

"My dear," he said, "I can assure you I am not mad. I should have prepared you, I know...."

She looked at him wild eyed. Then she glanced at the phial, gripped in her hand.

"Oh!" she exclaimed, and going swiftly to the window emptied out the contents of the little bottle. He realized what she was doing too late to prevent her.

"Don't waste that!" he cried, and stepping forward caught hold of her wrist. The phial fell from her white fingers, and crashed upon the rough paved garden path below.

"My dear," he cried, "my dear. You do not understand."

They stood face to face. "It was a tonic," he said. "I have been ill. I need it."

"It is a drug," she answered. "You have been uttering blasphemies."

He dropped her arm and walked half way across the room. Then he turned and faced her.

"They are not blasphemies," he said. "But I ought not to have surprised you and shocked you as I have done. I want to tell you of changes that have happened to my mind."

"Now!" she exclaimed, and then: "I will not hear them now. Until you are better. Until these fumes—"

Her manner changed. "Oh, Edward!" she cried, "why have you done this? Why have you taken things secretly? I know you have been sleepless, but I have been so ready to help you. I have been willing— you know I have been willing—for any help. My life is all to be of use to you...."

"Is there any reason," she pleaded, "why you should have hidden things from me?"

He stood remorseful and distressed. "I should have talked to you," he said lamely.

"Edward," she said, laying her hands on his shoulders, "will you do one thing for me? Will you try to eat a little breakfast? And stay here? I will go down to Mr. Whippham and arrange whatever is urgent with him. Perhaps if you rest—There is nothing really imperative until the confirmation in the afternoon.... I do not understand all this. For some time—I have felt it was going on. But of that we can talk. The thing now is that people should not know, that nothing should be seen.... Suppose for instance that horrible White Blackbird were to hear of it.... I implore you. If you rest here—And if I were to send for that young doctor who attended Miriam."

"I don't want a doctor," said the bishop.

"But you ought to have a doctor."

"I won't have a doctor," said the bishop.

It was with a perplexed but powerless dissent that the externalized perceptions of the bishop witnessed his agreement with the rest of Lady Ella's proposals so soon as this point about the doctor was conceded.

X

For the rest of that day until his breakdown in the cathedral the sense of being in two places at the same time haunted the bishop's mind. He stood beside the Angel in the great space amidst the stars, and at the same time he was back in his ordinary life, he was in his palace at Princhester, first resting in his bedroom and talking to his wife and presently taking up the routines of his duties again in his study downstairs.

His chief task was to finish his two addresses for the confirmation services of the day. He read over his notes, and threw them aside and remained for a time thinking deeply. The Greek tags at the end of Likeman's letter came into his thoughts; they assumed a quality of peculiar relevance to this present occasion. He repeated the words: "Epitelesei. Epiphausei."

He took his little Testament to verify them. After some slight trouble he located the two texts. The first, from Philippians, ran in the old version, "He that hath begun a good work in you will perform it"; the second was expressed thus: "Christ shall give thee light." He was dissatisfied with these renderings and resorted to the revised version, which gave "perfect" instead of "perform," and "shall shine upon you" for "give thee light." He reflected profoundly for a time.

Then suddenly his addresses began to take shape in his mind, and these little points lost any significance. He began to write rapidly, and as he wrote he felt the Angel stood by his right hand and read and approved what he was writing. There were moments when his mind seemed to be working entirely beyond his control. He had a transitory questioning whether this curious intellectual automatism was not perhaps what people meant by "inspiration."

XI

The bishop had always been sensitive to the secret fount of pathos that is hidden in the spectacle of youth. Long years ago when he and Lady Ella had been in Florence he had been moved to tears by the beauty of the fresh faced eager Tobit who runs beside the great angel in the picture of Botticelli. And suddenly and almost as uncontrollably, that feeling returned at the sight of the young congregation below him, of all these scores of neophytes who were gathered to make a public acknowledgment of God. The war has invested all youth now with the shadow of tragedy; before it came many of us were a little envious of youth and a little too assured of its certainty of happiness. All that has changed. Fear and a certain tender solicitude mingle in our regard for every child; not a lad we pass in the street but may presently be called to face such pain and stress and danger as no ancient hero ever knew. The patronage, the insolent condescension of age, has vanished out of the world. It is dreadful to look upon the young.

He stood surveying the faces of the young people as the rector read the Preface to the confirmation service. How simple they were, how innocent! Some were a little flushed by the excitement of the occasion; some a little pallid. But they were all such tender faces, so soft in outline, so fresh and delicate in texture and colour. They had soft credulous mouths. Some glanced sideways at one another; some listened with a forced intentness. The expression of one good looking boy, sitting in a corner scat, struck the bishop as being curiously defiant. He stood very erect, he blinked his eyes as though they smarted, his lips were compressed bitterly. And then it seemed to the bishop that the Angel stood beside him and gave him understanding.

"He is here," the bishop knew, "because he could not avoid coming. He tried to excuse himself. His mother wept. What could he do? But the church's teaching nowadays fails even to grip the minds of boys."

The rector came to the end of his Preface: "They will evermore endeavour themselves faithfully to observe such things as they by their own confession have assented unto."

"Like a smart solicitor pinning them down," said the bishop to himself, and then roused himself, unrolled the little paper in his hand, leant forward, and straightway began his first address.

Nowadays it is possible to say very unorthodox things indeed in an Anglican pulpit unchallenged. There remains no alert doctrinal criticism in the church congregations. It was possible, therefore, for the bishop to say all that follows without either hindrance or disturbance. The only opposition, indeed, came from within, from a sense of dreamlike incongruity between the place and the occasion and the things that he found himself delivering.

"All ceremonies," he began, "grow old. All ceremonies are tainted even from the first by things less worthy than their first intention, and you, my dear sons and daughters, who have gathered to day in this worn and ancient building, beneath these monuments to ancient vanities and these symbols of forgotten or abandoned theories about the mystery of God, will do well to distinguish in your minds between what is essential and what is superfluous and confusing in this dedication you make of yourselves to God our Master and King. For that is the real thing you seek to do today, to give yourselves to God. This is your spiritual coming of age, in which you set aside your childish dependence upon teachers and upon taught phrases, upon rote and direction, and stand up to look your Master in the face. You profess a great brotherhood when you do that, a brotherhood that goes round the earth, that numbers men of every race and nation and country, that aims to bring God into all the affairs of this world and make him not only the king of your individual lives but the king— in place of all the upstarts, usurpers, accidents, and absurdities who bear crowns and sceptres today—of an united mankind."

He paused, and in the pause he heard a little rustle as though the congregation before him was sitting up in its places, a sound that always nerves and reassures an experienced preacher.

"This, my dear children, is the reality of this grave business to day, as indeed it is the real and practical end of all true religion. This is your sacrament urn, your soldier's oath. You salute and give your fealty to the coming Kingdom of God. And upon that I would have you fix your minds to the exclusion of much that, I know only too well, has been narrow and evil and sectarian in your preparation for this solemn rite. God is like a precious jewel found among much rubble; you must cast the rubble from you. The crowning triumph of the human mind is simplicity; the supreme significance of God lies in his unity and universality. The God you salute to day is the God of the Jews and Gentiles alike, the God of Islam, the God of the Brahmo Somaj, the unknown God of many a righteous unbeliever. He is not the God of those felted theologies and inexplicable doctrines with which your teachers may have confused your minds. I would have it very clear in your minds that having drunken the draught you should not reverence unduly the cracked old vessel that has brought it to your lips. I should be falling short of my duty if I did not make that and everything I mean by that altogether plain to you."

He saw the lad whose face of dull defiance he had marked before, sitting now with a startled interest in his eyes. The bishop leant over the desk before him, and continued in the persuasive tone of a man who speaks of things too manifest for laboured argument.

"In all ages religion has come from God through broad minded creative men, and in all ages it has fallen very quickly into the hands of intense and conservative men. These last—narrow, fearful, and suspicious—have sought in every age to save the precious gift of religion by putting it into a prison of formulae and asseverations. Bear that in mind when you are pressed to definition. It is as if you made a box hermetically sealed to save the treasure of a fresh breeze from the sea. But they have sought out exact statements and tortuous explanations of the plain truth of God, they have tried to take down God in writing, to commit him to documents, to embalm his living faith as though it would otherwise corrupt. So they have lost God and fallen into endless differences, disputes, violence, and darkness about insignificant things. They have divided religion between this creed and teacher and that. The corruption of the best is the worst, said Aristotle; and the great religions of the world, and especially this Christianity of ours, are the ones most darkened and divided and wasted by the fussings and false exactitudes of the creed monger and the sectary. There is no lie so bad as a stale disfigured truth. There is no heresy so damnable as a narrow orthodoxy. All religious associations carry this danger of the over statement that misstates and the over emphasis that divides and betrays. Beware of that danger. Do not imagine, because you are gathered in this queerly beautiful old building today, because I preside here in this odd raiment of an odder compromise, because you see about you in coloured glass and carven stone the emblems of much vain disputation, that thereby you cut yourselves off and come apart from the great world of faith, Catholic, Islamic, Brahministic, Buddhistic, that grows now to a common consciousness of the near Advent of God our King. You enter that waiting world fraternity now, you do not leave it. This place, this church of ours, should be to you not a seclusion and a fastness but a door.

"I could quote you a score of instances to establish that this simple universalism was also the teaching of Christ. But now I will only remind you that it was Mary who went to her lord simply, who was commended, and not Martha who troubled about many things. Learn from the Mary of Faith and not from these Marthas of the Creeds. Let us abandon the presumptions of an ignorant past. The perfection of doctrine is not for finite men. Give yourselves to God. Give yourselves to God. Not to churches and uses, but to God. To God simply. He is the first word of religion and the last. He is Alpha; he is Omega. Epitelesei; it is He who will finish the good work begun."

The bishop ended his address in a vivid silence. Then he began his interrogation.

"Do you here, in the presence of God, and of this congregation, renew the solemn promise and vow that was made in your name at your Baptism; ratifying and confirming the same in your own persons, and acknowledging yourselves—"

He stopped short. The next words were: "bound to believe and do all those things, which your Godfathers and Godmothers then undertook for you."

He could not stand those words. He hesitated, and then substituted: "acknowledge yourselves to be the true servants of the one God, who is the Lord of Mankind?"

For a moment silence hung in the cathedral. Then one voice, a boy's voice, led a ragged response. "I do."

Then the bishop: "Our help is in the Name of the Lord."

The congregation answered doubtfully, with a glance at its prayer books: "Who hath made heaven and earth."

The bishop: "Blessed be the name of the Lord."

The congregation said with returning confidence: "Henceforth, world without end."

XII

Before his second address the bishop had to listen to Veni Creator Spiritus, in its English form, and it seemed to him the worst of all possible hymns. Its defects became monstrously exaggerated to his hypersensitive mind. It impressed him in its Englished travesty as a grotesque, as a veritable Charlie Chaplin among hymns, and in truth it does stick out most awkward feet, it misses its accusatives, it catches absurdly upon points of abstruse doctrine. The great Angel stood motionless and ironical at the bishop's elbow while it was being sung. "Your church," he seemed to say.

"We must end this sort of thing," whispered the bishop. "We must end this sort of thing—absolutely." He glanced at the faces of the singers, and it became beyond all other things urgent, that he should lift them once for all above the sectarian dogmatism of that hymn to a simple vision of God's light....

He roused himself to the touching business of the laying on of hands. While he did so the prepared substance of his second address was running through his mind. The following prayer and collects he read without difficulty, and so came to his second address. His disposition at first was explanatory.

"When I spoke to you just now," he began, "I fell unintentionally into the use of a Greek word, epitelesei. It was written to me in a letter from a friend with another word that also I am now going to quote to you. This letter touched very closely upon the things I want to say to you now, and so these two words are very much in my mind. The former one was taken from the Epistle to the Philippians; it signifies, 'He will complete the work begun'; the one I have now in mind comes from the Epistle to the Ephesians; it is Epiphausei—or, to be fuller, epiphausei soi ho Christos, which signifies that He will shine upon us. And this is very much in my thoughts now because I do believe that this world, which seemed so very far from God a little while ago, draws near now to an unexampled dawn. God is at hand.

"It is your privilege, it is your grave and terrible position, that you have been born at the very end and collapse of a negligent age, of an age of sham kingship, sham freedom, relaxation, evasion, greed, waste, falsehood, and sinister preparation. Your lives open out in the midst of the breakdown for which that age prepared. To you negligence is no longer possible. There is cold and darkness, there is the heat of the furnace before you; you will live amidst extremes such as our youth never knew; whatever betide, you of your generation will have small chance of living untempered lives. Our country is at war and half mankind is at war; death and destruction trample through the world;

men rot and die by the million, food diminishes and fails, there is a wasting away of all the hoarded resources, of all the accumulated well being of mankind; and there is no clear prospect yet of any end to this enormous and frightful conflict. Why did it ever arise? What made it possible? It arose because men had forgotten God. It was possible because they worshipped simulacra, were loyal to phantoms of race and empire, permitted themselves to be ruled and misled by idiot princes and usurper kings. Their minds were turned from God, who alone can rule and unite mankind, and so they have passed from the glare and follies of those former years into the darkness and anguish of the present day. And in darkness and anguish they will remain until they turn to that King who comes to rule them, until the sword and indignation of God have overthrown their misleaders and oppressors, and the Justice of God, the Kingdom of God set high over the republics of mankind, has brought peace for ever to the world. It is to this militant and imminent God, to this immortal Captain, this undying Law giver, that you devote yourselves to day.

"For he is imminent now. He comes. I have seen in the east and in the west, the hearts and the minds and the wills of men turning to him as surely as when a needle is magnetized it turns towards the north. Even now as I preach to you here, God stands over us all, ready to receive us...."

And as he said these words, the long nave of the cathedral, the shadows of its fretted roof, the brown choir with its golden screen, the rows of seated figures, became like some picture cast upon a flimsy and translucent curtain. Once more it seemed to the bishop that he saw God plain. Once more the glorious effulgence poured about him, and the beautiful and wonderful conquest of men's hearts and lives was manifest to him.

He lifted up his hands and cried to God, and with an emotion so profound, an earnestness so commanding, that very many of those who were present turned their faces to see the figure to which he looked and spoke. And some of the children had a strange persuasion of a presence there, as of a divine figure militant, armed, and serene....

"Oh God our Leader and our Master and our Friend," the bishop prayed, "forgive our imperfection and our little motives, take us and make us one with thy great purpose, use us and do not reject us, make us all here servants of thy kingdom, weave our lives into thy struggle to conquer and to bring peace and union to the world. We are small and feeble creatures, we are feeble in speech, feebler still in action, nevertheless let but thy light shine upon us and there is not one of us who cannot be lit by thy fire, and who cannot lose himself in thy salvation. Take us into thy purpose, O God. Let thy kingdom come into our hearts and into this world."

His voice ceased, and he stood for a measurable time with his arms extended and his face upturned....

The golden clouds that whirled and eddied so splendidly in his brain thinned out, his sense of God's immediacy faded and passed, and he was left aware of the cathedral pulpit in which he stood so strangely posed, and of the astonished congregation below him. His arms sank to his side. His eyes fell upon the book in front of him and he felt for and gripped the two upper corners of it and, regardless of the common order and practice, read out the Benediction, changing the words involuntarily as he read:

"The Blessing of God who is the Father, the Son, the Spirit and the King of all Mankind, be upon you and remain with you for ever. Amen."

Then he looked again, as if to look once more upon that radiant vision of God, but now he saw only the clear cool space of the cathedral vault and the coloured glass and tracery of the great rose window. And then, as the first notes of the organ came pealing above the departing stir of the congregation, he turned about and descended slowly, like one who is still half dreaming, from the pulpit.

XIII

In the vestry he found Canon Bliss. "Help me to take off these garments," the bishop said. "I shall never wear them again."

"You are ill," said the canon, scrutinizing his face.

"Not ill. But the word was taken out of my mouth. I perceive now that I have been in a trance, a trance in which the truth is real. It is a fearful thing to find oneself among realities. It is a dreadful thing when God begins to haunt a priest.... I can never minister in the church again."

Whippham thrust forward a chair for the bishop to sit down. The bishop felt now extraordinarily fatigued. He sat down heavily, and rested his wrists on the arms of the chair. "Already," he resumed presently, "I begin to forget what it was I said."

"You became excited," said Bliss, "and spoke very loudly and clearly."

"What did I say?"

"I don't know what you said; I have forgotten. I never want to remember. Things about the Second Advent. Dreadful things. You said God was close at hand. Happily you spoke partly in Greek. I doubt if any of those children understood. And you had a kind of lapse—an aphasia. You mutilated the interrogation and you did not pronounce the benediction properly. You changed words and you put in words. One sat frozen—waiting for what would happen next."

"We must postpone the Pringle confirmation," said Whippham. "I wonder to whom I could telephone."

Lady Ella appeared, and came and knelt down by the bishop's chair. "I never ought to have let this happen," she said, taking his wrists in her hands. "You are in a fever, dear."

"It seemed entirely natural to say what I did," the bishop declared.

Lady Ella looked up at Bliss.

"A doctor has been sent for," said the canon to Lady Ella.

"I must speak to the doctor," said Lady Ella as if her husband could not hear her. "There is something that will make things clearer to the doctor. I must speak to the doctor for a moment before he sees him."

Came a gust of pretty sounds and a flash of bright colour that shamed the rich vestments at hand. Over the shoulder of the rector and quite at the back, appeared Lady Sunderbund resolutely invading the vestry. The rector intercepted her, stood broad with extended arms.

"I must come in and speak to him. If it is only fo' a moment."

The bishop looked up and saw Lady Ella's expression. Lady Ella was sitting up very stiffly, listening but not looking round.

A vague horror and a passionate desire to prevent the entry of Lady Sunderbund at any cost, seized upon the bishop. She would, he felt, be the last overwhelming complication. He descended to a base subterfuge. He lay back in his chair slowly as though he unfolded himself, he covered his eyes with his hand and then groaned aloud.

"Leave me alone!" he cried in a voice of agony. "Leave me alone! I can see no one.... I can—no more."

There was a momentous silence, and then the tumult of Lady Sunderbund receded.

CHAPTER THE EIGHTH

THE NEW WORLD

I

That night the bishop had a temperature of a hundred and a half. The doctor pronounced him to be in a state of intense mental excitement, aggravated by some drug. He was a doctor modern and clear minded enough to admit that he could not identify the drug. He overruled, every one overruled, the bishop's declaration that he had done with the church, that he could never mock God with his episcopal ministrations again, that he must proceed at once with his resignation. "Don't think of these things," said the doctor. "Banish them from your mind until your temperature is down to ninety eight. Then after a rest you may go into them."

Lady Ella insisted upon his keeping his room. It was with difficulty that he got her to admit Whippham, and Whippham was exasperatingly in order. "You need not trouble about anything now, my lord," he said. "Everything will keep until you are ready to attend to it. It's well we're through with Easter. Bishop Buncombe of Eastern Blowdesia was coming here anyhow. And there is Canon Bliss. There's only two ordination candidates because of the war. We'll get on swimmingly."

The bishop thought he would like to talk to those two ordination candidates, but they prevailed upon him not to do so. He lay for the best part of one night confiding remarkable things to two imaginary ordination candidates.

He developed a marked liking for Eleanor's company. She was home again now after a visit to some friends. It was decided that the best thing to do with him would be to send him away in her charge. A journey abroad was impossible. France would remind him too dreadfully of the war. His own mind turned suddenly to the sweet air of Hunstanton. He had gone there at times to read, in the old Cambridge days. "It is a terribly ugly place," he said, "but it is wine in the veins."

Lady Ella was doubtful about Zeppelins. Thrice they had been right over Hunstanton already. They came in by the easy landmark of the Wash.

"It will interest him," said Eleanor, who knew her father better.

II

One warm and still and sunny afternoon the bishop found himself looking out upon the waters of the Wash. He sat where the highest pebble layers of the beach reached up to a little cliff of sandy earth perhaps a foot high, and he looked upon sands and sea and sky and saw that they were beautiful.

He was a little black gaitered object in a scene of the most exquisite and delicate colour. Right and left of him stretched the low grey salted shore, pale banks of marly earth surmounted by green grey wiry grass that held and was half buried in fine blown sand. Above, the heavens made a complete hemisphere of blue in which a series of remote cumulus clouds floated and dissolved. Before him spread the long levels of the sands, and far away at its utmost ebb was the sea. Eleanor had gone to explore the black ribs of a wrecked fishing boat that lay at the edge of a shallow lagoon. She was a little pink footed figure, very bright and apparently transparent. She had reverted for a time to shameless childishness; she had hidden her stockings among the reeds of the bank, and she was running to and fro, from star fish to razor shell and from cockle to weed. The shingle was pale drab and purple close at hand, but to the westward, towards Hunstanton, the sands became brown and purple, and were presently broken up into endless skerries of low flat weed covered boulders and little intensely blue pools. The sea was a band of sapphire that became silver to the west; it met the silver shining sands in one delicate breathing edge of intensely white foam. Remote to the west, very small and black and clear against the afternoon sky, was a cart, and about it was a score or so of mussel gatherers. A little nearer, on an apparently empty stretch of shining wet sand, a multitude of gulls was mysteriously busy. These two groups of activities and Eleanor's flitting translucent movements did but set off and emphasize the immense and soothing tranquillity.

For a long time the bishop sat passively receptive to this healing beauty. Then a little flow of thought began and gathered in his mind. He had come out to think over two letters that he had brought with him. He drew these now rather reluctantly from his pocket, and after a long pause over the envelopes began to read them.

He reread Likeman's letter first.

Likeman could not forgive him.

"My dear Scrope," he wrote, "your explanation explains nothing. This sensational declaration of infidelity to our mother church, made under the most damning and distressing circumstances in the presence of young and tender minds entrusted to your ministrations, and in defiance of the honourable engagements implied in the confirmation service, confirms my worst apprehensions of the weaknesses of your character. I have always felt the touch of theatricality in your temperament, the peculiar craving to be pseudo deeper, pseudo simpler than us all, the need of personal excitement. I know that you were never quite contented to believe in God at second hand. You wanted to be taken notice of—personally. Except for some few hints to you, I have never breathed a word of these doubts to any human being; I have always hoped that the ripening that comes with years and experience would give you an increasing strength against the dangers of emotionalism and against your strong, deep, quiet sense of your exceptional personal importance...."

The bishop read thus far, and then sat reflecting.

Was it just?

He had many weaknesses, but had he this egotism? No; that wasn't the justice of the case. The old man, bitterly disappointed, was endeavouring to wound. Scrope asked himself whether he was to blame for that disappointment. That was a more difficult question....

He dismissed the charge at last, crumpled up the letter in his hand, and after a moment's hesitation flung it away.... But he remained acutely sorry, not so much for himself as for the revelation of Likeman this letter made. He had had a great affection for Likeman and suddenly it was turned into a wound.

III

The second letter was from Lady Sunderbund, and it was an altogether more remarkable document. Lady Sunderbund wrote on a notepaper that was evidently the result of a perverse research, but she wrote a letter far more coherent than her speech, and without that curious falling away of the r's that flavoured even her gravest observations with an unjust faint aroma of absurdity. She wrote with a thin pen in a rounded boyish handwriting. She italicized with slashes of the pen.

He held this letter in both hands between his knees, and considered it now with an expression that brought his eyebrows forward until they almost met, and that tucked in the corners of his mouth.

"My dear Bishop," it began.

"I keep thinking and thinking and thinking of that wonderful service, of the wonderful, wonderful things you said, and the wonderful choice you made of the moment to say them—when all those young lives were coming to the great serious thing in life. It was most beautifully done. At any rate, dear Bishop and Teacher, it was most beautifully begun. And now we all stand to you like creditors because you have given us so much that you owe us ever so much more. You have started us and you have to go on with us. You have broken the shell of the old church, and here we are running about with nowhere to go. You have to make the shelter of a new church now for us, purged of errors, looking straight to God. The King of Mankind!—what a wonderful, wonderful phrase that is. It says everything. Tell us more of him and more. Count me first—not foremost, but just the little one that runs in first—among your disciples. They say you are resigning your position in the church. Of course that must be true. You are coming out of it—what did you call it?—coming out of the cracked old vessel from which you have poured the living waters. I called on Lady Ella yesterday. She did not tell me very much; I think she is a very reserved as well as a very dignified woman, but she said that you intended to go to London. In London then I suppose you will set up the first altar to the Divine King. I want to help.

"Dear Bishop and Teacher, I want to help tremendously—with all my heart and all my soul. I want to be let do things for you." (The "you" was erased by three or four rapid slashes, and "our King" substituted.)

"I want to be privileged to help build that First Church of the World Unified under God. It is a dreadful thing to says but, you see, I am very rich; this dreadful war has made me ever so much richer—steel and shipping and things—it is my trustees have done it. I am ashamed to be so rich. I want to give. I want to give and help this great beginning of yours. I want you to let me help on the temporal side, to make it easy for you to stand forth and deliver your message, amidst suitable surroundings and without any horrid worries on account of the sacrifices you have made. Please do not turn my offering aside. I have never wanted anything so much in all my life as I want to make this gift. Unless I can make it I feel that for me there is no salvation! I shall stick with my loads and loads of stocks and shares and horrid possessions outside the Needle's Eye. But if I could build a temple for God, and just live somewhere near it so as to be the poor woman who sweeps out the chapels, and die perhaps and be buried under its floor! Don't smile at me. I mean every word of it. Years ago I thought of such a thing. After I had visited the Certosa di Pavia—do you know it? So beautiful, and those two still alabaster figures—recumbent. But until now I could never see my way to any such service. Now I do. I am all afire to do it. Help me! Tell me! Let me stand behind you and make your mission possible. I feel I have come to the most wonderful phase in my life. I feel my call has come....

"I have written this letter over three times, and torn each of them up. I do so want to say all this, and it is so desperately hard to say. I am full of fears that you despise me. I know there is a sort of high colour about me. My passion for brightness. I am absurd. But inside of me is a soul, a real, living, breathing soul. Crying out to you: 'Oh, let me help! Let me help!' I will do anything, I will endure anything if only I can keep hold of the vision splendid you gave me in the cathedral. I see it now day and night, the dream of the place I can make for you—and you preaching! My fingers itch to begin. The day before yesterday I said to myself, 'I am quite unworthy, I am a worldly woman, a rich, smart, decorated woman. He will never accept me as I am.' I took off all my jewels, every one, I looked through all my clothes, and at last I decided I would have made for me a very simple straight grey dress, just simple and straight and grey. Perhaps you will think that too is absurd of me, too self conscious. I would not tell of it to you if I did not want you to understand how alive I am to my utter impossibilities, how resolved I am to do anything so that I may be able to serve. But never mind about silly me; let me tell you how I see the new church.

"I think you ought to have some place near the centre of London; not too west, for you might easily become fashionable, not too east because you might easily be swallowed up in merely philanthropic work, but somewhere between the two. There must be vacant sites still to be got round about Kingsway. And there we must set up your tabernacle, a very plain, very simple, very beautifully proportioned building in which you can give your message. I know a young man, just the very young man to do something of the sort, something quite new, quite modern, and yet solemn and serious. Lady Ella seemed to think you wanted to live somewhere in the north west of London—but she would tell me very little. I seem to see you not there at all, not in anything between west end and suburb, but yourself as central as your mind, in a kind of clergy house that will be part of the building. That is how it is in my dream anyhow. All that though can be settled afterwards. My imagination and my desire is running away with me. It is no time yet for premature plans. Not that I am not planning day and night. This letter is simply to offer. I just want to offer. Here I am and all my worldly goods. Take me, I pray you. And not only pray you. Take me, I demand of you, in the name of God our king. I have a right to be used. And you have no right to refuse me. You have to go on with your message, and it is your duty to take me—just as you are obliged to step on any steppingstone that lies on your way to do God service.... And so I am waiting. I shall be waiting—on thorns. I know you will take your time and think. But do not take too much time. Think of me waiting.

"Your servant, your most humble helper in God (your God),

"AGATHA SUNDERBUND."

And then scrawled along the margin of the last sheet:

"If, when you know—a telegram. Even if you cannot say so much as 'Agreed,' still such a word as 'Favourable.' I just hang over the Void until I hear.

"AGATHA S."

A letter demanding enormous deliberation. She argued closely in spite of her italics. It had never dawned upon the bishop before how light is the servitude of the disciple in comparison with the servitude of the master. In many ways this proposal repelled and troubled him, in many ways it attracted him. And the argument of his clear obligation to accept her co operation gripped him; it was a good argument.

And besides it worked in very conveniently with certain other difficulties that perplexed him.

IV

The bishop became aware that Eleanor was returning to him across the sands. She had made an end to her paddling, she had put on her shoes and stockings and become once more the grave and responsible young woman who had been taking care of him since his flight from Princhester. He replaced the two letters in his pocket, and sat ready to smile as she drew near; he admired her open brow, the toss of her hair, and the poise of her head upon her neck. It was good to note that her hard reading at Cambridge hadn't bent her shoulders in the least....

"Well, old Dad!" she said as she drew near. "You've got back a colour."

"I've got back everything. It's time I returned to Princhester."

"Not in this weather. Not for a day or so." She flung herself at his feet. "Consider your overworked little daughter. Oh, how good this is!"

"No," said the bishop in a grave tone that made her look up into his face. "I must go hack."

He met her clear gaze. "What do you think of all this business, Eleanor?" he asked abruptly. "Do you think I had a sort of fit in the cathedral?"

He winced as he asked the question.

"Daddy," she said, after a little pause; "the things you said and did that afternoon were the noblest you ever did in your life. I wish I had been there. It must have been splendid to be there. I've not told you before—I've been dying to.... I'd promised not to say a word—not to remind you. I promised the doctor. But now you ask me, now you are well again, I can tell you. Kitty Kingdom has told me all about it, how it felt. It was like light and order coming into a hopeless dark muddle. What you said was like what we have all been trying to think—I mean all of us young people. Suddenly it was all clear."

She stopped short. She was breathless with the excitement of her confession.

Her father too remained silent for a little while. He was reminded of his weakness; he was, he perceived, still a little hysterical. He felt that he might weep at her youthful enthusiasm if he did not restrain himself.

"I'm glad," he said, and patted her shoulder. "I'm glad, Norah."

She looked away from him out across the lank brown sands and water pools to the sea. "It was what we have all been feeling our way towards, the absolute simplification of religion, the absolute simplification of politics and social duty; just God, just God the King."

"But should I have said that—in the cathedral?"

She felt no scruples. "You had to," she said.

"But now think what it means," he said. "I must leave the church."

"As a man strips off his coat for a fight."

"That doesn't dismay you?"

She shook her head, and smiled confidently to sea and sky.

"I'm glad if you're with me," he said. "Sometimes—I think—I'm not a very self reliant man."

"You'll have all the world with you," she was convinced, "in a little time."

"Perhaps rather a longer time than you think, Norah. In the meantime—"

She turned to him once more.

"In the meantime there are a great many things to consider. Young people, they say, never think of the transport that is needed to win a battle. I have it in my mind that I should leave the church. But I can't just walk out into the marketplace and begin preaching there. I see the family furniture being carried out of the palace and put into vans. It has to go somewhere...."

"I suppose you will go to London."

"Possibly. In fact certainly. I have a plan. Or at least an opportunity.... But that isn't what I have most in mind. These things are not done without emotion and a considerable strain upon one's personal relationships. I do not think this—I do not think your mother sees things as we do."

"She will," said young enthusiasm, "when she understands."

"I wish she did. But I have been unlucky in the circumstances of my explanations to her. And of course you understand all this means risks—poverty perhaps—going without things—travel, opportunity, nice possessions—for all of us. A loss of position too. All this sort of thing," he stuck out a gaitered calf and smiled, "will have to go. People, some of them, may be disasagreeable to us...."

"After all, Daddy," she said, smiling, "it isn't so bad as the cross and the lions and burning pitch. And you have the Truth."

"You do believe—?" He left his sentence unfinished.

She nodded, her face aglow. "We know you have the Truth."

"Of course in my own mind now it is very clear. I had a kind of illumination...." He would have tried to tell her of his vision, and he was too shy. "It came to me suddenly that the whole world was in confusion because men followed after a thousand different immediate aims, when really it was quite easy, if only one could be simple it was quite easy, to show that nearly all men could only be fully satisfied and made happy in themselves by one single aim, which was also the aim that would make the whole world one great order, and that aim was to make God King of one's heart and the whole world. I saw that all this world, except for a few base monstrous spirits, was suffering hideous things because of this war, and before the war it was full of folly, waste, social injustice and suspicion for the same reason, because it had not realized the kingship of God. And that is so simple; the essence of God is simplicity. The sin of this war lies with men like myself, men who set up to tell people about God, more than it lies with any other class—"

"Kings?" she interjected. "Diplomatists? Finance?"

"Yes. Those men could only work mischief in the world because the priests and teachers let them. All things human lie at last at the door of the priest and teacher. Who differentiate, who qualify and complicate, who make mean unnecessary elaborations, and so divide mankind. If it were not for the weakness and wickedness of the priests, every one would know and understand God. Every one who was modest enough not to set up for particular knowledge. Men disputed whether God is Finite or Infinite, whether he has a triple or a single aspect. How should they know? All we need to know is the face he turns to us. They impose their horrible creeds and distinctions. None of those things matter. Call him Christ the God or call him simply God, Allah, Heaven; it does not matter. He comes to us, we know, like a Helper and Friend; that is all we want to know. You may speculate further if you like, but it is not religion. They dispute whether he can set aside nature. But that is superstition. He is either master of nature and he knows that it is good, or he is part of nature and must obey. That is an argument for hair splitting metaphysicians. Either answer means the same for us. It does not matter which way we come to believe that he does not idly set the course of things aside. Obviously he does not set the course of things aside. What he does do for certain is to give us courage and save us from our selfishness and the bitter hell it makes for us. And every one knows too what sort of things we want, and for what end we want to escape from ourselves. We want to do right. And right, if you think clearly, is just truth within and service without, the service of God's kingdom, which is mankind, the service of human needs and the increase of human power and experience. It is all perfectly plain, it is all quite easy for any one to understand, who isn't misled and chattered at and threatened and poisoned by evil priests and teachers."

"And you are going to preach that, Daddy?"

"If I can. When I am free—you know I have still to resign and give up—I shall make that my message."

"And so God comes."

"God comes as men perceive him in his simplicity.... Let men but see God simply, and forthwith God and his kingdom possess the world."

She looked out to sea in silence for awhile.

Then she turned to her father. "And you think that His Kingdom will come—perhaps in quite a little time—perhaps in our lifetimes? And that all these ridiculous or wicked little kings and emperors, and these political parties, and these policies and conspiracies, and this nationalist nonsense and all the patriotism and rowdyism, all the private profit seeking and every baseness in life, all the things that it is so horrible and disgusting to be young among and powerless among, you think they will fade before him?"

The bishop pulled his faith together.

"They will fade before him—but whether it will take a lifetime or a hundred lifetimes or a thousand lifetimes, my Norah—"

He smiled and left his sentence unfinished, and she smiled back at him to show she understood.

And then he confessed further, because he did not want to seem merely sentimentally hopeful.

"When I was in the cathedral, Norah—and just before that service, it seemed to me—it was very real.... It seemed that perhaps the Kingdom of God is nearer than we suppose, that it needs but the faith and courage of a few, and it may be that we may even live to see the dawning of his kingdom, even—who knows?—the sunrise. I am so full of faith and hope that I fear to be hopeful with you. But whether it is near or far—"

"We work for it," said Eleanor.

Eleanor thought, eyes downcast for a little while, and then looked up.

"It is so wonderful to talk to you like this, Daddy. In the old days, I didn't dream—Before I went to Newnham. I misjudged you. I thought Never mind what I thought. It was silly. But now I am so proud of you. And so happy to be back with you, Daddy, and find that your religion is after all just the same religion that I have been wanting."

CHAPTER THE NINTH

THE THIRD VISION

I

One afternoon in October, four months and more after that previous conversation, the card of Mr. Edward Scrope was brought up to Dr. Brighton Pomfrey. The name awakened no memories. The doctor descended to discover a man so obviously in unaccustomed plain clothes that he had a momentary disagreeable idea that he was facing a detective. Then he saw that this secular disguise draped the familiar form of his old friend, the former Bishop of Princhester. Scrope was pale and a little untidy; he had already acquired something of the peculiar, slightly faded quality one finds in a don who has gone to Hampstead and fallen amongst advanced thinkers and got mixed up with the Fabian Society. His anxious eyes and faintly propitiatory manner suggested an impending appeal.

Dr. Brighton Pomfrey had the savoir faire of a successful consultant; he prided himself on being all things to all men; but just for an instant he was at a loss what sort of thing he had to be here. Then he adopted the genial, kindly, but by no means lavishly generous tone advisable in the case of a man who has suffered considerable social deterioration without being very seriously to blame.

Dr. Brighton Pomfrey was a little round faced man with defective eyesight and an unsuitable nose for the glasses he wore, and he flaunted—God knows why—enormous side whiskers.

"Well," he said, balancing the glasses skilfully by throwing back his head, "and how are you? And what can I do for you? There's no external evidence of trouble. You're looking lean and a little pale, but thoroughly fit."

"Yes," said the late bishop, "I'm fairly fit—"

"Only—?" said the doctor, smiling his teeth, with something of the manner of an old bathing woman who tells a child to jump.

"Well, I'm run down and—worried."

"We'd better sit down," said the great doctor professionally, and looked hard at him. Then he pulled at the arm of a chair.

The ex bishop sat down, and the doctor placed himself between his patient and the light.

"This business of resigning my bishopric and so forth has involved very considerable strains," Scrope began. "That I think is the essence of the trouble. One cuts so many associations.... I did not realize how much feeling there would be.... Difficulties too of readjusting one's position."

"Zactly. Zactly. Zactly," said the doctor, snapping his face and making his glasses vibrate. "Run down. Want a tonic or a change?"

"Yes. In fact—I want a particular tonic."

Dr. Brighton Pomfrey made his eyes and mouth round and interrogative.

"While you were away last spring—"

"Had to go," said the doctor, "unavoidable. Gas gangrene. Certain enquiries. These young investigators all very well in their way. But we older reputations—Experience. Maturity of judgment. Can't do without us. Yes?"

"Well, I came here last spring and saw, an assistant I suppose he was, or a supply,—do you call them supplies in your profession?—named, I think—Let me see—D—?"

"Dale!"

The doctor as he uttered this word set his face to the unaccustomed exercise of expressing malignity. His round blue eyes sought to blaze, small cherubic muscles exerted themselves to pucker his brows. His colour became a violent pink. "Lunatic!" he said. "Dangerous Lunatic! He didn't do anything—anything bad in your case, did he?"

He was evidently highly charged with grievance in this matter. "That man was sent to me from Cambridge with the highest testimonials. The very highest. I had to go at twenty four hours' notice. Enquiry—gas gangrene. There was nothing for it but to leave things in his hands."

Dr. Brighton Pomfrey disavowed responsibility with an open, stumpy fingered hand.

"He did me no particular harm," said Scrope.

"You are the first he spared," said Dr. Brighton Pomfrey.

"Did he—? Was he unskilful?"

"Unskilful is hardly the word."

"Were his methods peculiar?"

The little doctor sprang to his feet and began to pace about the room. "Peculiar!" he said. "It was abominable that they should send him to me. Abominable!"

He turned, with all the round knobs that constituted his face, aglow. His side whiskers waved apart like wings about to flap. He protruded his face towards his seated patient. "I am glad that he has been killed," he said. "Glad! There!"

His glasses fell off—shocked beyond measure. He did not heed them. They swung about in front of him as if they sought to escape while he poured out his feelings.

"Fool!" he spluttered with demonstrative gestures. "Dangerous fool! His one idea—to upset everybody. Drugs, Sir! The most terrible drugs! I come back. Find ladies. High social position. Morphine maniacs. Others. Reckless use of the most dangerous expedients.... Cocaine not in it. Stimulants—violent stimulants. In the highest quarters. Terrible. Exalted persons. Royalty! Anxious to be given war work and become anonymous.... Horrible! He's been a terrible influence. One idea—to disturb soul and body. Minds unhinged. Personal relations deranged. Shattered the practice of years. The harm he has done! The harm!"

He looked as though he was trying to burst—as a final expression of wrath. He failed. His hands felt trembling to recover his pince nez. Then from his tail pocket he produced a large silk handkerchief and wiped the glasses. Replaced them. Wriggled his head in his collar, running his fingers round his neck. Patted his tie.

"Excuse this outbreak!" he said. "But Dr. Dale has inflicted injuries!"

Scrope got up, walked slowly to the window, clasping his hands behind his back, and turned. His manner still retained much of his episcopal dignity. "I am sorry. But still you can no doubt tell from your books what it was he gave me. It was a tonic that had a very great effect on me. And I need it badly now."

Dr. Brighton Pomfrey was quietly malignant. "He kept no diary at all," he said. "No diary at all."

"But

"If he did," said Dr. Brighton Pomfrey, holding up a flat hand and wagging it from side to side, "I wouldn't follow his treatment." He intensified with the hand going faster. "I wouldn't follow his treatment. Not under any circumstances."

"Naturally," said Scrope, "if the results are what you say. But in my case it wasn't a treatment. I was sleepless, confused in my mind, wretched and demoralized; I came here, and he just produced the stuff—It clears the head, it clears the mind. One seems to get away from the cloud of things, to get through to essentials and fundamentals. It straightened me out.... You must know such a stuff. Just now, confronted with all sorts of problems arising out of my resignation, I want that tonic effect again. I must have it. I have matters to decide—and I can't decide. I find myself uncertain, changeable from hour to hour. I don't ask you to take up anything of this man Dale's. This is a new occasion. But I want that drug."

At the beginning of this speech Dr. Brighton Pomfrey's hands had fallen to his hips. As Scrope went on the doctor's pose had stiffened. His head had gone a little on one side; he had begun to play with his glasses. At the end he gave vent to one or two short coughs, and then pointed his words with his glasses held out.

"Tell me," he said, "tell me." (Cough.) "Had this drug that cleared your head—anything to do with your resignation?"

And he put on his glasses disconcertingly, and threw his head back to watch the reply.

"It did help to clear up the situation."

"Exactly," said Dr. Brighton Pomfrey in a tone that defined his own position with remorseless clearness. "Exactly." And he held up a flat, arresting hand. .

"My dear Sir," he said. "How can you expect me to help you to a drug so disastrous?—even if I could tell you what it is."

"But it was not disastrous to me," said Scrope.

"Your extraordinary resignation—your still more extraordinary way of proclaiming it!"

"I don't think those were disasters."

"But my dear Sir!"

"You don't want to discuss theology with me, I know. So let me tell you simply that from my point of view the illumination that came to me—this drug of Dr. Dale's helping—has been the great release of my life. It crystallized my mind. It swept aside the confusing commonplace things about me. Just for a time I saw truth clearly.... I want to do so again."

"Why?"

"There is a crisis in my affairs—never mind what. But I cannot see my way clear."

Dr. Brighton Pomfrey was meditating now with his eyes on his carpet and the corners of his mouth tucked in. He was swinging his glasses pendulum wise. "Tell me," he said, looking sideways at Scrope, "what were the effects of this drug? It may have been anything. How did it give you this— this vision of the truth—that led to your resignation?"

Scrope felt a sudden shyness. But he wanted Dale's drug again so badly that he obliged himself to describe his previous experiences to the best of his ability.

"It was," he said in a matter of fact tone, "a golden, transparent liquid. Very golden, like a warm tinted Chablis. When water was added it became streaked and opalescent, with a kind of living quiver in it. I held it up to the light."

"Yes? And when you took it?"

"I felt suddenly clearer. My mind—I had a kind of exaltation and assurance."

"Your mind," Dr. Brighton Pomfrey assisted, "began to go twenty nine to the dozen."

"It felt stronger and clearer," said Scrope, sticking to his quest.

"And did things look as usual?" asked the doctor, protruding his knobby little face like a clenched fist.

"No," said Scrope and regarded him. How much was it possible to tell a man of this type?

"They differed?" said the doctor, relaxing.

"Yes.... Well, to be plain.... I had an immediate sense of God. I saw the world—as if it were a transparent curtain, and then God became—evident.... Is it possible for that to determine the drug?"

"God became—evident," the doctor said with some distaste, and shook his head slowly. Then in a sudden sharp cross examining tone: "You mean you had a vision? Actually saw 'um?"

"It was in the form of a vision." Scrope was now mentally very uncomfortable indeed.

The doctor's lips repeated these words noiselessly, with an effect of contempt. "He must have given you something—It's a little like morphia. But golden—opalescent? And it was this vision made you astonish us all with your resignation?"

"That was part of a larger process," said Scrope patiently. "I had been drifting into a complete repudiation of the Anglican positions long before that. All that this drug did was to make clear what was already in my mind. And give it value. Act as a developer."

The doctor suddenly gave way to a botryoidal hilarity. "To think that one should be consulted about visions of God—in Mount Street!" he said. "And you know, you know you half want to believe that vision was real. You know you do."

So far Scrope had been resisting his realization of failure. Now he gave way to an exasperation that made him reckless of Brighton Pomfrey's opinion. "I do think," he said, "that that drug did in some way make God real to me. I think I saw God."

Dr. Brighton Pomfrey shook his head in a way that made Scrope want to hit him.

"I think I saw God," he repeated more firmly. "I had a sudden realization of how great he was and how great life was, and how timid and mean and sordid were all our genteel, professional lives. I was seized upon, for a time I was altogether possessed by a passion to serve him fitly and recklessly, to make an end to compromises with comfort and self love and secondary things. And I want to hold to that. I want to get back to that. I am given to lassitudes. I relax. I am by temperament an easy going man. I want to buck myself up, I want to get on with my larger purposes, and I find myself tired, muddled, entangled.... The drug was a good thing. For me it was a good thing. I want its help again."

"I know no more than you do what it was."

"Are there no other drugs that you do know, that have a kindred effect? If for example I tried morphia in some form?"

"You'd get visions. They wouldn't be divine visions. If you took small quantities very discreetly you might get a temporary quickening. But the swift result of all repeated drug taking is, I can assure you, moral decay—rapid moral decay. To touch drugs habitually is to become hopelessly unpunctual, untruthful, callously selfish and insincere. I am talking mere textbook, mere everyday common places, to you when I tell you that."

"I had an idea. I had a hope...."

"You've a stiff enough fight before you," said the doctor, "without such a handicap as that."

"You won't help me?"

The doctor walked up and down his hearthrug, and then delivered himself with an extended hand and waggling fingers.

"I wouldn't if I could. For your good I wouldn't. And even if I would I couldn't, for I don't know the drug. One of his infernal brews, no doubt. Something—accidental. It's lost—for good—for your good, anyhow...."

II

Scrope halted outside the stucco portals of the doctor's house. He hesitated whether he should turn to the east or the west.

"That door closes," he said. "There's no getting back that way."...

He stood for a time on the kerb. He turned at last towards Park Lane and Hyde Park. He walked along thoughtfully, inattentively steering a course for his new home in Pembury Road, Notting Hill.

III

At the outset of this new phase in Scrope's life that had followed the crisis of the confirmation service, everything had seemed very clear before him. He believed firmly that he had been shown God, that he had himself stood in the presence of God, and that there had been a plain call to him to proclaim God to the world. He had realized God, and it was the task of every one who had realized God to help all mankind to the same realization. The proposal of Lady Sunderbund had fallen in with that idea. He had been steeling himself to a prospect of struggle and dire poverty, but her prompt loyalty had come as an immense relief to his anxiety for his wife and family. When he had talked to Eleanor upon the beach at Hunstanton it had seemed to him that his course was manifest, perhaps a little severe but by no means impossible. They had sat together in the sunshine, exalted by a sense of fine adventure and confident of success, they had looked out upon the future, upon the great near future in which the idea of God was to inspire and reconstruct the world.

It was only very slowly that this pristine clearness became clouded and confused. It had not been so easy as Eleanor had supposed to win over the sympathy of Lady Ella with his resignation. Indeed it had not been won over. She had become a stern and chilling companion, mute now upon the issue of his resignation, but manifestly resentful. He was secretly disappointed and disconcerted by her tone. And the same hesitation of the mind, instinctive rather than reasoned, that had prevented a frank explanation of his earlier doubts to her, now restrained him from telling her naturally and at once of the part that Lady Sunderbund was to play in his future ministry. In his own mind he felt assured about that part, but in order to excuse his delay in being frank with his wife, he told himself that he was not as yet definitely committed to Lady Sunderbund's project. And in accordance with that idea he set up housekeeping in London upon a scale that implied a very complete cessation of income. "As yet," he told Lady Ella, "we do not know where we stand. For a time we must not so much house ourselves as camp. We must take some quite small and modest house in some less expensive district. If possible I would like to take it for a year, until we know better how things are with us."

He reviewed a choice of London districts.

Lady Ella said her bitterest thing. "Does it matter where we hide our heads?"

That wrung him to: "We are not hiding our heads."

She repented at once. "I am sorry, Ted," she said. "It slipped from me."...

He called it camping, but the house they had found in Pembury Road, Notting Hill, was more darkened and less airy than any camp. Neither he nor his wife had ever had any experience of middle class house hunting or middle class housekeeping before, and they spent three of the most desolating days of their lives in looking for this cheap and modest shelter for their household possessions. Hitherto life had moved them from one established and comfortable home to another; their worst affliction had been the modern decorations of the Palace at Princhester, and it was altogether a revelation to them to visit house after house, ill lit, ill planned, with dingy paint and peeling wallpaper, kitchens for the most part underground, and either without bathrooms or with built out bathrooms that were manifestly grudging afterthoughts, such as harbour the respectable middle classes of London. The house agents perceived intimations of helplessness in their manner, adopted a "rushing" method with them strange to people who had hitherto lived in a glowing halo of episcopal dignity. "Take it or leave it," was the note of those gentlemen; "there are always people ready for houses." The line that property in land and houses takes in England, the ex bishop realized, is always to hold up and look scornful. The position of the land owning, house owning class in a crowded country like England is ultra regal. It is under no obligation to be of use, and people are obliged to get down to the land somewhere. They cannot conduct business and rear families in the air. England's necessity is the landlord's opportunity....

Scrope began to generalize about this, and develop a new and sincerer streak of socialism in his ideas. "The church has been very remiss," he said, as he and Lady Ella stared at the basement "breakfast room" of their twenty seventh dismal possibility. "It should have insisted far more than it has done upon the landlord's responsibility. No one should tolerate the offer of such a house as this—at such a rent—to decent people. It is unrighteous."

At the house agent's he asked in a cold, intelligent ruling class voice, the name of the offending landlord.

"It's all the property of the Ecclesiastical Commissioners that side of the railway," said the agent, picking his teeth with a pin. "Lazy lot. Dreadfully hard to get 'em to do anything. Own some of the worst properties in London."

Lady Ella saw things differently again. "If you had stayed in the church," she said afterwards, "you might have helped to alter such things as that."

At the time he had no answer.

"But," he said presently as they went back in the tube to their modest Bloomsbury hotel, "if I had stayed in the church I should never have realized things like that."

IV

But it does no justice to Lady Ella to record these two unavoidable expressions of regret without telling also of the rallying courage with which she presently took over the task of resettling herself and her stricken family. Her husband's change of opinion had fallen upon her out of a clear sky, without any premonition, in one tremendous day. In one day there had come clamouring upon her, with an effect of revelation after revelation, the ideas of drugs, of heresy and blasphemy, of an alien feminine influence, of the entire moral and material breakdown of the man who had been the centre of her life. Never was the whole world of a woman so swiftly and comprehensively smashed. All the previous troubles of her life seemed infinitesimal in comparison with any single item in this dismaying debacle. She tried to consolidate it in the idea that he was ill, "disordered." She assured herself that he would return from Hunstanton restored to health and orthodoxy, with all his threatenings of a resignation recalled; the man she had loved and trusted to succeed in the world and to do right always according to her ideas. It was only with extreme reluctance that she faced the fact that with the fumes of the drug dispelled and all signs of nervous exhaustion gone, he still pressed quietly but resolutely toward a severance from the church. She tried to argue with him and she found she could not argue. The church was a crystal sphere in which her life was wholly contained, her mind could not go outside it even to consider a dissentient proposition.

While he was at Hunstanton, every day she had prayed for an hour, some days she had prayed for several hours, in the cathedral, kneeling upon a harsh hassock that hurt her knees. Even in her prayers she could not argue nor vary. She prayed over and over again many hundreds of times: "Bring him back, dear Lord. Bring him back again."

In the past he had always been a very kind and friendly mate to her, but sometimes he had been irritable about small things, especially during his seasons of insomnia; now he came back changed, a much graver man, rather older in his manner, carefully attentive to her, kinder and more watchful, at times astonishingly apologetic, but rigidly set upon his purpose of leaving the church. "I know you do not think with me in this," he said. "I have to pray you to be patient with me. I have struggled with my conscience.... For a time it means hardship, I know. Poverty. But if you will trust me I think I shall be able to pull through. There are ways of doing my work. Perhaps we shall not have to undergo this cramping in this house for very long...."

"It is not the poverty I fear," said Lady Ella.

And she did face the worldly situation, if a little sadly, at any rate with the courage of practical energy. It was she who stood in one ungainly house after another and schemed how to make discomforts tolerable, while Scrope raged unhelpfully at landlordism and the responsibility of the church for economic disorder. It was she who at last took decisions into her hands when he was too jaded to do anything but generalize weakly, and settled upon the house in Pembury Road which became their London home. She got him to visit Hunstanton again for half a week while she and Miriam, who was the practical genius of the family, moved in and made the new home presentable. At the best it was barely presentable. There were many plain hardships. The girls had to share one of the chief bedrooms in common instead of their jolly little individual dens at Princhester.... One little room was all that could be squeezed out as a study for "father"; it was not really a separate room, it was merely cut off by closed folding doors from the dining room, folding doors that slowly transmitted the dinner flavours to a sensitive worker, and its window looked out upon a blackened and uneventful yard and the skylights of a populous, conversational, and high spirited millinery establishment that had been built over the corresponding garden of the house in Restharrow Street. Lady Ella had this room lined with open shelves, and Clementina (in the absence of Eleanor at Newuham) arranged the pick of her father's books. It is to be noted as a fact of psychological interest that this cramped, ill lit little room distressed Lady Ella more than any other of the discomforts of their new quarters. The bishop's writing desk filled a whole side of it. Parsimony ruled her mind, but she could not resist the impulse to get him at least a seemly reading lamp.

He came back from Hunstanton full of ideas for work in London. He was, he thought, going to "write something" about his views. He was very grateful and much surprised at what she had done to that forbidding house, and full of hints and intimations that it would not be long before they moved to something roomier. She was disposed to seek some sort of salaried employment for Clementina and Miriam at least, but he would not hear of that. "They must go on and get educated," he said, "if I have to give up smoking to do it. Perhaps I may manage even without that." Eleanor, it seemed, had a good prospect of a scholarship at the London School of Economics that would practically keep her. There would be no Cambridge for Clementina, but London University might still be possible with a little pinching, and the move to London had really improved the prospects of a good musical training for Miriam. Phoebe and Daphne, Lady Ella believed, might get in on special terms at the Notting Hill High School.

Scrope found it difficult to guess at what was going on in the heads of his younger daughters. None displayed such sympathy as Eleanor had confessed. He had a feeling that his wife had schooled them to say nothing about the change in their fortunes to him. But they quarrelled a good deal, he could hear, about the use of the one bathroom—there was never enough hot water after the second bath. And Miriam did not seem to enjoy playing the new upright piano in the drawing room as much as she had done the Princhester grand it replaced. Though she was always willing to play that thing he liked; he knew now that it was the Adagio of Of. 111; whenever he asked for it.

London servants, Lady Ella found, were now much more difficult to get than they had been in the Holy Innocents' days in St. John's Wood. And more difficult to manage when they were got. The households of the more prosperous clergy are much sought after by domestics of a serious and excellent type; an unfrocked clergyman's household is by no means so attractive. The first comers were young women of unfortunate dispositions; the first cook was reluctant and insolent, she went before her month was up; the second careless; she made burnt potatoes and cindered chops, underboiled and overboiled eggs; a "dropped" look about everything, harsh coffee and bitter tea seemed to be a natural aspect of the state of being no longer a bishop. He would often after a struggle with his nerves in the bedroom come humming cheerfully to breakfast, to find that Phoebe, who was a delicate eater, had pushed her plate away scarcely touched, while Lady Ella sat at the end of the table in a state of dangerous calm, framing comments for delivering downstairs that would be sure to sting and yet leave no opening for repartee, and trying at the same time to believe that a third cook, if the chances were risked again, would certainly be "all right."

The drawing room was papered with a morose wallpaper that the landlord, in view of the fact that Scrope in his optimism would only take the house on a yearly agreement, had refused to replace; it was a design of very dark green leaves and grey gothic arches; and the apartment was lit by a chandelier, which spilt a pool of light in the centre of the room and splashed useless weak patches elsewhere. Lady Ella had to interfere to prevent the monopolization of this centre by Phoebe and Daphne for their home work. This light trouble was difficult to arrange; the plain truth was that there was not enough illumination to go round. In the Princhester drawing room there had been a number of obliging little electric pushes. The size of the dining room, now that the study was cut off from it, forbade hospitality. As it was, with only the family at home, the housemaid made it a grievance that she could scarcely squeeze by on the sideboard side to wait.

The house vibrated to the trains in the adjacent underground railway. There was a lady next door but one who was very pluckily training a contralto voice that most people would have gladly thrown away. At the end of Restharrow Street was a garage, and a yard where chauffeurs were accustomed to "tune up" their engines. All these facts were persistently audible to any one sitting down in the little back study to think out this project of "writing something," about a change in the government of the whole world. Petty inconveniences no doubt all these inconveniences were, but they distressed a rather oversensitive mind which was also acutely aware that even upon this scale living would cost certainly two hundred and fifty pounds if not more in excess of the little private income available.

V

These domestic details, irrelevant as they may seem in a spiritual history, need to be given because they added an intimate keenness to Scrope's readiness for this private chapel enterprise that he was discussing with Lady Sunderbund. Along that line and along that line alone, he saw the way of escape from the great sea of London dinginess that threatened to submerge his family. And it was also, he felt, the line of his duty; it was his "call."

At least that was how he felt at first. And then matters began to grow complicated again.

Things had gone far between himself and Lady Sunderbund since that letter he had read upon the beach at Old Hunstanton. The blinds of the house with the very very blue door in Princhester had been drawn from the day when the first vanload of the renegade bishop's private possessions had departed from the palace. The lady had returned to the brightly decorated flat overlooking Hyde Park. He had seen her repeatedly since then, and always with a fairly clear understanding that she was to provide the chapel and pulpit in which he was to proclaim to London the gospel of the Simplicity and Universality of God. He was to be the prophet of a reconsidered faith, calling the whole world from creeds and sects, from egotisms and vain loyalties, from prejudices of race and custom, to the worship and service of the Divine King of all mankind. That in fact had been the ruling resolve in his mind, the resolve determining his relations not only with Lady Sunderbund but with Lady Ella and his family, his friends, enemies and associates. He had set out upon this course unchecked by any doubt, and overriding the manifest disapproval of his wife and his younger daughters. Lady Sunderbund's enthusiasm had been enormous and sustaining....

Almost imperceptibly that resolve had weakened. Imperceptibly at first. Then the decline had been perceived as one sometimes perceives a thing in the background out of the corner of one's eye.

In all his early anticipations of the chapel enterprise, he had imagined himself in the likeness of a small but eloquent figure standing in a large exposed place and calling this lost misled world back to God. Lady Sunderbund, he assumed, was to provide the large exposed place (which was dimly paved with pews) and guarantee that little matter which was to relieve him of sordid anxieties for his family, the stipend. He had agreed in an inattentive way that this was to be eight hundred a year, with a certain proportion of the subscriptions. "At first, I shall be the chief subscriber," she said. "Before the rush comes." He had been so content to take all this for granted and think no more about it—more particularly to think no more about it—that for a time he entirely disregarded the intense decorative activities into which Lady Sunderbund incontinently plunged. Had he been inclined to remark them he certainly might have done so, even though a considerable proportion was being thoughtfully veiled for a time from his eyes.

For example, there was the young architect with the wonderful tie whom he met once or twice at lunch in the Hyde Park flat. This young man pulled the conversation again and again, Lady Sunderbund aiding and abetting, in the direction of the "ideal church." It was his ambition, he said, someday, to build an ideal church, "divorced from tradition."

Scrope had been drawn at last into a dissertation. He said that hitherto all temples and places of worship had been conditioned by orientation due to the seasonal aspects of religion, they pointed to the west or—as in the case of the Egyptian temples—to some particular star, and by sacramentalism, which centred everything on a highly lit sacrificial altar. It was almost impossible to think of a church built upon other lines than that. The architect would be so free that—

"Absolutely free," interrupted the young architect. "He might, for example, build a temple like a star."

"Or like some wondyful casket," said Lady Sunderbund....

And also there was a musician with fuzzy hair and an impulsive way of taking the salted almonds, who wanted to know about religious music.

Scrope hazarded the idea that a chanting people was a religious people. He said, moreover, that there was a fine religiosity about Moussorgski, but that the most beautiful single piece of music in the world was Beethoven's sonata, Opus 111,—he was thinking, he said, more particularly of the Adagio at the end, molto semplice e cantabile. It had a real quality of divinity.

The musician betrayed impatience at the name of Beethoven, and thought, with his mouth appreciatively full of salted almonds, that nowadays we had got a little beyond that anyhow.

"We shall be superhuman before we get beyond either Purcell or Beethoven," said Scrope.

Nor did he attach sufficient importance to Lady Sunderbund's disposition to invite Positivists, members of the Brotherhood Church, leaders among the Christian Scientists, old followers of the Rev. Charles Voysey, Swedenborgians, Moslem converts, Indian Theosophists, psychic phenomena and so forth, to meet him. Nevertheless it began to drift into his mind that he was by no means so completely in control of the new departure as he had supposed at first. Both he and Lady Sunderbund professed universalism; but while his was the universalism of one who would simplify to the bare fundamentals of a common faith, hers was the universalism of the collector. Religion to him was something that illuminated the soul, to her it was something that illuminated prayer books. For a considerable time they followed their divergent inclinations without any realization of their divergence. None the less a vague doubt and dissatisfaction with the prospect before him arose to cloud his confidence.

At first there was little or no doubt of his own faith. He was still altogether convinced that he had to confess and proclaim God in his life. He was as sure that God was the necessary king and saviour of mankind and of a man's life, as he was of the truth of the Binomial Theorem. But what began first to fade was the idea that he had been specially called to proclaim the True God to all the world. He would have the most amiable conference with Lady Sunderbund, and then as he walked back to Notting Hill he would suddenly find stuck into his mind like a challenge, Heaven knows how: "Another prophet?" Even if he succeeded in this mission enterprise, he found himself asking, what would he be but just a little West end Mahomet? He would have founded another sect, and we have to make an end to all sects. How is there to be an end to sects, if there are still to be chapels—richly decorated chapels—and congregations, and salaried specialists in God?

That was a very disconcerting idea. It was particularly active at night. He did his best to consider it with a cool detachment, regardless of the facts that his private income was just under three hundred pounds a year, and that his experiments in cultured journalism made it extremely improbable that the most sedulous literary work would do more than double this scanty sum. Yet for all that these nasty, ugly, sordid facts were entirely disregarded, they did somehow persist in coming in and squatting down, shapeless in a black corner of his mind—from which their eyes shone out, so to speak—whenever his doubt whether he ought to set up as a prophet at all was under consideration.

VI

Then very suddenly on this October afternoon the situation had come to a crisis.

He had gone to Lady Sunderbund's flat to see the plans and drawings for the new church in which he was to give his message to the world. They had brought home to him the complete realization of Lady Sunderbund's impossibility. He had attempted upon the spur of the moment an explanation of just how much they differed, and he had precipitated a storm of extravagantly perplexing emotions....

She kept him waiting for perhaps ten minutes before she brought the plans to him. He waited in the little room with the Wyndham Lewis picture that opened upon the balcony painted with crazy squares of livid pink. On a golden table by the window a number of recently bought books were lying, and he went and stood over these, taking them up one after another. The first was "The Countess of Huntingdon and Her Circle," that bearder of lightminded archbishops, that formidable harbourer of Wesleyan chaplains. For some minutes he studied the grim portrait of this inspired lady standing with one foot ostentatiously on her coronet and then turned to the next volume. This was a life of Saint Teresa, that energetic organizer of Spanish nunneries. The third dealt with Madame Guyon. It was difficult not to feel that Lady Sunderbund was reading for a part.

She entered.

She was wearing a long simple dress of spangled white with a very high waist; she had a bracelet of green jade, a waistband of green silk, and her hair was held by a wreath of artificial laurel, very stiff and green. Her arms were full of big rolls of cartridge paper and tracing paper. "I'm so pleased," she said. "It's 'eady at last and I can show you."

She banged the whole armful down upon a vivid little table of inlaid black and white wood. He rescued one or two rolls and a sheet of tracing paper from the floor.

"It's the Temple," she panted in a significant whisper. "It's the Temple of the One T'ue God!"

She scrabbled among the papers, and held up the elevation of a strange square building to his startled eyes. "Iszi't it just pe'fect?" she demanded.

He took the drawing from her. It represented a building, manifestly an enormous building, consisting largely of two great, deeply fluted towers flanking a vast archway approached by a long flight of steps. Between the towers appeared a dome. It was as if the Mosque of Saint Sophia had produced this offspring in a mesalliance with the cathedral of Wells. Its enormity was made manifest by the minuteness of the large automobiles that were driving away in the foreground after "setting down." "Here is the plan," she said, thrusting another sheet upon him before he could fully take in the quality of the design. "The g'eat Hall is to be pe'fectly 'ound, no aisle, no altar, and in lettas of sapphiah, 'God is ev'ywhe'.'"

She added with a note of solemnity, "It will hold th'ee thousand people sitting down."

"But—!" said Scrope.

"The'e's a sort of g'andeur," she said. "It's young Venable's wo'k. It's his fl'st g'ate oppo'tunity."

"But—is this to go on that little site in Aldwych?"

"He says the' isn't 'oom the'!" she explained. "He wants to put it out at Golda's G'een."

"But—if it is to be this little simple chapel we proposed, then wasn't our idea to be central?"

"But if the' isn't 'oem!" she said—conclusively. "And isn't this—isn't it rather a costly undertaking, rather more costly—"

"That doesn't matta. I'm making heaps and heaps of money. Half my p'ope'ty is in shipping and a lot of the 'eat in munitions. I'm 'icher than eva. Isn't the' a sort of g'andeur?" she pressed.

He put the elevation down. He took the plan from her hands and seemed to study it. But he was really staring blankly at the whole situation.

"Lady Sunderbund," he said at last, with an effort, "I am afraid all this won't do."

"Won't do!"

"No. It isn't in the spirit of my intention. It isn't in a great building of this sort—so—so ornate and imposing, that the simple gospel of God's Universal Kingdom can be preached."

"But oughtn't so gate a message to have as g'ate a pulpit?"

And then as if she would seize him before he could go on to further repudiations, she sought hastily among the drawings again.

"But look," she said. "It has ev'ything! It's not only a p'eaching place; it's a headquarters for ev'ything."

With the rapid movements of an excited child she began to thrust the remarkable features and merits of the great project upon him. The preaching dome was only the heart of it. There were to be a library, "'efecto'ies," consultation rooms, classrooms, a publication department, a big underground printing establishment. "Nowadays," she said, "ev'y gate movement must p'int." There was to be music, she said, "a gate invisible o'gan," hidden amidst the architectural details, and pouring out its sounds into the dome, and then she glanced in passing at possible "p'ocessions" round the preaching dome. This preaching dome was not a mere shut in drum for spiritual reverberations, around it ran great open corridors, and in these corridors there were to be "chapels."

"But what for?" he asked, stemming the torrent. "What need is there for chapels? There are to be no altars, no masses, no sacraments?"

"No," she said, "but they are to be chapels for special int'ests; a chapel for science, a chapel for healing, a chapel for gov'ment. Places for peoples to sit and think about those things—with paintings and symbols."

"I see your intention," he admitted. "I see your intention."

"The' is to be a gate da'k blue 'ound chapel for sta's and atoms and the myst'ry of matta." Her voice grew solemn. "All still and deep and high. Like a k'ystal in a da'k place. You will go down steps to it. Th'ough a da'k 'ounded a'ch ma'ked with mathematical symbols and balances and scientific app'atus.... And the ve'y next to it, the ve'y next, is to be a little b'ight chapel for bi'ds and flowas!"

"Yes," he said, "it is all very fine and expressive. It is, I see, a symbolical building, a great artistic possibility. But is it the place for me? What I have to say is something very simple, that God is the king of the whole world, king of the ha'penny newspaper and the omnibus and the vulgar everyday things, and that they have to worship him and serve him as their leader in every moment of their lives. This isn't that. This is the old religions over again. This is taking God apart. This is putting him into a fresh casket instead of the old one. And.... I don't like it."

"Don't like it," she cried, and stood apart from him with her chin in the air, a tall astonishment and dismay.

"I can't do the work I want to do with this."

"But—Isn't it you' idea?"

"No. It is not in the least my idea. I want to tell the whole world of the one God that can alone unite it and save it—and you make this extravagant toy."

He felt as if he had struck her directly he uttered that last word.

"Toy!" she echoed, taking it in, "you call it a Toy!"

A note in her voice reminded him that there were two people who might feel strongly in this affair.

"My dear Lady Sunderbund," he said with a sudden change of manner, "I must needs follow the light of my own mind. I have had a vision of God, I have seen him as a great leader towering over the little lives of men, demanding the little lives of men, prepared to take them and guide them to the salvation of mankind and the conquest of pain and death. I have seen him as the God of the human affair, a God of politics, a God of such muddy and bloody wars as this war, a God of economics, a God of railway junctions and clinics and factories and evening schools, a God in fact of men. This God—this God here, that you want to worship, is a God of artists and poets—of elegant poets, a God of bric a brac, a God of choice allusions. Oh, it has its grandeur! I don't want you to think that what you are doing may not be altogether fine and right for you to do. But it is not what I have to do.... I cannot—indeed I cannot—go on with this project—upon these lines."

He paused, flushed and breathless. Lady Sunderbund had heard him to the end. Her bright face was brightly flushed, and there were tears in her eyes. It was like her that they should seem tears of the largest, most expensive sort, tears of the first water.

"But," she cried, and her red delicate mouth went awry with dismay and disappointment, and her expression was the half incredulous expression of a child suddenly and cruelly disappointed: "You won't go on with all this?"

"No," he said. "My dear Lady Sunderbund—"

"Oh! don't Lady Sunderbund me!" she cried with a novel rudeness. "Don't you see I've done it all for you?"

He winced and felt boorish. He had never liked and disapproved of Lady Sunderbund so much as he did at that moment. And he had no words for her.

"How can I stop it all at once like this?"

And still he had no answer.

She pursued her advantage. "What am I to do?" she cried.

She turned upon him passionately. "Look what you've done!" She marked her points with finger upheld, and gave odd suggestions in her face of an angry coster girl. "Eva' since I met you, I've wo'shipped you. I've been 'eady to follow you anywhe'—to do anything. Eva' since that night when you sat so calm and dignified, and they baited you and wo'id you. When they we' all vain and cleva, and you—you thought only of God and 'iligion and didn't mind fo' you'self.... Up to then—I'd been living—oh! the emptiest life..."

The tears ran. "Pe'haps I shall live it again...." She dashed her grief away with a hand beringed with stones as big as beetles.

"I said to myself, this man knows something I don't know. He's got the seeds of ete'nal life su'ely. I made up my mind then and the' I'd follow you and back you and do all I could fo' you. I've lived fo' you. Eve' since. Lived fo' you. And now when all my little plans are 'ipe, you—! Oh!"

She made a quaint little gesture with pink fists upraised, and then stood with her hand held up, staring at the plans and drawings that were littered over the inlaid table. "I've planned and planned. I said, I will build him a temple. I will be his temple se'vant.... Just a me' se'vant...."

She could not go on.

"But it is just these temples that have confused mankind," he said.

"Not my temple," she said presently, now openly weeping over the gay rejected drawings. "You could have explained...."

"Oh!" she said petulantly, and thrust them away from her so that they went sliding one after the other on to the floor. For some long drawn moments there was no sound in the room but the slowly accelerated slide and flop of one sheet of cartridge paper after another.

"We could have been so happy," she wailed, "se'ving oua God."

And then this disconcerting lady did a still more disconcerting thing. She staggered a step towards Scrape, seized the lapels of his coat, bowed her head upon his shoulder, put her black hair against his cheek, and began sobbing and weeping.

"My dear lady!" he expostulated, trying weakly to disengage her.

"Let me k'y," she insisted, gripping more resolutely, and following his backward pace. "You must let me k'y. You must let me k'y."

His resistance ceased. One hand supported her, the other patted her shining hair. "My dear child!" he said. "My dear child! I had no idea. That you would take it like this...."

VII

That was but the opening of an enormous interview. Presently he had contrived in a helpful and sympathetic manner to seat the unhappy lady on a sofa, and when after some cramped discourse she stood up before him, wiping her eyes with a wet wonder of lace, to deliver herself the better, a newborn appreciation of the tactics of the situation made him walk to the other side of the table under colour of picking up a drawing.

In the retrospect he tried to disentangle the threads of a discussion that went to and fro and contradicted itself and began again far back among things that had seemed forgotten and disposed of. Lady Sunderbund's mind was extravagantly untrained, a wild grown mental thicket. At times she reproached him as if he were a heartless God; at times she talked as if he were a recalcitrant servant. Her mingling of utter devotion and the completest disregard for his thoughts and wishes dazzled and distressed his mind. It was clear that for half a year her clear, bold, absurd will had been crystallized upon the idea of giving him exactly what she wanted him to want. The crystal sphere of those ambitions lay now shattered between them.

She was trying to reconstruct it before his eyes.

She was, she declared, prepared to alter her plans in any way that would meet his wishes. She had not understood. "If it is a Toy," she cried, "show me how to make it not a Toy! Make it 'eal!"

He said it was the bare idea of a temple that made it impossible. And there was this drawing here; what did it mean? He held it out to her. It represented a figure, distressingly like himself, robed as a priest in vestments.

She snatched the offending drawing from him and tore it to shreds.

"If you don't want a Temple, have a meeting house. You wanted a meeting house anyhow."

"Just any old meeting house," he said. "Not that special one. A place without choirs and clergy."

"If you won't have music," she responded, "don't have music. If God doesn't want music it can go. I can't think God does not app'ove of music, but—that is for you to settle. If you don't like the' being o'naments, we'll make it all plain. Some g'ate g'ey Dome—all g'ey and black. If it isn't to be beautiful, it can be ugly. Yes, ugly. It can be as ugly"—she sobbed—"as the City Temple. We will get some otha a'chitect—some City a'chitect. Some man who has built B'anch Banks or 'ailway stations. That's if you think it pleases God.... B'eak young Venable's hea't.... Only why should you not let me make a place fo' you' message? Why shouldn't it be me? You must have a place. You've got 'to p'each somewhe'."

"As a man, not as a priest."

"Then p'each as a man. You must still wea' something."

"Just ordinary clothes."

"O'dina'y clothes a' clothes in the fashion," she said. "You would have to go to you' taila for a new p'eaching coat with b'aid put on dif'ently, or two buttons instead of th'ee...."

"One needn't be fashionable."

"Ev'ybody is fash'nable. How can you help it? Some people wea' old fashions; that's all.... A cassock's an old fashion. There's nothing so plain as a cassock."

"Except that it's a clerical fashion. I want to be just as I am now."

"If you think that—that owoble suit is o'dina'y clothes!" she said, and stared at him and gave way to tears of real tenderness.

"A cassock," she cried with passion. "Just a pe'fectly plain cassock. Fo' deecency!... Oh, if you won't—not even that!"

VIII

As he walked now after his unsuccessful quest of Dr. Brighton Pomfrey towards the Serpentine he acted that stormy interview with Lady Sunderbund over again. At the end, as a condition indeed of his departure, he had left things open. He had assented to certain promises. He was to make her understand better what it was he needed. He was not to let anything that had happened affect that "spi'tual f'enship." She was to abandon all her plans, she was to begin again "at the ve'y beginning." But he knew that indeed there should be no more beginning again with her. He knew that quite beyond these questions of the organization of a purified religion, it was time their association ended. She had wept upon him; she had clasped both his hands at parting and prayed to be forgiven. She was drawing him closer to her by their very dissension. She had infected him with the softness of remorse; from being a bright and spirited person, she had converted herself into a warm and touching person. Her fine, bright black hair against his cheek and the clasp of her hand on his shoulder was now inextricably in the business. The perplexing, the astonishing thing in his situation was that there was still a reluctance to make a conclusive breach.

He was not the first of men who have tried to find in vain how and when a relationship becomes an entanglement. He ought to break off now, and the riddle was just why he should feel this compunction in breaking off now. He had disappointed her, and he ought not to have disappointed her; that was the essential feeling. He had never realized before as he realized now this peculiar quality of his own mind and the gulf into which it was leading him. It came as an illuminating discovery.

He was a social animal. He had an instinctive disposition to act according to the expectations of the people about him, whether they were reasonable or congenial expectations or whether they were not. That, he saw for the first time, had been the ruling motive of his life; it was the clue to him. Man is not a reasonable creature; he is a socially responsive creature trying to be reasonable in spite of that fact. From the days in the rectory nursery when Scrope had tried to be a good boy on the whole and just a little naughty sometimes until they stopped smiling, through all his life of school, university, curacy, vicarage and episcopacy up to this present moment, he perceived now that he had acted upon no authentic and independent impulse. His impulse had always been to fall in with people and satisfy them. And all the painful conflicts of those last few years had been due to a growing realization of jarring criticisms, of antagonized forces that required from him incompatible things. From which he had now taken refuge—or at any rate sought refuge—in God. It was paradoxical, but manifestly in God he not only sank his individuality but discovered it.

It was wonderful how much he had thought and still thought of the feelings and desires of Lady Sunderbund, and how little he thought of God. Her he had been assiduously propitiating, managing, accepting, for three months now. Why? Partly because she demanded it, and there was a quality in her demand that had touched some hidden spring—of vanity perhaps it was—in him, that made him respond. But partly also it was because after the evacuation of the palace at Princhester he had felt more and more, felt but never dared to look squarely in the face, the catastrophic change in the worldly circumstances of his family. Only this chapel adventure seemed likely to restore those fallen and bedraggled fortunes. He had not anticipated a tithe of the dire quality of that change. They were not simply uncomfortable in the Notting Hill home. They were miserable. He fancied they looked to him with something between reproach and urgency. Why had he brought them here? What next did he propose to do? He wished at times they would say it out instead of merely looking it. Phoebe's failing appetite chilled his heart.

That concern for his family, he believed, had been his chief motive in clinging to Lady Sunderbund's projects long after he had realized how little they would forward the true service of God. No doubt there had been moments of flattery, moments of something, something rather in the nature of an excited affection; some touch of the magnificent in her, some touch of the infantile,—both appealed magnetically to his imagination; but the real effective cause was his habitual solicitude for his wife and children and his consequent desire to prosper materially. As his first dream of being something between Mohammed and Peter the Hermit in a new proclamation of God to the world lost colour and life in his mind, he realized more and more clearly that there was no way of living in a state of material prosperity and at the same time in a state of active service to God. The Church of the One True God (by favour of Lady Sunderbund) was a gaily coloured lure.

And yet he wanted to go on with it. All his imagination and intelligence was busy now with the possibility of in some way subjugating Lady Sunderbund, and modifying her and qualifying her to an endurable proposition. Why?

Why?

There could be but one answer, he thought. Brought to the test of action, he did not really believe in God! He did not believe in God as he believed in his family. He did not believe in the reality of either his first or his second vision; they had been dreams, autogenous revelations, exaltations of his own imaginations. These beliefs were upon different grades of reality. Put to the test, his faith in God gave way; a sword of plaster against a reality of steel.

And yet he did believe in God. He was as persuaded that there was a God as he was that there was another side to the moon. His intellectual conviction was complete. Only, beside the living, breathing—occasionally coughing—reality of Phoebe, God was something as unsubstantial as the Binomial Theorem....

Very like the Binomial Theorem as one thought over that comparison.

By this time he had reached the banks of the Serpentine and was approaching the grey stone bridge that crosses just where Hyde Park ends and Kensington Gardens begins. Following upon his doubts of his religious faith had come another still more extraordinary question: "Although there is a God, does he indeed matter more in our ordinary lives than that same demonstrable Binomial Theorem? Isn't one's duty to Phoebe plain and clear?" Old Likeman's argument came back to him with novel and enhanced powers. Wasn't he after all selfishly putting his own salvation in front of his plain duty to those about him? What did it matter if he told lies, taught a false faith, perjured and damned himself, if after all those others were thereby saved and comforted?

"But that is just where the whole of this state of mind is false and wrong," he told himself. "God is something more than a priggish devotion, an intellectual formula. He has a hold and a claim—he should have a hold and a claim—exceeding all the claims of Phoebe, Miriam, Daphne, Clementina— all of them.... But he hasn't'!..."

It was to that he had got after he had left Lady Sunderbund, and to that he now returned. It was the thinness and unreality of his thought of God that had driven him post haste to Brighton Pomfrey in search for that drug that had touched his soul to belief.

Was God so insignificant in comparison with his family that after all with a good conscience he might preach him every Sunday in Lady Sunderbund's church, wearing Lady Sunderbund's vestments?

Before him he saw an empty seat. The question was so immense and conclusive, it was so clearly a choice for all the rest of his life between God and the dear things of this world, that he felt he could not decide it upon his legs. He sat down, threw an arm along the back of the seat and drummed with his fingers.

If the answer was "yes" then it was decidedly a pity that he had not stayed in the church. It was ridiculous to strain at the cathedral gnat and then swallow Lady Sunderbund's decorative Pantechnicon.

For the first time, Scrope definitely regretted his apostasy.

A trivial matter, as it may seem to the reader, intensified that regret. Three weeks ago Borrowdale, the bishop of Howeaster, had died, and Scrope would have been the next in rotation to succeed him on the bench of bishops. He had always looked forward to the House of Lords, intending to take rather a new line, to speak more, and to speak more plainly and fully upon social questions than had hitherto been the practice of his brethren. Well, that had gone....

IX

Regrets were plain now. The question before his mind was growing clear; whether he was to persist in this self imposed martyrdom of himself and his family or whether he was to go back upon his outbreak of visionary fanaticism and close with this last opportunity that Lady Sunderbund offered of saving at least the substance of the comfort and social status of his wife and daughters. In which case it was clear to him he would have to go to great lengths and exercise very considerable subtlety—and magnetism—in the management of Lady Sunderbund....

He found himself composing a peculiar speech to her, very frank and revealing, and one that he felt would dominate her thoughts.... She attracted him oddly.... At least this afternoon she had attracted him....

And repelled him....

A wholesome gust of moral impatience stirred him. He smacked the back of the seat hard, as though he smacked himself.

No. He did not like it....

A torn sunset of purple and crimson streamed raggedly up above and through the half stripped trecs of Kensington Gardens, and he found himself wishing that Heaven would give us fewer sublimities in sky and mountain and more in our hearts. Against the background of darkling trees and stormily flaming sky a girl was approaching him. There was little to be seen of her but her outline. Something in her movement caught his eye and carried his memory back to a sundown at Hunstanton. Then as she came nearer he saw that it was Eleanor.

It was odd to see her here. He had thought she was at Newnham.

But anyhow it was very pleasant to see her. And there was something in Eleanor that promised an answer to his necessity. The girl had a kind of instinctive wisdom. She would understand the quality of his situation better perhaps than any one. He would put the essentials of that situation as fully and plainly as he could to her. Perhaps she, with that clear young idealism of hers, would give him just the lift and the light of which he stood in need. She would comprehend both sides of it, the points about Phoebe as well as the points about God.

When first he saw her she seemed to be hurrying, but now she had fallen to a loitering pace. She looked once or twice behind her and then ahead, almost as though she expected some one and was not sure whether this person would approach from east or west. She did not observe her father until she was close upon him.

Then she was so astonished that for a moment she stood motionless, regarding him. She made an odd movement, almost as if she would have walked on, that she checked in its inception. Then she came up to him and stood before him. "It's Dad," she said.

"I didn't know you were in London, Norah," he began.

"I came up suddenly."

"Have you been home?"

"No. I wasn't going home. At least—not until afterwards."

Then she looked away from him, east and then west, and then met his eye again.

"Won't you sit down, Norah?"

"I don't know whether I can."

She consulted the view again and seemed to come to a decision. "At least, I will for a minute."

She sat down. For a moment neither of them spoke....

"What are you doing here, little Norah?"

She gathered her wits. Then she spoke rather volubly. "I know it looks bad, Daddy. I came up to meet a boy I know, who is going to France to morrow. I had to make excuses—up there. I hardly remember what excuses I made."

"A boy you know?"

"Yes."

"Do we know him?"

"Not yet."

For a time Scrope forgot the Church of the One True God altogether. "Who is this boy?" he asked.

With a perceptible effort Eleanor assumed a tone of commonsense conventionality. "He's a boy I met first when we were skating last year. His sister has the study next to mine."

Father looked at daughter, and she met his eyes. "Well?"

"It's all happened so quickly, Daddy," she said, answering all that was implicit in that "Well?" She went on, "I would have told you about him if he had seemed to matter. But it was just a friendship. It didn't seem to matter in any serious way. Of course we'd been good friends—and talked about all sorts of things. And then suddenly you see,"—her tone was offhand and matter of fact—"he has to go to France."

She stared at her father with the expression of a hostess who talks about the weather. And then the tears gathered and ran down her cheek.

She turned her face to the Serpentine and clenched her fist.

But she was now fairly weeping. "I didn't know he cared. I didn't know I cared."

His next question took a little time in coming.

"And it's love, little Norah?" he asked.

She was comfortably crying now, the defensive altogether abandoned. "It's love, Daddy.... Oh! love!.... He's going tomorrow." For a minute or so neither spoke. Scrope's mind was entirely made up in the matter. He approved altogether of his daughter. But the traditions of parentage, his habit of restrained decision, made him act a judicial part. "I'd like just to see this boy," he said, and added: "If it isn't rather interfering...."

"Dear Daddy!" she said. "Dear Daddy!" and touched his hand. "He'll be coming here...."

"If you could tell me a few things about him," said Scrope. "Is he an undergraduate?"

"You see," began Eleanor and paused to marshal her facts. "He graduated this year. Then he's been in training at Cambridge. Properly he'd have a fellowship. He took the Natural Science tripos, zoology chiefly. He's good at philosophy, but of course our Cambridge philosophy is so silly—McTaggart blowing bubbles.... His father's a doctor, Sir Hedley Riverton."

As she spoke her eyes had been roving up the path and down. "He's coming," she interrupted. She hesitated. "Would you mind if I went and spoke to him first, Daddy?"

"Of course go to him. Go and warn him I'm here," said Scrope.

Eleanor got up, and was immediately greeted with joyful gestures by an approaching figure in khaki. The two young people quickened their paces as they drew nearer one another. There was a rapid greeting; they stood close together and spoke eagerly. Scrope could tell by their movements when he became the subject of their talk. He saw the young man start and look over Eleanor's shoulder, and he assumed an attitude of philosophical contemplation of the water, so as to give the young man the liberty of his profile.

He did not look up until they were quite close to him, and when he did he saw a pleasant, slightly freckled fair face a little agitated, and very honest blue eyes. "I hope you don't think, Sir, that it's bad form of me to ask Eleanor to come up and see me as I've done. I telegraphed to her on an impulse, and it's been very kind of her to come up to me."

"Sit down," said Scrope, "sit down. You're Mr. Riverton?"

"Yes, Sir," said the young man. He had the frequent "Sir" of the subaltern. Scrope was in the centre of the seat, and the young officer sat down on one side of him while Eleanor took up a watching position on her father's other hand. "You see, Sir, we've hardly known each other—I mean we've been associated over a philosophical society and all that sort of thing, but in a more familiar way, I mean...."

He hung for a moment, just a little short of breath. Scrope helped him with a grave but sympathetic movement of the head. "It's a little difficult to explain," the young man apologized.

"We hadn't understood, I think, either of us very much. We'd just been friendly—and liked each other. And so it went on even when I was training. And then when I found I had to go out—I'm going out a little earlier than I expected—I thought suddenly I wouldn't ever go to Cambridge again at all perhaps—and there was something in one of her letters.... I thought of it a lot, Sir, I thought it all over, and I thought it wasn't right for me to do anything and I didn't do anything until this morning. And then I sort of had to telegraph. I know it was frightful cheek and bad form and all that, Sir. It is. It would be worse if she wasn't different—I mean, Sir, if she was just an ordinary girl.... But I had a sort of feeling—just wanting to see her. I don't suppose you've ever felt anything, Sir, as I felt I wanted to see her—and just hear her speak to me...."

He glanced across Scrope at Eleanor. It was as if he justified himself to them both.

Scrope glanced furtively at his daughter who was leaning forward with tender eyes on her lover, and his heart went out to her. But his manner remained judicial.

"All this is very sudden," he said.

"Or you would have heard all about it, Sir," said young Riverton. "It's just the hurry that has made this seem furtive. All that there is between us, Sir, is just the two telegrams we've sent, hers and mine. I hope you won't mind our having a little time together. We won't do anything very committal. It's as much friendship as anything. I go by the evening train to morrow."

"Mm," said Serope with his eye on Eleanor.

"In these uncertain times," he began.

"Why shouldn't I take a risk too, Daddy?" said Eleanor sharply.

"I know there's that side of it," said the young man. "I oughtn't to have telegraphed," he said.

"Can't I take a risk?" exclaimed Eleanor. "I'm not a doll. I don't want to live in wadding until all the world is safe for me."

Scrope looked at the glowing face of the young man.

"Is this taking care of her?" he asked.

"If you hadn't telegraphed—!" she cried with a threat in her voice, and left it at that.

"Perhaps I feel about her—rather as if she was as strong as I am—in those ways. Perhaps I shouldn't. I could hardly endure myself, Sir—cut off from her. And a sort of blank. Nothing said."

"You want to work out your own salvation," said Scrope to his daughter.

"No one else can," she answered. "I'm—I'm grown up."

"Even if it hurts?"

"To live is to be hurt somehow," she said. "This—This—" She flashed her love. She intimated by a gesture that it is better to be stabbed with a clean knife than to be suffocated or poisoned or to decay....

Scrope turned his eyes to the young man again. He liked him. He liked the modelling of his mouth and chin and the line of his brows. He liked him altogether. He pronounced his verdict slowly. "I suppose, after all," he said, "that this is better than the tender solicitude of a safe and prosperous middleaged man. Eleanor, my dear, I've been thinking to day that a father who stands between his children and hardship, by doing wrong, may really be doing them a wrong. You are a dear girl to me. I won't stand between you two. Find your own salvation." He got up. "I go west," he said, "presently. You, I think, go east."

"I can assure you, Sir," the young man began.

Scrope held his hand out. "Take your life in your own way," he said.

He turned to Eleanor. "Talk as you will," he said.

She clasped his hand with emotion. Then she turned to the waiting young man, who saluted.

"You'll come back to supper?" Scrope said, without thinking out the implications of that invitation.

She assented as carelessly. The fact that she and her lover were to go, with their meeting legalized and blessed, excluded all other considerations. The two young people turned to each other.

Scrope stood for a moment or so and then sat down again.

For a time he could think only of Eleanor.... He watched the two young people as they went eastward. As they walked their shoulders and elbows bumped amicably together.

X

Presently he sought to resume the interrupted thread of his thoughts. He knew that he had been dealing with some very tremendous and urgent problem when Eleanor had appeared. Then he remembered that Eleanor at the time of her approach had seemed to be a solution rather than an interruption. Well, she had her own life. She was making her own life. Instead of solving his problems she was solving her own. God bless those dear grave children! They were nearer the elemental things than he was. That eastward path led to Victoria—and thence to a very probable death. The lad was in the infantry and going straight into the trenches.

Love, death, God; this war was bringing the whole world back to elemental things, to heroic things. The years of comedy and comfort were at an end in Europe; the age of steel and want was here. And he had been thinking—What had he been thinking?

He mused, and the scheme of his perplexities reshaped itself in his mind. But at that time he did not realize that a powerful new light was falling upon it now, cast by the tragic illumination of these young lovers whose love began with a parting. He did not see how reality had come to all things through that one intense reality. He reverted to the question as he had put it to himself, before first he recognized Eleanor. Did he believe in God? Should he go on with this Sunderbund adventure in which he no longer believed? Should he play for safety and comfort, trusting to God's toleration? Or go back to his family and warn them of the years of struggle and poverty his renunciation cast upon them?

Somehow Lady Sunderbund's chapel was very remote and flimsy now, and the hardships of poverty seemed less black than the hardship of a youthful death.

Did he believe in God? Again he put that fundamental question to himself.

He sat very still in the sunset peace, with his eyes upon the steel mirror of the waters. The question seemed to fill the whole scene, to wait, even as the water and sky and the windless trees were waiting....

And then by imperceptible degrees there grew in Scrope's mind the persuasion that he was in the presence of the living God. This time there was no vision of angels nor stars, no snapping of bow strings, no throbbing of the heart nor change of scene, no magic and melodramatic drawing back of the curtain from the mysteries; the water and the bridge, the ragged black trees, and a distant boat that broke the silvery calm with an arrow of black ripples, all these things were still before him. But God was there too. God was everywhere about him. This persuasion was over him and about him; a dome of protection, a power in his nerves, a peace in his heart. It was an exalting beauty; it was a perfected conviction.... This indeed was the coming of God, the real coming of God. For the first time

Scrope was absolutely sure that for the rest of his life he would possess God. Everything that had so perplexed him seemed to be clear now, and his troubles lay at the foot of this last complete realization like a litter of dust and leaves in the foreground of a sunlit, snowy mountain range.

It was a little incredible that he could ever have doubted.

XI

It was a phase of extreme intellectual clairvoyance. A multitude of things that hitherto had been higgledy piggledy, contradictory and incongruous in his mind became lucid, serene, full and assured. He seemed to see all things plainly as one sees things plainly through perfectly clear still water in the shadows of a summer noon. His doubts about God, his periods of complete forgetfulness and disregard of God, this conflict of his instincts and the habits and affections of his daily life with the service of God, ceased to be perplexing incompatibilities and were manifest as necessary, understandable aspects of the business of living.

It was no longer a riddle that little immediate things should seem of more importance than great and final things. For man is a creature thrusting his way up from the beast to divinity, from the blindness of individuality to the knowledge of a common end. We stand deep in the engagements of our individual lives looking up to God, and only realizing in our moments of exaltation that through God we can escape from and rule and alter the whole world wide scheme of individual lives. Only in phases of illumination do we realize the creative powers that lie ready to man's hand. Personal affections, immediate obligations, ambitions, self seeking, these are among the natural and essential things of our individual lives, as intimate almost as our primordial lusts and needs; God, the true God, is a later revelation, a newer, less natural thing in us; a knowledge still remote, uncertain, and confused with superstition; an apprehension as yet entangled with barbaric traditions of fear and with ceremonial surgeries, blood sacrifices, and the maddest barbarities of thought. We are only beginning to realize that God is here; so far as our minds go he is still not here continually; we perceive him and then again we are blind to him. God is the last thing added to the completeness of human life. To most His presence is imperceptible throughout their lives; they know as little of him as a savage knows of the electric waves that beat through us for ever from the sun. All this appeared now so clear and necessary to Scrope that he was astonished he had ever found the quality of contradiction in these manifest facts.

In this unprecedented lucidity that had now come to him, Scrope saw as a clear and simple necessity that there can be no such thing as a continuous living presence of God in our lives. That is an unreasonable desire. There is no permanent exaltation of belief. It is contrary to the nature of life. One cannot keep actively believing in and realizing God round all the twenty four hours any more than one can keep awake through the whole cycle of night and day, day after day. If it were possible so to apprehend God without cessation, life would dissolve in religious ecstasy. But nothing human has ever had the power to hold the curtain of sense continually aside and retain the light of God always. We must get along by remembering our moments of assurance. Even Jesus himself, leader of all those who have hailed the coming kingdom of God, had cried upon the cross, "My God, my God, why hast thou forsaken me?" The business of life on earth, life itself, is a thing curtained off, as it were, from such immediate convictions. That is in the constitution of life. Our ordinary state of belief, even when we are free from doubt, is necessarily far removed from the intuitive certainty of sight and hearing. It is a persuasion, it falls far short of perception....

"We don't know directly," Scrope said to himself with a checking gesture of the hand, "we don't see. We can't. We hold on to the remembered glimpse, we go over our reasons."...

And it was clear too just because God is thus manifest like the momentary drawing of a curtain, sometimes to this man for a time and sometimes to that, but never continuously to any, and because the perception of him depends upon the ability and quality of the perceiver, because to the intellectual man God is necessarily a formula, to the active man a will and a commandment, and to the emotional man love, there can be no creed defining him for all men, and no ritual and special forms of service to justify a priesthood. "God is God," he whispered to himself, and the phrase seemed to him the discovery of a sufficient creed. God is his own definition; there is no other definition of God. Scrope had troubled himself with endless arguments whether God was a person, whether he was concerned with personal troubles, whether he loved, whether he was finite. It were as reasonable to argue whether God was a frog or a rock or a tree. He had imagined God as a figure of youth and courage, had perceived him as an effulgence of leadership, a captain like the sun. The vision of his drug quickened mind had but symbolized what was otherwise inexpressible. Of that he was now sure. He had not seen the invisible but only its sign and visible likeness. He knew now that all such presentations were true and that all such presentations were false. Just as much and just as little was God the darkness and the brightness of the ripples under the bows of the distant boat, the black beauty of the leaves and twigs of those trees now acid clear against the flushed and deepening sky. These riddles of the profundities were beyond the compass of common living. They were beyond the needs of common living. He was but a little earth parasite, sitting idle in the darkling day, trying to understand his infinitesimal functions on a minor planet. Within the compass of terrestrial living God showed himself in its own terms. The life of man on earth was a struggle for unity of spirit and for unity with his kind, and the aspect of God that alone mattered to man was a unifying kingship without and within. So long as men were men, so would they see God. Only when they reached the crest could they begin to look beyond. So we knew God, so God was to us; since we struggled, he led our struggle, since we were finite and mortal he defined an aim, his personality was the answer to our personality; but God, except in so far as he was to us, remained inaccessible, inexplicable, wonderful, shining through beauty, shining beyond research, greater than time or space, above good and evil and pain and pleasure.

XII

Serope's mind was saturated as it had never been before by his sense of the immediate presence of God. He floated in that realization. He was not so much thinking now as conversing starkly with the divine interlocutor, who penetrated all things and saw into and illuminated every recess of his mind. He spread out his ideas to the test of this presence; he brought out his hazards and interpretations that this light might judge them.

There came back to his mind the substance of his two former visions; they assumed now a reciprocal quality, they explained one another and the riddle before him. The first had shown him the personal human aspect of God, he had seen God as the unifying captain calling for his personal service, the second had set the stage for that service in the spectacle of mankind's adventure. He had been shown a great multitude of human spirits reaching up at countless points towards the conception of the racial unity under a divine leadership, he had seen mankind on the verge of awakening to the kingdom of God. "That solves no mystery," he whispered, gripping the seat and frowning at the water; "mysteries remain mysteries; but that is the reality of religion. And now, now, what is my place? What have I to do? That is the question I have been asking always; the question that this moment now will answer; what have I to do?..."

God was coming into the life of all mankind in the likeness of a captain and a king; all the governments of men, all the leagues of men, their debts and claims and possessions, must give way to the world republic under God the king. For five troubled years he had been staring religion in the face, and now he saw that it must mean this—or be no more than fetishism, Obi, Orphic mysteries or ceremonies of Demeter, a legacy of mental dirtiness, a residue of self mutilation and superstitious sacrifices from the cunning, fear haunted, ape dog phase of human development. But it did mean this. And every one who apprehended as much was called by that very apprehension to the service of God's kingdom. To live and serve God's kingdom on earth, to help to bring it about, to propagate the idea of it, to establish the method of it, to incorporate all that one made and all that one did into its growing reality, was the only possible life that could be lived, once that God was known.

He sat with his hands gripping his knees, as if he were holding on to his idea. "And now for my part," he whispered, brows knit, "now for my part."

Ever since he had given his confirmation addresses he had been clear that his task, or at least a considerable portion of his task, was to tell of this faith in God and of this conception of service in his kingdom as the form and rule of human life and human society. But up to now he had been floundering hopelessly in his search for a method and means of telling. That, he saw, still needed to be thought out. For example, one cannot run through the world crying, "The Kingdom of God is at hand." Men's minds were still so filled with old theological ideas that for the most part they would understand by that only a fantasy of some great coming of angels and fiery chariots and judgments, and hardly a soul but would doubt one's sanity and turn scornfully away. But one must proclaim God not to confuse but to convince men's minds. It was that and the habit of his priestly calling that had disposed him towards a pulpit. There he could reason and explain. The decorative genius of Lady Sunderbund had turned that intention into a vast iridescent absurdity.

This sense he had of thinking openly in the sight of God, enabled him to see the adventure of Lady Sunderbund without illusion and without shame. He saw himself at once honest and disingenuous, divided between two aims. He had no doubt now of the path he had to pursue. A stronger man of permanently clear aims might possibly turn Lady Sunderbund into a useful opportunity, oblige her to provide the rostrum he needed; but for himself, he knew he had neither the needed strength nor clearness; she would smother him in decoration, overcome him by her picturesque persistence. It might be ridiculous to run away from her, but it was necessary. And he was equally clear now that for him there must be no idea of any pulpit, of any sustained mission. He was a man of intellectual moods; only at times, he realized, had he the inspiration of truth; upon such uncertain snatches and glimpses he must live; to make his life a ministry would be to face phases when he would simply be "carrying on," with his mind blank and his faith asleep.

His thought spread out from this perennial decision to more general things again. Had God any need of organized priests at all? Wasn't that just what had been the matter with religion for the last three thousand years?

His vision and his sense of access to God had given a new courage to his mind; in these moods of enlightenment he could see the world as a comprehensible ball, he could see history as an understandable drama. He had always been on the verge of realizing before, he realized now, the two entirely different and antagonistic strands that interweave in the twisted rope of contemporary religion; the old strand of the priest, the fetishistic element of the blood sacrifice and the obscene rite, the element of ritual and tradition, of the cult, the caste, the consecrated tribe; and interwoven with this so closely as to be scarcely separable in any existing religion was the new strand, the religion of the prophets, the unidolatrous universal worship of the one true God. Priest religion is the antithesis to prophet religion. He saw that the founders of all the great existing religions of the world had been like himself—only that he was a weak and commonplace man with no creative force, and they had been great men of enormous initiative—men reaching out, and never with a complete definition, from the old kind of religion to the new. The Hebrew prophets, Jesus, whom the priests killed when Pilate would have spared him, Mohammed, Buddha, had this much in common that they had sought to lead men from temple worship, idol worship, from rites and ceremonies and the rule of priests, from anniversaryism and sacramentalism, into a direct and simple relation to the simplicity of God. Religious progress had always been liberation and simplification. But none of these efforts had got altogether clear. The organizing temper in men, the disposition to dogmatic theorizing, the distrust of the discretion of the young by the wisdom of age, the fear of indiscipline which is so just in warfare and so foolish in education, the tremendous power of the propitiatory tradition, had always caught and crippled every new gospel before it had run a score of years. Jesus for example gave man neither a theology nor a church organization; His sacrament was an innocent feast of memorial; but the fearful, limited, imitative men he left to carry on his work speedily restored all these three abominations of the antiquated religion, theology, priest, and sacrifice. Jesus indeed, caught into identification with the ancient victim of the harvest sacrifice and turned from a plain teacher into a horrible blood bath and a mock cannibal meal, was surely the supreme feat of the ironies of chance....

"It is curious how I drift back to Jesus," said Scrope. "I have never seen how much truth and good there was in his teaching until I broke away from Christianity and began to see him plain. If I go on as I am going, I shall end a Nazarene...."

He thought on. He had a feeling of temerity, but then it seemed as if God within him bade him be of good courage.

Already in a glow of inspiration he had said practically as much as he was now thinking in his confirmation address, but now he realized completely what it was he had then said. There could be no priests, no specialized ministers of the one true God, because every man to the utmost measure of his capacity was bound to be God's priest and minister. Many things one may leave to specialists: surgery, detailed administration, chemistry, for example; but it is for every man to think his own philosophy and think out his own religion. One man may tell another, but no man may take charge of another. A man may avail himself of electrician or gardener or what not, but he must stand directly before God; he may suffer neither priest nor king. These other things are incidental, but God, the kingdom of God, is what he is for.

"Good," he said, checking his reasoning. "So I must bear witness to God—but neither as priest nor pastor. I must write and talk about him as I can. No reason why I should not live by such writing and talking if it does not hamper my message to do so. But there must be no high place, no ordered congregation. I begin to see my way...."

The evening was growing dark and chill about him now, the sky was barred with deep bluish purple bands drawn across a chilly brightness that had already forgotten the sun, the trees were black and dim, but his understanding of his place and duty was growing very definite.

"And this duty to bear witness to God's kingdom and serve it is so plain that I must not deflect my witness even by a little, though to do so means comfort and security for my wife and children. God comes first...."

"They must not come between God and me...."

"But there is more in it than that."

He had come round at last through the long clearing up of his mind, to his fundamental problem again. He sat darkly reluctant.

"I must not play priest or providence to them," he admitted at last. "I must not even stand between God and them."

He saw now what he had been doing; it had been the flaw in his faith that he would not trust his family to God. And he saw too that this distrust has been the flaw in the faith of all religious systems hitherto....

XIII

In this strange voyage of the spirit which was now drawing to its end, in which Scrope had travelled from the confused, unanalyzed formulas and assumptions and implications of his rectory upbringing to his present stark and simple realization of God, he had at times made some remarkable self identifications. He was naturally much given to analogy; every train of thought in his mind set up induced parallel currents. He had likened himself to the Anglican church, to the whole Christian body, as, for example, in his imagined second conversation with the angel of God. But now he found himself associating himself with a still more far reaching section of mankind. This excess of solicitude was traceable perhaps in nearly every one in all the past of mankind who had ever had the vision of God. An excessive solicitude to shield those others from one's own trials and hardships, to preserve the exact quality of the revelation, for example, had been the fruitful cause of crippling errors, spiritual tyrannies, dogmatisms, dissensions, and futilities. "Suffer little children to come unto me"; the text came into his head with an effect of contribution. The parent in us all flares out at the thought of the younger and weaker minds; we hide difficulties, seek to spare them from the fires that temper the spirit, the sharp edge of the truth that shapes the soul. Christian is always trying to have a carriage sent back from the Celestial City for his family. Why, we ask, should they flounder dangerously in the morasses that we escaped, or wander in the forest in which we lost ourselves? Catch these souls young, therefore, save them before they know they exist, kidnap them to heaven; vaccinate them with a catechism they may never understand, lull them into comfort and routine. Instinct plays us false here as it plays the savage mother false when she snatches her fevered child from the doctor's hands. The last act of faith is to trust those we love to God....

Hitherto he had seen the great nets of theological overstatement and dogma that kept mankind from God as if they were the work of purely evil things in man, of pride, of self assertion, of a desire to possess and dominate the minds and souls of others. It was only now that he saw how large a share in the obstruction of God's Kingdom had been played by the love of the elder and the parent, by the carefulness, the fussy care, of good men and women. He had wandered in wildernesses of unbelief, in dangerous places of doubt and questioning, but he had left his wife and children safe and secure in the self satisfaction of orthodoxy. To none of them except to Eleanor had he ever talked with any freedom of his new apprehensions of religious reality. And that had been at Eleanor's initiative. There was, he saw now, something of insolence and something of treachery in this concealment. His ruling disposition throughout the crisis had been to force comfort and worldly well being upon all those dependants even at the price of his own spiritual integrity. In no way had he consulted them upon the bargain.... While we have pottered, each for the little good of his own family, each for the lessons and clothes and leisure of his own children, assenting to this injustice, conforming to that dishonest custom, being myopically benevolent and fundamentally treacherous, our accumulated folly has achieved this catastrophe. It is not so much human wickedness as human weakness that has permitted the youth of the world to go through this hell of blood and mud and fire. The way to the kingdom of God is the only way to the true safety, the true wellbeing of the children of men....

It wasn't fair to them. But now he saw how unfair it was to them in a light that has only shone plainly upon European life since the great interlude of the armed peace came to an end in August, 1914. Until that time it had been the fashion to ignore death and evade poverty and necessity for the young. We can shield our young no longer, death has broken through our precautions and tender evasions—and his eyes went eastward into the twilight that had swallowed up his daughter and her lover.

The tumbled darkling sky, monstrous masses of frowning blue, with icy gaps of cold light, was like the great confusions of the war. All our youth has had to go into that terrible and destructive chaos—because of the kings and churches and nationalities sturdier souled men would have set aside.

Everything was sharp and clear in his mind now. Eleanor after all had brought him his solution.

He sat quite still for a little while, and then stood up and turned northward towards Notting Hill.

The keepers were closing Kensington Gardens, and he would have to skirt the Park to Victoria Gate and go home by the Bayswater Road....

XIV

As he walked he rearranged in his mind this long overdue apology for his faith that he was presently to make to his family. There was no one to interrupt him and nothing to embarrass him, and so he was able to set out everything very clearly and convincingly. There was perhaps a disposition to digress into rather voluminous subordinate explanations, on such themes, for instance, as sacramentalism, whereon he found himself summarizing Frazer's Golden Bough, which the Chasters' controversy had first obliged him to read, and upon the irrelevance of the question of immortality to the process of salvation. But the reality of his eclaircissement was very different from anything he prepared in these anticipations.

Tea had been finished and put away, and the family was disposed about the dining room engaged in various evening occupations; Phoebe sat at the table working at some mathematical problem, Clementina was reading with her chin on her fist and a frown on her brow; Lady Ella, Miriam and Daphne were busy making soft washing cloths for the wounded; Lady Ella had brought home the demand for them from the Red Cross centre in Burlington House. The family was all downstairs in the dining room because the evening was chilly, and there were no fires upstairs yet in the drawing room. He came into the room and exchanged greetings with Lady Ella. Then he stood for a time surveying his children. Phoebe, he noted, was a little flushed; she put passion into her work; on the whole she was more like Eleanor than any other of them. Miriam knitted with a steady skill. Clementina's face too expressed a tussle. He took up one of the rough knit washing cloths upon the side table, and asked how many could be made in an hour. Then he asked some idle obvious question about the fire upstairs. Clementina made an involuntary movement; he was disturbing her. He hovered for a moment longer. He wanted to catch his wife's eye and speak to her first. She looked up, but before he could convey his wish for a private conference with her, she smiled at him and then bent over her work again.

He went into the back study and lit his gas fire. Hitherto he had always made a considerable explosion when he did so, but this time by taking thought and lighting his match before he turned on the gas he did it with only a gentle thud. Then he lit his reading lamp and pulled down the blind—pausing for a time to look at the lit dressmaker's opposite. Then he sat down thoughtfully before the fire. Presently Ella would come in and he would talk to her. He waited a long time, thinking only weakly and inconsecutively, and then he became restless. Should he call her?

But he wanted their talk to begin in a natural seeming way. He did not want the portentousness of "wanting to speak" to her and calling her out to him. He got up at last and went back into the other room. Clementina had gone upstairs, and the book she had been reading was lying closed on the sideboard. He saw it was one of Chasters' books, he took it up, it was "The Core of Truth in Christianity," and he felt an irrational shock at the idea of Clementina reading it. In spite of his own immense changes of opinion he had still to revise his conception of the polemical Chasters as an evil influence in religion. He fidgeted past his wife to the mantel in search of an imaginary mislaid pencil. Clementina came down with some bandage linen she was cutting out. He hung over his wife in a way that he felt must convey his desire for a conversation. Then he picked up Chasters' book again. "Does any one want this?" he asked.

"Not if I may have it again," consented Clementina.

He took it back with him and began to read again those familiar controversial pages. He read for the best part of an hour with his knees drying until they smoked over the gas. What curious stuff it was! How it wrangled! Was Chasters a religious man? Why did he write these books? Had he really a passion for truth or only a Swift like hatred of weakly thinking people? None of this stuff in his books was really wrong, provided it was religious spirited. Much of it had been indeed destructively illuminating to its reader. It let daylight through all sorts of walls. Indeed, the more one read the more vividly true its acid bit lines became.... And yet, and yet, there was something hateful in the man's tone. Scrope held the book and thought. He had seen Chasters once or twice. Chasters had the sort of face, the sort of voice, the sort of bearing that made one think of his possibly saying upon occasion, rudely and rejoicing, "More fool you!" Nevertheless Scrope perceived now with an effort of discovery that it was from Chasters that he had taken all the leading ideas of the new faith that was in him. Here was the stuff of it. He had forgotten how much of it was here. During those months of worried study while the threat of a Chasters prosecution hung over him his mind had assimilated almost unknowingly every assimilable element of the Chasters doctrine; he had either assimilated and transmuted it by the alchemy of his own temperament, or he had reacted obviously and filled in Chasters' gaps and pauses. Chasters could beat a road to the Holy of Holies, and shy at entering it. But in spite of all the man's roughness, in spite of a curious flavour of baseness and malice about him, the spirit of truth had spoken through him. God has a use for harsh ministers. In one man God lights the heart, in another the reason becomes a consuming fire. God takes his own where he finds it. He does not limit himself to nice people. In these matters of evidence and argument, in his contempt for amiable, demoralizing compromise, Chasters served God as Scrope could never hope to serve him. Scrope's new faith had perhaps been altogether impossible if the Chasters controversy had not ploughed his mind.

For a time Scrope dwelt upon this remarkable realization. Then as he turned over the pages his eyes rested on a passage of uncivil and ungenerous sarcasm. Against old Likeman of all people!...

What did a girl like Clementina make of all this? How had she got the book? From Eleanor? The stuff had not hurt Eleanor. Eleanor had been able to take the good that Chasters taught, and reject the evil of his spirit....

He thought of Eleanor, gallantly working out her own salvation. The world was moving fast to a phase of great freedom—for the young and the bold.... He liked that boy....

His thoughts came back with a start to his wife. The evening was slipping by and he had momentous things to say to her. He went and just opened the door.

"Ella!" he said.

"Did you want me?"

"Presently."

She put a liberal interpretation upon that "presently," so that after what seemed to him a long interval he had to call again, "Ella!"

"Just a minute," she answered.

XV

Lady Ella was still, so to speak, a little in the other room when she came to him.

"Shut that door, please," he said, and felt the request had just that flavour of portentousness he wished to avoid.

"What is it?" she asked.

"I wanted to talk to you—about some things. I've done something rather serious to day. I've made an important decision."

Her face became anxious. "What do you mean?" she asked.

"You see," he said, leaning upon the mantelshelf and looking down at the gas flames, "I've never thought that we should all have to live in this crowded house for long."

"All!" she interrupted in a voice that made him look up sharply. "You're not going away, Ted?"

"Oh, no. But I hoped we should all be going away in a little time. It isn't so."

"I never quite understood why you hoped that."

"It was plain enough."

"How?"

"I thought I should have found something to do that would have enabled us to live in better style. I'd had a plan."

"What plan?"

"It's fallen through."

"But what plan was it?"

"I thought I should be able to set up a sort of broad church chapel. I had a promise."

Her voice was rich with indignation. "And she has betrayed you?"

"No," he said, "I have betrayed her."

Lady Ella's face showed them still at cross purposes. He looked down again and frowned. "I can't do that chapel business," he said. "I've had to let her down. I've got to let you all down. There's no help for it. It isn't the way. I can't have anything to do with Lady Sunderbund and her chapel."

"But," Lady Ella was still perplexed.

"It's too great a sacrifice."

"Of us?"

"No, of myself. I can't get into her pulpit and do as she wants and keep my conscience. It's been a horrible riddle for me. It means plunging into all this poverty for good. But I can't work with her, Ella. She's impossible."

"You mean—you're going to break with Lady Sunderbund?"

"I must."

"Then, Teddy!"—she was a woman groping for flight amidst intolerable perplexities—"why did you ever leave the church?"

"Because I have ceased to believe—"

"But had it nothing to do with Lady Sunderbund?"

He stared at her in astonishment.

"If it means breaking with that woman," she said.

"You mean," he said, beginning for the first time to comprehend her, "that you don't mind the poverty?"

"Poverty!" she cried. "I cared for nothing but the disgrace."

"Disgrace?"

"Oh, never mind, Ted! If it isn't true, if I've been dreaming...."

Instead of a woman stunned by a life sentence of poverty, he saw his wife rejoicing as if she had heard good news.

Their minds were held for a minute by the sound of some one knocking at the house door; one of the girls opened the door, there was a brief hubbub in the passage and then they heard a cry of "Eleanor!" through the folding doors.

"There's Eleanor," he said, realizing he had told his wife nothing of the encounter in Hyde Park.

They heard Eleanor's clear voice: "Where's Mummy? Or Daddy?" and then: "Can't stay now, dears. Where's Mummy or Daddy?"

"I ought to have told you," said Scrope quickly. "I met Eleanor in the Park. By accident. She's come up unexpectedly. To meet a boy going to the front. Quite a nice boy. Son of Riverton the doctor. The parting had made them understand one another. It's all right, Ella. It's a little irregular, but I'd stake my life on the boy. She's very lucky."

Eleanor appeared through the folding doors. She came to business at once.

"I promised you I'd come back to supper here, Daddy," she said. "But I don't want to have supper here. I want to stay out late."

She saw her mother look perplexed. "Hasn't Daddy told you?"

"But where is young Riverton?"

"He's outside."

Eleanor became aware of a broad chink in the folding doors that was making the dining room an auditorium for their dialogue. She shut them deftly.

"I have told Mummy," Scrope explained. "Bring him in to supper. We ought to see him."

Eleanor hesitated. She indicated her sisters beyond the folding doors. "They'll all be watching us, Mummy," she said. "We'd be uncomfortable. And besides—"

"But you can't go out and dine with him alone!"

"Oh, Mummy! It's our only chance."

"Customs are changing," said Scrope.

"But can they?" asked Lady Ella.

"I don't see why not."

The mother was still doubtful, but she was in no mood to cross her husband that night. "It's an exceptional occasion," said Scrope, and Eleanor knew her point was won. She became radiant. "I can be late?"

Scrope handed her his latch key without a word.

"You dear kind things," she said, and went to the door. Then turned and came back and kissed her father. Then she kissed her mother. "It is so kind of you," she said, and was gone. They listened to her passage through a storm of questions in the dining room.

"Three months ago that would have shocked me," said Lady Ella.

"You haven't seen the boy," said Scrope.

"But the appearances!"

"Aren't we rather breaking with appearances?" he said.

"And he goes to morrow—perhaps to get killed," he added. "A lad like a schoolboy. A young thing. Because of the political foolery that we priests and teachers have suffered in the place of the Kingdom of God, because we have allowed the religion of Europe to become a lie; because no man spoke the word of God. You see—when I see that—see those two, those children of one and twenty, wrenched by tragedy, beginning with a parting.... It's like a knife slashing at all our appearances and discretions.... Think of our lovemaking...."

The front door banged.

He had some idea of resuming their talk. But his was a scattered mind now.

"It's a quarter to eight," he said as if in explanation.

"I must see to the supper," said Lady Ella.

XVI

There was an air of tension at supper as though the whole family felt that momentous words impended. But Phoebe had emerged victorious from her mathematical struggle, and she seemed to eat with better appetite than she had shown for some time. It was a cold meat supper; Lady Ella had found it impossible to keep up the regular practice of a cooked dinner in the evening, and now it was only on Thursdays that the Scropes, to preserve their social tradition, dressed and dined; the rest of the week they supped. Lady Ella never talked very much at supper; this evening was no exception. Clementina talked of London University and Bedford College; she had been making enquiries; Daphne described some of the mistresses at her new school. The feeling that something was expected had got upon Scrope's nerves. He talked a little in a flat and obvious way, and lapsed into thoughtful silences. While supper was being cleared away he went back into his study.

Thence he returned to the dining room hearthrug as his family resumed their various occupations.

He tried to speak in a casual conversational tone.

"I want to tell you all," he said, "of something that has happened to day."

He waited. Phoebe had begun to figure at a fresh sheet of computations. Miriam bent her head closer over her work, as though she winced at what was coming. Daphne and Clementina looked at one another. Their eyes said "Eleanor!" But he was too full of his own intention to read that glance. Only his wife regarded him attentively.

"It concerns you all," he said.

He looked at Phoebe. He saw Lady Ella's hand go out and touch the girl's hand gently to make her desist. Phoebe obeyed, with a little sigh.

"I want to tell you that to day I refused an income that would certainly have exceeded fifteen hundred pounds a year."

Clementina looked up now. This was not what she expected. Her expression conveyed protesting enquiry.

"I want you all to understand why I did that and why we are in the position we are in, and what lies before us. I want you to know what has been going on in my mind."

He looked down at the hearthrug, and tried to throw off a memory of his Princhester classes for young women, that oppressed him. His manner he forced to a more familiar note. He stuck his hands into his trouser pockets.

"You know, my dears, I had to give up the church. I just simply didn't believe any more in orthodox Church teaching. And I feel I've never explained that properly to you. Not at all clearly. I want to explain that now. It's a queer thing, I know, for me to say to you, but I want you to understand that I am a religious man. I believe that God matters more than wealth or comfort or position or the respect of men, that he also matters more than your comfort and prosperity. God knows I have cared for your comfort and prosperity. I don't want you to think that in all these changes we have been through lately, I haven't been aware of all the discomfort into which you have come—the relative discomfort. Compared with Princhester this is dark and crowded and poverty stricken. I have never felt crowded before, but in this house I know you are horribly crowded. It is a house that seems almost contrived for small discomforts. This narrow passage outside; the incessant going up and down stairs. And there are other things. There is the blankness of our London Sundays. What is the good of pretending? They are desolating. There's the impossibility too of getting good servants to come into our dug out kitchen. I'm not blind to all these sordid consequences. But all the same, God has to be served first. I had to come to this. I felt I could not serve God any longer as a bishop in the established church, because I did not believe that the established church was serving God. I struggled against that conviction—and I struggled against it largely for your sakes. But I had to obey my conviction.... I haven't talked to you about these things as much as I should have done, but partly at least that is due to the fact that my own mind has been changing and reconsidering, going forward and going back, and in that fluid state it didn't seem fair to tell you things that I might presently find mistaken. But now I begin to feel that I have really thought out things, and that they are definite enough to tell you...."

He paused and resumed. "A number of things have helped to change the opinions in which I grew up and in which you have grown up. There were worries at Princhester; I didn't let you know much about them, but there were. There was something harsh and cruel in that atmosphere. I saw for the first time—it's a lesson I'm still only learning—how harsh and greedy rich people and employing people are to poor people and working people, and how ineffective our church was to make things better. That struck me. There were religious disputes in the diocese too, and they shook me. I thought my faith was built on a rock, and I found it was built on sand. It was slipping and sliding long before the war. But the war brought it down. Before the war such a lot of things in England and Europe seemed like a comedy or a farce, a bad joke that one tolerated. One tried half consciously, half avoiding the knowledge of what one was doing, to keep one's own little circle and life civilized.

The war shook all those ideas of isolation, all that sort of evasion, down. The world is the rightful kingdom of God; we had left its affairs to kings and emperors and suchlike impostors, to priests and profit seekers and greedy men. We were genteel condoners. The war has ended that. It thrusts into all our lives. It brings death so close—A fortnight ago twenty seven people were killed and injured within a mile of this by Zeppelin bombs.... Every one loses some one.... Because through all that time men like myself were going through our priestly mummeries, abasing ourselves to kings and politicians, when we ought to have been crying out: 'No! No! There is no righteousness in the world, there is no right government, except it be the kingdom of God.'"

He paused and looked at them. They were all listening to him now. But he was still haunted by a dread of preaching in his own family. He dropped to the conversational note again.

"You see what I had in mind. I saw I must come out of this, and preach the kingdom of God. That was my idea. I don't want to force it upon you, but I want you to understand why I acted as I did. But let me come to the particular thing that has happened to day. I did not think when I made my final decision to leave the church that it meant such poverty as this we are living in—permanently. That is what I want to make clear to you. I thought there would be a temporary dip into dinginess, but that was all. There was a plan; at the time it seemed a right and reasonable plan; for setting up a chapel in London, a very plain and simple undenominational chapel, for the simple preaching of the world kingdom of God. There was some one who seemed prepared to meet all the immediate demands for such a chapel."

"Was it Lady Sunderbund?" asked Clementina.

Scrope was pulled up abruptly. "Yes," he said. "It seemed at first a quite hopeful project."

"We'd have hated that," said Clementina, with a glance as if for assent, at her mother. "We should all have hated that."

"Anyhow it has fallen through."

"We don't mind that," said Clementina, and Daphne echoed her words.

"I don't see that there is any necessity to import this note of—hostility to Lady Sunderbund into this matter." He addressed himself rather more definitely to Lady Ella. "She's a woman of a very extraordinary character, highly emotional, energetic, generous to an extraordinary extent...."

Daphne made a little noise like a comment.

A faint acerbity in her father's voice responded.

"Anyhow you make a mistake if you think that the personality of Lady Sunderbund has very much to do with this thing now. Her quality may have brought out certain aspects of the situation rather more sharply than they might have been brought out under other circumstances, but if this chapel enterprise had been suggested by quite a different sort of person, by a man, or by a committee, in the end I think I should have come to the same conclusion. Leave Lady Sunderbund out. Any chapel was impossible. It is just this specialization that has been the trouble with religion. It is just this tendency to make it the business of a special sort of man, in a special sort of building, on a special day—Every man, every building, every day belongs equally to God. That is my conviction. I think that the only possible existing sort of religions meeting is something after the fashion of the Quaker meeting. In that there is no professional religious man at all; not a trace of the sacrifices to the ancient gods.... And no room for a professional religions man...." He felt his argument did a little escape him. He snatched, "That is what I want to make clear to you. God is not a speciality; he is a universal interest."

He stopped. Both Daphne and Clementina seemed disposed to say something and did not say anything.

Miriam was the first to speak. "Daddy," she said, "I know I'm stupid. But are we still Christians?"

"I want you to think for yourselves."

"But I mean," said Miriam, "are we—something like Quakers—a sort of very broad Christians?"

"You are what you choose to be. If you want to keep in the church, then you must keep in the church. If you feel that the Christian doctrine is alive, then it is alive so far as you are concerned."

"But the creeds?" asked Clementina.

He shook his head. "So far as Christianity is defined by its creeds, I am not a Christian. If we are going to call any sort of religious feeling that has a respect for Jesus, Christianity, then no doubt I am a Christian. But so was Mohammed at that rate. Let me tell you what I believe. I believe in God, I believe in the immediate presence of God in every human life, I believe that our lives have to serve the Kingdom of God...."

"That practically is what Mr. Chasters calls 'The Core of Truth in Christianity.'"

"You have been reading him?"

"Eleanor lent me the book. But Mr. Chasters keeps his living."

"I am not Chasters," said Scrope stiffly, and then relenting: "What he does may be right for him. But I could not do as he does."

Lady Ella had said no word for some time.

"I would be ashamed," she said quietly, "if you had not done as you have done. I don't mind—The girls don't mind—all this.... Not when we understand—as we do now."

That was the limit of her eloquence.

"Not now that we understand, Daddy," said Clementina, and a faint flavour of Lady Sunderbund seemed to pass and vanish.

There was a queer little pause. He stood rather distressed and perplexed, because the talk had not gone quite as he had intended it to go. It had deteriorated towards personal issues. Phoebe broke the awkwardness by jumping up and coming to her father. "Dear Daddy," she said, and kissed him.

"We didn't understand properly," said Clementina, in the tone of one who explains away much—that had never been spoken....

"Daddy," said Miriam with an inspiration, "may I play something to you presently?"

"But the fire!" interjected Lady Ella, disposing of that idea.

"I want you to know, all of you, the faith I have," he said.

Daphne had remained seated at the table.

"Are we never to go to church again?" she asked, as if at a loss.

XVII

Scrope went back into his little study. He felt shy and awkward with his daughters now. He felt it would be difficult to get back to usualness with them. To night it would be impossible. To morrow he must come down to breakfast as though their talk had never occurred.... In his rehearsal of this deliverance during his walk home he had spoken much more plainly of his sense of the coming of God to rule the world and end the long age of the warring nations and competing traders, and he had intended to speak with equal plainness of the passionate subordination of the individual life to this great common purpose of God and man, an aspect he had scarcely mentioned at all. But in that little room, in the presence of those dear familiar people, those great horizons of life had vanished. The room with its folding doors had fixed the scale. The wallpaper had smothered the Kingdom of God; he had been, he felt, domestic; it had been an after supper talk. He had been put out, too, by the mention of Lady Sunderbund and the case of Chasters....

In his study he consoled himself for this diminution of his intention. It had taken him five years, he reflected, to get to his present real sense of God's presence and to his personal subordination to God's purpose. It had been a little absurd, he perceived, to expect these girls to leap at once to a complete understanding of the halting hints, the allusive indications of the thoughts that now possessed his soul. He tried like some maiden speaker to recall exactly what it was he had said and what it was he had forgotten to say.... This was merely a beginning, merely a beginning.

After the girls had gone to bed, Lady Ella came to him and she was glowing and tender; she was in love again as she had not been since the shadow had first fallen between them. "I was so glad you spoke to them," she said. "They had been puzzled. But they are dear loyal girls."

He tried to tell her rather more plainly what he felt about the whole question of religion in their lives, but eloquence had departed from him.

"You see, Ella, life cannot get out of tragedy—and sordid tragedy—until we bring about the Kingdom of God. It's no unreality that has made me come out of the church."

"No, dear. No," she said soothingly and reassuringly. "With all these mere boys going to the most dreadful deaths in the trenches, with death, hardship and separation running amok in the world—"

"One has to do something," she agreed.

"I know, dear," he said, "that all this year of doubt and change has been a dreadful year for you."

"It was stupid of me," she said, "but I have been so unhappy. It's over now—but I was wretched. And there was nothing I could say.... I prayed.... It isn't the poverty I feared ever, but the disgrace. Now—I'm happy. I'm happy again.

"But how far do you come with me?"

"I'm with you."

"But," he said, "you are still a churchwoman?"

"I don't know," she said. "I don't mind."

He stared at her.

"But I thought always that was what hurt you most, my breach with the church."

"Things are so different now," she said.

Her heart dissolved within her into tender possessiveness. There came flooding into her mind the old phrases of an ancient story: "Whither thou goest I will go... thy people shall be my people and thy God my God.... The Lord do so to me and more also if aught but death part thee and me."

Just those words would Lady Ella have said to her husband now, but she was capable of no such rhetoric.

"Whither thou goest," she whispered almost inaudibly, and she could get no further. "My dear," she said.

XVIII

At two o'clock the next morning Scrope was still up. He was sitting over the snoring gas fire in his study. He did not want to go to bed. His mind was too excited, he knew, for any hope of sleep. In the last twelve hours, since he had gone out across the park to his momentous talk with Lady Sunderbund, it seemed to him that his life had passed through its cardinal crisis and come to its crown and decision. The spiritual voyage that had begun five years ago amidst a stormy succession of theological nightmares had reached harbour at last. He was established now in the sure conviction of God's reality, and of his advent to unify the lives of men and to save mankind. Some unobserved process in his mind had perfected that conviction, behind the cloudy veil of his vacillations and moods. Surely that work was finished now, and the day's experience had drawn the veil and discovered God established for ever.

He contrasted this simple and overruling knowledge of God as the supreme fact in a practical world with that vague and ineffective subject for sentiment who had been the "God" of his Anglican days. Some theologian once spoke of God as "the friend behind phenomena"; that Anglican deity had been rather a vague flummery behind court and society, wealth, "respectability," and the comfortable life. And even while he had lived in lipservice to that complaisant compromise, this true God had been here, this God he now certainly professed, waiting for his allegiance, waiting to take up the kingship of this distraught and bloodstained earth. The finding of God is but the stripping of bandages from the eyes. Seek and ye shall find....

He whispered four words very softly: "The Kingdom of God!"

He was quite sure he had that now, quite sure.

The Kingdom of God!

That now was the form into which all his life must fall. He recalled his vision of the silver sphere and of ten thousand diverse minds about the world all making their ways to the same one conclusion. Here at last was a king and emperor for mankind for whom one need have neither contempt nor resentment; here was an aim for which man might forge the steel and wield the scalpel, write and paint and till and teach. Upon this conception he must model all his life. Upon this basis he must found friendships and co operations. All the great religions, Christianity, Islam, in the days of their power and honesty, had proclaimed the advent of this kingdom of God. It had been their common inspiration. A religion surrenders when it abandons the promise of its Millennium. He had recovered that ancient and immortal hope. All men must achieve it, and with their achievement the rule of God begins. He muttered his faith. It made it more definite to put it into words and utter it. "It comes. It surely comes. To morrow I begin. I will do no work that goes not Godward. Always now it shall be the truth as near as I can put it. Always now it shall be the service of the commonweal as well as I can do it. I will live for the ending of all false kingship and priestcraft, for the eternal growth of the spirit of man...."

He was, he knew clearly, only one common soldier in a great army that was finding its way to enlistment round and about the earth. He was not alone. While the kings of this world fought for dominion these others gathered and found themselves and one another, these others of the faith that grows plain, these men who have resolved to end the bloodstained chronicles of the Dynasts and the miseries of a world that trades in life, for ever. They were many men, speaking divers tongues. He was but one who obeyed the worldwide impulse. He could smile at the artless vanity that had blinded him to the import of his earlier visions, that had made him imagine himself a sole discoverer, a new Prophet, that had brought him so near to founding a new sect. Every soldier in the new host was a recruiting sergeant according to his opportunity.... And none was leader. Only God was leader....

"The achievement of the Kingdom of God;" this was his calling. Henceforth this was his business in life....

For a time he indulged in vague dreams of that kingdom of God on earth of which he would be one of the makers; it was a dream of a shadowy splendour of cities, of great scientific achievements, of a universal beauty, of beautiful people living in the light of God, of a splendid adventure, thrusting out at last among the stars. But neither his natural bent nor his mental training inclined him to mechanical or administrative explicitness. Much more was his dream a vision of men inwardly ennobled and united in spirit. He saw history growing reasonable and life visibly noble as mankind realized the divine aim. All the outward peace and order, the joy of physical existence finely conceived, the mounting power and widening aim were but the expression and verification of the growth of God within. Then we would bear children for finer ends than the blood and mud of battlefields. Life would tower up like a great flame. By faith we reached forward to that. The vision grew more splendid as it grew more metaphorical. And the price one paid for that; one gave sham dignities, false honour, a Levitical righteousness, immediate peace, one bartered kings and churches for God.... He looked at the mean, poverty struck room, he marked the dinginess and tawdriness of its detail and all the sordid evidences of ungracious bargaining and grudging service in its appointments. For all his life now he would have to live in such rooms. He who had been one of the lucky ones.... Well, men were living in dug outs and dying gaily in muddy trenches, they had given limbs and lives, eyes and the joy of movement, prosperity and pride, for a smaller cause and a feebler assurance than this that he had found....

Presently his thoughts were brought back to his family by the sounds of Eleanor's return. He heard her key in the outer door; he heard her move about in the hall and then slip lightly up to bed. He did not go out to speak to her, and she did not note the light under his door.

He would talk to her later when this discovery of her own emotions no longer dominated her mind. He recalled her departing figure and how she had walked, touching and looking up to her young mate, and he a little leaning to her....

"God bless them and save them," he said....

He thought of her sisters. They had said but little to his clumsy explanations. He thought of the years and experience that they must needs pass through before they could think the fulness of his present thoughts, and so he tempered his disappointment. They were a gallant group, he felt. He had to thank Ella and good fortune that so they were. There was Clementina with her odd quick combatant sharpness, a harder being than Eleanor, but nevertheless a fine spirited and even more independent. There was Miriam, indefatigably kind. Phoebe too had a real passion of the intellect and Daphne an innate disposition to service. But it was strange how they had taken his proclamation of a conclusive breach with the church as though it was a command they must, at least outwardly, obey. He had expected them to be more deeply shocked; he had thought he would have to argue against objections and convert them to his views. Their acquiescence was strange. They were content he should think all this great issue out and give his results to them. And his wife, well as he knew her, had surprised him. He thought of her words: "Whither thou goest—"

He was dissatisfied with this unconditional agreement. Why could not his wife meet God as he had met God? Why must Miriam put the fantastic question—as though it was not for her to decide: "Are we still Christians?" And pursuing this thought, why couldn't Lady Sunderbund set up in religion for herself without going about the world seeking for a priest and prophet. Were women Undines who must get their souls from mortal men? And who was it tempted men to set themselves up as priests? It was the wife, the disciple, the lover, who was the last, the most fatal pitfall on the way to God.

He began to pray, still sitting as he prayed.

"Oh God!" he prayed. "Thou who has shown thyself to me, let me never forget thee again. Save me from forgetfulness. And show thyself to those I love; show thyself to all mankind. Use me, O God, use me; but keep my soul alive. Save me from the presumption of the trusted servant; save me from the vanity of authority...."

"And let thy light shine upon all those who are so dear to me.... Save them from me. Take their dear loyalty...."

He paused. A flushed, childishly miserable face that stared indignantly through glittering tears, rose before his eyes. He forgot that he had been addressing God.

"How can I help you, you silly thing?" he said. "I would give my own soul to know that God had given his peace to you. I could not do as you wished. And I have hurt you!... You hurt yourself.... But all the time you would have hampered me and tempted me—and wasted yourself. It was impossible.... And yet you are so fine!"

He was struck by another aspect.

"Ella was happy—partly because Lady Sunderbund was hurt and left desolated...."

"Both of them are still living upon nothings. Living for nothings. A phantom way of living...."

He stared blankly at the humming blue gas jets amidst the incandescent asbestos for a space.

"Make them understand," he pleaded, as though he spoke confidentially of some desirable and reasonable thing to a friend who sat beside him. "You see it is so hard for them until they understand. It is easy enough when one understands. Easy—" He reflected for some moments—"It is as if they could not exist—except in relationship to other definite people. I want them to exist—as now I exist—in relationship to God. Knowing God...."

But now he was talking to himself again.

"So far as one can know God," he said presently.

For a while he remained frowning at the fire. Then he bent forward, turned out the gas, arose with the air of a man who relinquishes a difficult task. "One is limited," he said. "All one's ideas must fall within one's limitations. Faith is a sort of tour de force. A feat of the imagination. For such things as we are. Naturally—naturally.... One perceives it clearly only in rare moments.... That alters nothing...."

H G WELLS – A SHORT BIOGRAPHY

Herbert George Wells was born on September 21st, 1866 at Atlas House, 46 High Street, Bromley, Kent. He was the youngest of four siblings and his family affectionately knew him as 'Bertie'.

At the time of his birth his father, Joseph Wells, was a professional cricketer playing for the Kent county team. While this afforded him some seasonal income, it was far too little to raise a family and so he and his wife Sarah, a former domestic servant, acquired a shop on Bromley high street selling sporting goods and chinaware. It was in their accommodation above this shop that H. G. Wells was born.

The first few years of his childhood were spent fairly quietly, and Wells didn't display much literary interest until, in 1874, he accidentally broke his leg and was left to recover in bed, largely entertained by the library books his father regularly brought him. Through these Wells found he could escape the boredom and misery of his bed and convalescence by exploring the new worlds he encountered in these books.

Very quickly his vivid and fertile imagination began an interest in creating his own worlds, and from then on he was motivated to write.

Later that year the young Wells entered Thomas Morley's Commercial Academy, a private school. An earlier version of the school had gone bankrupt some years before. And perhaps not without good reason; the teaching was erratic, the curriculum mostly focused, as Wells later said, on producing copperplate handwriting and doing the sort of sums useful to tradesmen. However, despite that, Wells remained a pupil there for six years until 1880.

In 1877, his father fractured his thigh and effectively put an end to Joseph's career as a cricketer. His subsequent earnings as a shopkeeper were not enough to compensate for the loss of the primary source of family income.

No longer able to support themselves financially, the family instead sought to place their sons as apprentices in various occupations. From 1880 to 1883, Wells had a miserable apprenticeship as a draper at the Southsea Drapery Emporium, Hyde's. The hours were long, usually thirteen hours a day, and board was provided by a dormitory shared with the other apprentices. These experiences were valuable in one respect. They would later inspire such classic novels as *The Wheels of Chance* and *Kipps*, which portray the life of a draper's apprentice as well as providing much of the factual evidence for his writings on society's unequal distribution of wealth.

Wells' parents had a turbulent marriage, mainly caused by the friction of his mother being a Protestant and his father a freethinker. When his mother returned to work as a lady's maid (at Uppark, a country house in Sussex), one of the conditions of work was that she would not be permitted to have living space for her husband and children. Thereafter, she and Joseph lived separate lives, though they never divorced and remained faithful to each other. As a probable extension of this the young Well's personal troubles increased as he subsequently failed as a draper and also, later, as a chemist's assistant.

Fortunately for him Uppark had a magnificent well stocked library in which he immersed himself, reading many from the many classic works; from Plato's Republic to More's Utopia.

In October 1879 Sarah secured Wells a position through a distant relative as pupil-teacher at the National School at Wookey, in Somerset, where, as a senior pupil of the school, he would teach the younger children. This was a regular practice at the time and, for Wells, a valuable experience.

But the career plan did not go as hoped. A few months later in December his relative, Arthur Williams, was dismissed for "irregularities in his qualifications" and so Wells was also dismissed. It was yet another obstacle for him to overcome.

He moved to Midhurst Grammar School, though his time there was brief lasting only a year.

Whilst there he gained a scholarship to the Normal School of Science, which would later become the Royal College of Science in South Kensington.

Here he studied biology under the tuition of Thomas Henry Huxley, the famous advocate of the theory of evolution and known as "Darwin's Bulldog" for his ferocity.

The scholarship also gave him twenty-one shillings per week upon which to live, and helped him to remain at the College until 1887. The College also had a debating society which quickly aroused Wells's interest, and he joined it within his first year.

Drawing on his learnings from his time in the library at Uppark, he soon became interested and involved with societal matters, including that of reformation and revolution. Though his initial involvement was founded on his understanding of *The Republic*, it wasn't long before he began to consider socialist matters from a more contemporary perspective, encouraged by his fellows and recently expressed by the Fabian Society, a newly established socialist organism seeking reform by gradualist means. He attended lectures given at the home of the artist and socialist William Morris at Kelmscott House.

Wells was numbered amongst the co-founders of *The Science School Journal*, for which he began to write about his own views on society, and literature. The journal also provided an environment in which he could relatively safely experiment with fiction writing, and the earliest version of *The Time Machine* (1895) was published in the journal, under the name *The Chronic Argonauts*.

Unfortunately for Wells he experienced another obstacle when he lost his scholarship in 1887 when he failed to pass his geology exams, owing to a marked lack of interest, though he had successfully passed exams in biology and physics.

Wells moved to Stoke-on-Trent in 1888, staying in both Basford and in Burslem in the Leopard Hotel. In a letter to a friend he wrote that "the district made an immense impression on me", and it is widely thought that he took inspiration from the Potteries, the furnaces and industry of the area in his imagining of the landscape of *The War of the Worlds*. While here he wrote *The Cone*, a macabre short story, which was published in 1895 alongside *The Time Machine*. It is set in the north of Stoke-on-Trent.

He spent some time teaching at Henley House School where he taught A.A. Milne (the future and famed author of Winnie the Pooh), and after some time decided to further his knowledge of the methodology and principles of the practice of education. In order to do so, he enrolled at the College of Preceptors, now the College of Teachers, and went on to receive his Licentiate and Fellowship FCP diplomas.

Two years later, in 1890, Wells finally received a Bachelor of Science degree, in zoology, from the University of London External Programme.

Having now left London he found himself without accommodation until he moved to his aunt Mary's house, where he courted his cousin, Isabel Mary Wells, whom he married in 1891.

Wells was still teaching at Henley House School throughout the courtship and marriage, and gradually he became romantically interested with Amy Catherine Robbins, one of his students. Wells separated from Isabel in favour of Amy, who later became known as Jane, and they married in 1895.

The same year saw the publication of *The Time Machine*. Interestingly, Wells was initially expecting to reuse the material from *The Chronic Argonauts*, the first version he had written for his College journal, in a series of articles for the *Pall Mall Gazette*. However, upon that magazine's publisher's request he instead expanded and serialised the novel on the agreement of a sum of £100 on publication by Heinemann (this is roughly equivalent today to £10,000), was significantly more money than he expected or had, and he readily agreed.

It ran from January to May in *The New Review*, and then was published in its first book edition by Henry Holt and Company in New York on May 7th of the same year. Shortly thereafter Heinemann produced an English book edition, which became available on May 29th. The two editions differ slightly, but the English version has now established itself as the preferred version.

In this classic book Wells first uses the term 'time machine', and introduces and popularises the concept of purposeful and deliberate travel through time. Along with the novel's significance for the genre of science fiction is its importance as a text of social commentary and criticism, exploring Wells's views of abundance and the industrial revolution. Written at the time of a growing British

Empire where great strides were being made in real life across many fields it tunes in to his unique ability to slightly distort reality and make our fears and dreams believable and achievable.

Buoyed by his success with *The Time Machine*, Wells proceeded with his next major work, *The Wonderful Visit*. It was published in the same year, by MacMillan and Co., to critical acclaim. It is purportedly based on a famous quotation from John Ruskin, the painter and critic, who wrote that, were an angel to appear in Victorian England, it would be shot on sight. Wells introduces themes of contemporary fantasy and satire, and was highly praised for the book; Joseph Conrad wrote to him praising his "imagination so unbounded and so brilliant". Alongside these two more prominent works of 1895 were two others, *Select Conversations With An Uncle* and *The Stolen Bacillus and Other Incidents*.

In 1896 *The Island of Doctor Moreau*, was published by Heinemann, Stone and Kimball. In it Wells imagines our narrator, Edward Prendrick, marooned on the island of Doctor Moreau who uses the vivisection of animals to construct macabre representations of human beings. Using this model Wells is able to explore a number of philosophical ideas about morality, ethics and pain. The book was written at a time of increasing and vested interest in vivisection across Europe, and in the succeeding few years several interest groups were established, notable amongst which was the British Union for the Abolition of Vivisection.

In a change of literary direction and tone Wells finished 1896 with *The Wheels of Chance*, a satirical comedy, much in the vein of Jerome K. Jerome's more famous and celebrated *Three Men in a Boat*. It was written at the height of the cycling craze in Great Britain, when bicycles became cheap to manufacture and available to the masses, and imagines the escapist holiday of a frustrated draper whose calamitous expedition by bicycle to the South coast to explore new areas of his country. Indeed a famous Wells quote of the time was "Every time I see an adult on a bicycle, I no longer despair for the future of the human race."

The next year saw his published work return to its more philosophical grandeur with the publication by C. Arthur Pearson of *The Invisible Man*. Firmly in his now established vein of early science fiction, it explores the moral and social implications of scientific experiment and the consequences when the experiment malfunctions.

This same year, 1897, Wells completed what is arguably his most famous, most influential and most recognisable work, *The War of the Worlds*. He had been working on the idea since 1895, and when it was published it was classified along with his earlier work, *The Time Machine,* as 'scientific romance'.

Romance seems a stretch as the Martian invasion lays waste to southern England. But Wells was able to explore some of the popular superstitions of Victorian society as well as ideas about British Imperialism as the Empire approached its zenith.

Though it had been serialised the year before in *Pearson's Magazine*, for which he was paid £200 on the condition that he tell the publisher how it ends before receipt of payment, it was more successful the following year when it was published in book form by Heinemann. It has become a never ending source of media inventions, from books to Radio, TV and of course, film.

Part of its success is arguably attributable to the fascination with an increasing interest by the general population in what has become known as 'invasion literature', this genre, most prominent between 1871 and 1914, had a focus largely directed towards the increasing hostilities between the British Empire and her European rivals, and the ramifications of the widespread nature of the British Empire both commercial, culturally and military.

Between 1898 and 1899, Wells serialised a novel entitled *When The Sleeper Awakes*, concerning a man who, after experimenting with drugs to alleviate his insomnia, enters a sort of coma for 203 years and wakes up in the year 2100 to find that his wealth, with compound interest from the bank, accumulated to such an extent over the course of his coma that he is now the richest man in the world. Meanwhile, a sinister organisation called the White Council has invested his money and used his status as a demi-god to justify their actions in order to establish a plutocracy. Graham awakes and is presented with a dystopian reality over which he effectively has dominion. The novel sought to explore the nature of greed and oppression and, though it was fairly successful in its time, Wells revisited it in 1910 to far greater commercial and critical acclaim with *The Sleeper Awakes*. Wells followed the first version of this novel with *Love and Mr Lewisham*, a departure from his now established science fiction genre, and with a protagonist who bears striking resemblance to Wells in several ways. Mr Lewisham is a teacher at the age of eighteen, he falls in love in circumstances which cause the loss of his teaching post, and he progresses to study at the Normal School of Science, where Wells himself had studied. Wells himself spoke of the differences between this and his earlier work, stating that "the writing was an altogether more serious undertaking than I have ever done before".

In 1901, and with his health poor, Wells moved near Folkestone to Sandgate where he built a large home, which he named Spade House, for his family in anticipation of his first son, George Philip, who was born in the same year on July 17th.

H G Wells had by now established himself as a significant proponent of the scientific romance genre, now becoming better known as science fiction, his works reaching and thrilling a wide commercial audience as did those of Jules Verne who, although in his last days, was equally instrumental in bringing life to this new literary genre.

Wells wrote a novel almost every year until 1941 when he published his last novel, *You Can't Be Too Careful*, and in each he explores his various progressive, and progressing, political and social ideas.

Alongside his significant output of serialised novels, he was a prolific writer of shorter stories and non-fiction, whether that be social and political commentary or scientific journalism, literary criticism or autobiography. His attendance at the Fabian Society continued, and it was through connections made there that he had several affairs, with Jane's consent, with writers, political thinkers and most ironically an American birth control activist named Margaret Sanger.

Despite these affairs, his marriage to Jane continued and remained strong enough that they had another child, Frank Richard, in 1903, and the marriage continued until 1927 when Jane died. Some of the affairs seemed rather more complicated and, given society's morals at the time, must have caused problems with his wife. Having met the parents of novelist Amber Reeves at the Fabian Society, he began an affair with her which resulted in a child, born in 1909, named Anna-Jane. Five years later, in 1914, he had a son, Anthony West, with the feminist and novelist Rebecca West, who at the time was twenty-six years younger than him. Wells remained in fairly regular contact with his lovers and his children.

While continuing to write at his regular pace of one or two novels, short stories or essays per year, a glance at the bibliography below will give some idea of the scope, quality and output he was able to write with.

Wells also managed to put more time into politics and religion, though he was increasingly outspoken in his criticism of the Catholic church in his final years.

He ran as a Labour Party candidate for London University in the 1922 and 1923 general elections though it appears his views on the Party were diverging from theirs at the time.

In 1933 Wells predicted in *The Shape of Things to Come* that the world war he feared would begin in January 1940. It was another example of his predictive skills that had brought so many new ideas once thought fantastic to become almost everyday events.

By now Wells had become widely read almost everywhere both in the English language and through the myriad of translated works also in print through many other languages. With the rise of the Nazi party and his direct and confrontational criticism of it on May 10th, 1933, Wells' books were burned by the Nazi youth in Berlin's Opernplatz, and his works banned from libraries and bookstores.

Wells, who was president of PEN International (Poets, Essayists, Novelists), further angered the Nazis by overseeing the expulsion of the German PEN club from the international body in 1934 following the German PEN's refusal to admit non-Aryan writers to its membership.

It was later discovered after the war that he was one of almost three thousand names listed in "The Black Book" and slated for immediate arrest by the SS should the invasion of Britain have been successful.

Having suffered from diabetes throughout his life, in 1934 he decided to set up the charity which became Diabetes UK, which has now become the UK's leading diabetes charity.

On October 28th, 1940, on radio station KTSA in San Antonio, Texas, Wells took part in a radio interview with his near namesake, Orson Welles, who two years previously had performed a famous radio adaptation of *The War of the Worlds* which had caused utter panic and mass evacuation in America. During the interview Wells admitted his surprise at the events that resulted from the broadcast, but acknowledged his debt to Welles for increasing sales of one of his "more obscure" titles.

An immense talent Wells not only wrote prolifically and to a large audience but he was always much admired both for this thinking on various subjects including social issues, such as governments and race relations, but also for his literary ideas which pushed the boundaries for both contemporary science and future generations.

Additionally, his work received major recognition by being nominated for the Nobel Prize in Literature in 1921, 1932, 1935, and 1946.

Herbert George Wells died at home, 13 Hanover Terrace, Regent's Park, London, August 13th, 1946. His death is recorded as being of 'unspecified causes'. He was 79 years of age.

Wells had stated that his epitaph should be: "I told you so. You damned fools".

He was cremated at Golders Green Crematorium on August 16th, 1946, his ashes scattered at sea near Old Harry Rocks at Handfast Point, on the Isle of Purbeck in Dorset

The literary papers and correspondence from his estate were purchased in 1954 by the University of Illinois at Urbana–Champaign.

Novels

The Time Machine (1895)
The Wonderful Visit (1895)
The Island of Doctor Moreau (1896)
The Wheels of Chance (1896)
The Invisible Man (1897)
The War of the Worlds (1898)
When the Sleeper Wakes (1899)
Love and Mr Lewisham (1900)
The First Men in the Moon (1901)
The Sea Lady (1902)
The Food of the Gods and How It Came to Earth (1904)
Kipps (1905)
A Modern Utopia (1905)
In the Days of the Comet (1906)
The War in the Air (1908)
Tono-Bungay (1909)
Ann Veronica (1909)
The History of Mr Polly (1910)
The Sleeper Awakes (1910) – revised edition of When the Sleeper Wakes (1899)
The New Machiavelli (1911)
Marriage (1912)
The Passionate Friends (1913)
The Wife of Sir Isaac Harman (1914)
The World Set Free (1914)
Bealby: A Holiday (1915)
Boon (1915)
The Research Magnificent (1915)
Mr Britling Sees It Through (1916)
The Soul of a Bishop (1917)
Joan and Peter: The Story of an Education (1918)
The Undying Fire (1919)
The Secret Places of the Heart (1922)
Men Like Gods (1923)
The Dream (1924)
Christina Alberta's Father (1925)
The World of William Clissold (1926)
Meanwhile (1927)
Mr. Blettsworthy on Rampole Island (1928)
The Autocracy of Mr. Parham (1930)
The Bulpington of Blup (1932)
The Shape of Things to Come (1933)
The Croquet Player (1936)
Brynhild (1937)
Star Begotten (1937)
The Camford Visitation (1937)
Apropos of Dolores (1938)
The Brothers (1938)

The Holy Terror (1939)
Babes in the Darkling Wood (1940)
All Aboard for Ararat (1940)
You Can't Be Too Careful (1941)

Cover of Little Wars (1913).
Text-Book of Biology (1893)
Honours Physiography (1893) – with R. A. Gregory
Certain Personal Matters (1897)
Anticipations of the Reactions of Mechanical and Scientific Progress upon Human Life and Thought (1901)
Mankind in the Making (1903)
The Future in America (1906)
This Misery of Boots (1907)
Will Socialism Destroy the Home? (1907)
New Worlds for Old (1908)
First and Last Things (1908)
Floor Games (1911)
The Great State (1912)
Great Thoughts From H. G. Wells (1912)
Thoughts From H. G. Wells (1912)
Little Wars (1913)
The War That Will End War (1914)
An Englishman Looks at the World (1914); US title: Social Forces in England and America
The War and Socialism (1915)
The Peace of the World (1915)
What is Coming? (1916)
The Elements of Reconstruction (1916) – published under the pseudonym D. P.
God the Invisible King (1917)
War and the Future (a.k.a. Italy, France and Britain at War) (1917)
Introduction to Nocturne (1917)
In the Fourth Year (1918)
The Idea of a League of Nations (1919) – with Viscount Edward Grey, Lionel Curtis, William Archer, H. Wickham Steed, A. E. Zimmern, J. A. Spender, Viscount Bryce and Gilbert Murray
The Way to the League of Nations (1919) – with Viscount Edward Grey, Lionel Curtis, William Archer, H. Wickham Steed, A. E. Zimmern, J. A. Spender, Viscount Bryce and Gilbert Murray
The Outline of History (1920)
Russia in the Shadows (1920)
Frank Swinnerton (1920) – with Arnold Bennett, Grant Overton
The Salvaging of Civilization (1921)
A Short History of the World (1922)
Washington and the Hope of Peace (aka Washington and the Riddle of Peace) (1922)
Socialism and the Scientific Motive (1923)
The Story of a Great Schoolmaster: Being a Plain Account of the Life and Ideas of Sanderson of Oundle (1924) – a biography of Frederick William Sanderson
A Year of Prophesying (1925)
A Short History of Mankind (1925)
Mr. Belloc Objects to "The Outline of History" (1926)
Wells' Social Anticipations (1927)

The Way the World is Going (1928)
The Book of Catherine Wells (1928)
The Open Conspiracy (aka What Are We To Do With Our Lives?) (1928)
The Science of Life (1930) – with Julian S. Huxley and G. P. Wells
Divorce as I See It (1930)
Points of View (1930)
The Work, Wealth and Happiness of Mankind (1931)
The New Russia (1931)
Selections From the Early Prose Works of H. G. Wells (1931)
After Democracy (1932)
Experiment in Autobiography (1934)
The New America: The New World (1935)
The Anatomy of Frustration (1936)
World Brain (1938)
The Fate of Homo Sapiens (a.k.a. The Fate of Man) (1939)
The New World Order (1939)
Travels of a Republican Radical in Search of Hot Water (1939)
The Common Sense of War and Peace (1940)
The Rights of Man (1940)
The Pocket History of the World (1941)
Guide to the New World (1941)
The Outlook for Homo Sapiens (1942)
The Conquest of Time (1942)
Modern Russian and English Revolutionaries (1942) – with Lev Uspensky
Phoenix: A Summary of the Inescapable Conditions of World Reorganization (1942)
Crux Ansata: An Indictment of the Roman Catholic Church (1943)
'42 to '44: A Contemporary Memoir (1944)
Reshaping Man's Heritage (1944) – with J. B. S. Haldane, Julian S. Huxley
The Happy Turning (1945)
Mind at the End of Its Tether (1945)
Marxism vs Liberalism (1945) – with J. V. Stalin
H.G. Wells: Early Writings in Science and Science Fiction (1975)

Stories
A Family Elopement (1884)
A Tale of the Twentieth Century (1887)
A Talk with Gryllotalpa (1887) – published under the pseudonym Septimus Browne
A Vision of the Past (1887)
The Chronic Argonauts (1888)
The Devotee of Art (1888)
The Flying Man (aka The Advent of the Flying Man) (1893)
Æpyornis Island (1894)
A Deal in Ostriches (1894)
The Diamond Maker (1894)
The Flowering of the Strange Orchid (aka The Strange Orchid) (1894)
The Hammerpond Park Burglary (1894)
The Lord of the Dynamos (1894)
How Gabriel Became Thompson (1894)
In the Avu Observatory (1894)
In the Modern Vein: An Unsympathetic Love Story (aka A Bardlet's Romance) (1894)

The Jilting of Jane (1894)
The Man With a Nose (1894)
A Misunderstood Artist (1894)
Mr. Ledbetter's Vacation (1894) (aka Mr. Leadbetter's Vacation)
The Stolen Bacillus (1894)
The Thing in No. 7 (1894)
Through a Window (aka At a Window) (1894)
The Thumbmark (1894)
The Treasure in the Forest (1894)
The Triumphs of a Taxidermist (1894)
The Argonauts of the Air (1895)
A Catastrophe (1895)
The Cone (1895)
How Pingwill Was Routed (1895)
Le Mari Terrible (1895)
The Moth" (aka A Moth – Genus Novo) (1895)
Our Little Neighbour (1895)
Pollock and the Porroh Man (1895)
The Reconciliation (aka The Bulla) (1895)
The Remarkable Case of Davidson's Eyes (aka The Story of Davidson's Eyes) (1895)
The Sad Story of a Dramatic Critic (aka The Obliterated Man) (1895)
The Temptation of Harringay (1895)
Wayde's Essence (1895)
The Apple (1896)
In the Abyss (1896)
The Plattner Story (1896)
The Purple Pileus (1896)
The Rajah's Treasure (1896)
The Red Room (1896) (aka The Ghost of Fear)
The Sea Raiders (1896)
A Slip Under the Microscope (1896)
The Story of the Late Mr. Elvesham (1896)
Under the Knife (aka Slip Under the Knife) (1896)
The Crystal Egg (1897)
The Lost Inheritance (1897)
Mr Marshall's Doppelganger (1897)
A Perfect Gentleman on Wheels (1897)
The Presence by the Fire (1897)
The Star (1897)
A Story of the Days To Come (1897)
A Story of the Stone Age (aka. Stories of the Stone Age) (1897)
Jimmy Goggles the God (1898)
The Man Who Could Work Miracles (1898)
Miss Winchelsea's Heart (1898)
The Stolen Body (1898)
Walcote (1898)
Mr. Brisher's Treasure (1899)
A Vision of Judgment (1899)
A Dream of Armageddon (1901)
Filmer (1901)
Mr. Skelmersdale in Fairyland (1901)

The New Accelerator (1901)
The Inexperienced Ghost (aka The Story of the Inexperienced Ghost) (1902)
The Loyalty of Esau Common (1902)
The Land Ironclads (1903)
The Magic Shop (1903)
The Truth About Pyecraft (1903)
The Valley of Spiders (1903)
The Country of the Blind (1904)
The Empire of the Ants (1905)
The Door in the Wall (1906)
The Beautiful Suit (aka. A Moonlight Fable) (1909)
Little Mother Up the Morderberg (1910)
My First Aeroplane (1910)
The Story of the Last Trump (1915)
The Wild Asses of the Devil (1915)
Peter Learns Arithmetic (1918)
The Grisly Folk (1921)
The Pearl of Love (1924)
The Queer Story of Brownlow's Newspaper (1932)
Answer to Prayer (1937)
The Country of the Blind (revised) (1939)

Story Collections
Select Conversations with an Uncle (Now Extinct) and Two Other Reminscences (1895)
The Stolen Bacillus and Other Incidents (1895)
The Red Room (1896)
Thirty Strange Stories (1897)
The Plattner Story and Others (1897)
Tales of Space and Time (1899)
A Cure For Love (1899)
Twelve Stories and a Dream (1903)
The Country of the Blind and Other Stories (1911)
The Door in the Wall and Other Stories (1911)
The Star (1913)
Boon, The Mind of the Race, The Wild Asses of the Devil, and The Last Trump (1915) – first edition
published under the pseudonym Reginald Bliss
Tales of the Unexpected (1922)
Tales of Wonder (1923)
Tales of Life and Adventure (1923)
The Empire of the Ants and Other Stories (1925)
The Short Stories of H. G. Wells (1927)
Selected Short Stories (1927)
The Adventures of Tommy (1929)
The Valley of Spiders (1930)
The Stolen Body and Other Tales of the Unexpected (1931)
The Famous Short Stories of H. G. Wells (aka The Favorite Short Stories of H. G. Wells) (1937)
Short Stories by H. G. Wells (1940)
The Inexperienced Ghost (1943)
The Land Ironclads (1943)
The New Accelerator (1943)

The Truth About Pyecraft and Other Short Stories (1943)
Twenty-Eight Science Fiction Stories (1952)
Seven Stories (1953)
Three Prophetic Science Fiction Novels of H. G. Wells (1960)
The Cone (1965)

Published versions of film scripts and scenarios written by Wells
The King Who Was a King: The Book of a Film (1929 – scenario for a film which was never made)
Things to Come (1935 – adaptation of The Shape of Things to Come and The Work, Wealth and Happiness of Mankind)
The Man Who Could Work Miracles (1936)
The New Faust (in Nash's Pall Magazine, December 1936 – adaptation of The Story of the Late Mr Elvesham)

Zoological Retrogression (1891)
The Rediscovery of the Unique (1891)
Ancient Experiments in Co-Operation (1892)
On Extinction (1893)
The Man of the Year Million (1893)
The Sun God and the Holy Stars (1894)
Province of Pain (1894)
Life in the Abyss (1894)
Another Basis for Life (1894)
The Rate of Change in Species (1894)
The Biological Problem of To-day (1894)
The 'Cyclic' Delusion (1894)
Flat Earth Again (1894)
Bio-Optimism (1895)
Bye-Products in Evolution (1895)
Death (1895)
The Duration of Life (1895)
The Visibility of Change in the Moon (1895)
The Limits of Individual Plasticity (1895)
Human Evolution, an Artificial Process (1896)
Intelligence on Mars (1896)
Concerning Skeletons (1896)
The Possible Individuality of Atoms (1896)
Morals and Civilisation (1897)
On Comparative Theology (1898)
The Discovery of the Future (1902)
The English House of the Future (1903; several other authors)
Skepticism of the Instrument (1903)
The Things that Live on Mars (illustrated by William Robinson Leigh) (1908)
The Grisly Folk (1921)
Mr. Wells and Mr. Vowles (1926)
The Red Dust a Fact! (1927)
Democracy Under Revision (1927)

Wells Speaks Some Plain Words to us, New York Times, October 16, 1927
Common Sense of World Peace (1929)
Foretelling the Future (1938)